Praise for Nibi Soto's

Beyond the Map's Boundary

A Timely Sort of Adventure

"Beyond the Map's Boundary is somehow both charming and tense, and the world the characters inhabit is deep and complicated, perfect for realistic fantasy. The action is riveting, and the plot will absolutely draw the reader in. The level of detail demands that this story be re-read and appreciated for its nuances."

– J. Blackmore – Allbook Reviews

Allbook Reviews – Featured Book of the Month ★★★★★

"Soto offers mystery, romance, science fiction, family reunions, and a hearty dose of humor. Readers will get the feeling that she's having a lot of fun with her writing, and the result is true entertainment. Her characters are vibrant and well-defined and will appeal to a wide range of ages from young teenagers to adults who harbor a sense of adventure."

– Andi Diehn – ForeWord Reviews★★★★

Praise from Adventurers of All Ages

"I loved the book. Once I started to read it I was in my own little world and wanted to find out what happened next! I told my teacher at school how much I had read and she was amazed. I read 250 minutes in one day and just wanted to keep reading it, but I had to do my chores. I loved how Kash and Trevor kept freaking each other out. It is so funny!"

A. Hansen (Age 11)

"I loved this book. I couldn't put it down! It is completely original and the plot makes you eager to read what's going to happen next. If there was a sequel to this book I would try to get it A.S.A.P. It's an amazing book!"

L. Skaggs (Age 13)

"I enjoy reading a lot and get excited when I discover a new author that inserts as many twists as I found from Nibi Soto. "Beyond the Map's Boundary" has been one of the most fun books I've ever read. It was hard to put down. I look forward to the next book and can hardly wait to see where the adventure will go and what magical powers are yet to be discovered by Mattie."

M. Jones (Age 18)

"Beyond the Map's Boundary is a captivating read that will absorb you from the first page. It is full of suspense and excitement and keeps you guessing until the very end. There are moments of laughter as well as touching poignant ones. Nibi Soto has proven herself to be an author with excellent insight into the human spirit. I can't wait for the next installment!

K. Hammock (Age 35)

"Beyond the Map's Boundary is a fantastical time-traveling adventure. Once I opened the book, I was hooked. The twists and turns kept me guessing and excited to read more. I can't wait for the next book to see "where in time" Nibi's story will continue."

E. Rasmussen (Age 38)

"Fun, fresh and endearing! Once you start reading it's like a race you've got to run and finish."

S. Rammell (Age 45)

"Wow!! What a page turner! I could hardly put "Beyond the Map's Boundary" down. In the same spirit as "Harry Potter," young and old will be avid fans of Nibi Soto's creative masterpiece."

C. Lindquist (Age 62)

"As a former teacher, principal and superintendent of schools, I want to encourage every reader, library, and school to enjoy Nibi Soto's new book, "Beyond the Map's Boundary." I can promise you an unforgettable journey beyond your imagination! You will become part of an odyssey that will bend and roll your mind through untold adventure. The audio version also provides an exciting interpretation of this extraordinary novel. Mattie and Trevor come alive with unpredictable powers that will surprise and excite you. I look forward to the next book being available and I'm sure you will, too."

S. Mecham (Age 70)

"At my age it's hard to get me excited about reading anything! However, as I was getting involved in listening to the audio book I could hardly wait to hear the next chapter. It was both exciting and entertaining and kept me guessing. I recommend "Beyond the Map's Boundary" to readers of all ages. I can hardly wait for book two to see what will happen next!"

W. Thornock (Age 81)

Thornock
International
Productions, Inc.
USA

ISBN-13: 978-0-615-28825-3
ISBN-10: 0-6152882-51
LCCN: 2009903301

Printed in the U.S.A.

First printing, March 2010

Dedicated to O. Wayne and EuVola M. Thornock

The adventurer and the heart…

Special thanks to:

Wayne, Carl, Audrie, Chrissa, Annalyn, Megan, Elizabeth

Stefan, Lauren, Lori, Kelly, Carol, Emily

and *Poola, Poola, Poola.*

Preface

This novel is the first in a series of four or more that will follow the lives of an extraordinary family of time travelers as they work together to maintain the true course of the future. It is my intention with these books to give the reader a charming, but tense experience of realistic fantasy, magic, riveting action and plots that draw them in to valuable lessons of life taught in inconspicuous ways. I hope to supply readers between the ages of ten to twenty (and really, readers of all ages) with an experience that not only entertains them, but teaches them many of the much needed moral values that are beginning to disappear in our world today.

My intention for my characters is to make them family oriented and simple to relate to for young readers. Though not everyone in this long family line of Trekkers has good intensions in dealing with their completely out-of-the-ordinary experiences, they ultimately make it through their trials in life by coming together and supporting one another to the end.

I hope you will come to love these fictitious characters as I have. Each one has taken on a life and personality that continues to surprise me as I write about them and the challenges they face.

I do hope that you will enjoy the adventure; that the strange, new words will become a part of your vocabulary and the complicated world my characters live in will spark your own imagination for what might come next.

May your dreams be full of Divvies that bring the magic in you to life and may you come to discover the tremendous possibilities for adventure every day. Learn to look for the good in people and their intensions and seek to serve others like the Trekkers are sworn to do. Therein you will find true happiness, ensuring that your own journey through life will be as beautiful as a song as you travel life's higher ways.

Contents

Contents

Beyond the Map's Boundary

A Timely Sort of Adventure

by

Nibi Soto

Illustrations and Cover Art by Chris Humpherys

Chapter 1

The Premonition

February 21, 1992 – 11:00 A.M. –Post Office - Benten, CA

“Afternoon, Mrs. Bott…” the postman said flatly. He had about as much personality as white paint. Amber had never seen him smile once in all the years she had lived in Benten.

“Mr. Hail; you’re looking well today.”

“Hmm,” he grunted. “Got another one of them funny little packages fer me ta send do ya?”

“I do. How’d you guess?” Amber replied sweetly. She smiled and winked at the postman. Grouchy as he always was, she knew he liked her teasing nature and if he didn’t, she still enjoyed doing it anyway; it was part of who she was.

“Oh…I spoze after ten years, perty-near every week, one oughta catch on. I ain’t dumb, ya know?

“…course not Mr. Hail.”

“Used ta keep me up at nights fer the longest time thinkin’ bout’ them blinkin’ little brown boxes you mail!”

"But not anymore?" Amber asked politely as she opened her purse and started digging through it.

"Nah, finally figur'd it's none of ma business anyways," he grumbled. "Need a pen?"

"Yes, thank you."

Amber pulled the package out of her pocket and wrote a different name and number as usual, but always the same address:

Amber Graham Bott – 022192

Box 53, Route 1

Seaport, California 93302

– Fragile, Handle with Care -

Mr. Hail noticed the package was different this time. "Yer sendin' a package to yersef?"

Amber's eyes wandered off to the side as though she were deep in thought. "Well, yeah. Today is the day!" she mumbled.

"What about today?" A ripple of puzzlement rolled across Mr. Hail's face. "What's gonna happen today?"

Amber didn't respond. She began rummaging through her purse again as though she were looking for something else.

The postman could see that Amber didn't want to talk about it. Finally he shook his head in dissatisfaction and said, "Yer one strange lady; Mrs. Bott. That'll be 98 cents."

"Yes…well…the price has gone up hasn't it?" Amber said, further diverting the conversation.

Mr. Hail glared at Amber with a smug expression of satisfaction on his face. He tilted his head side to side and said, "Yip! Highway robbery id'n it? But, I don't have no choice—I don't set them r-r-rates now do I?"

"Oh, I know, Mr. Hail," she said in a distracted tone. "Thank you!"

Amber turned and started walking towards the front door.

"Good day then, Mrs. Bott!"

"Yes yes…good day, Mr. Hail."

Amber waved goodbye over her shoulder as she headed for the exit. "*Strange little man*," she thought, pushing aside the squeaking post office door. The air was always stale inside and it was nice to get out. "I think I'm going to actually miss that old guy," she muttered to herself and hurried on her way.

She walked towards the car automatically as her mind ran through a checklist for the picnic. Something bright flashed briefly on the ground in front of her that reminded her of a red footprint. It vanished almost instantly, before she could get a good look at it. She stopped abruptly, staring at the spot where the print had appeared, blinking her eyes several times.

"Red…just like Mattie said!" she said quietly to herself. She was deep in thought when she was rudely startled back to the present by the blast of a car horn.

"Why don't you find a place to park that piece of junk that's actually legal," bellowed Fran Schnettle, the town gossip, shaking her finger at Amber out the window, "…instead of double parking every time you come to town?"

Hardly anyone came in to town on Friday morning and the streets were far from busy, but Fran could never resist an opportunity to pick at Amber. She had been the impatient, snoopy neighbor for most of Amber's married life. Since the day Fran and her mumbling, recluse-of-a-husband had moved in she had been a pain to get along with. She had a nasty habit of driving people away from her. All, but one, of her friends had given up on her many years ago. But today, it didn't even bother Amber because she had a lot more serious issues on her mind.

"Oh…sorry; I'm so sorry Mrs. Schnettle. I'll get out of your way."

Amber hurried over to her car and reached for the handle when she noticed the small, rectangular window on the passenger side of the old Chevy had been smashed out. There were several finger prints on the front window; mostly smeared, but one was exceptionally clear. She got in and checked around to see if anything was missing. Her sweater was still there and her hairbrush was lying on the seat where she had left it. However, the glove box was open. At first glance it didn't appear as though anything had been taken. She immediately reached underneath the passenger seat and felt around. When her fingers touched the object she sought she let out a big sigh of relief

"That's odd, it smells like chocolate in here?" she thought.

Amber noticed the stick shift was kind of slippery. When she bent over to get a closer look, she could see a fine smattering of brown powder on it that smelled like chocolate. On the floor beneath it she saw a small crumpled piece of Scotch tape. She was experienced with taking fingerprints since she had done it herself almost every couple of weeks for the past 10 years. Who and why would anyone want to do that to her? Amber reached in the glove box and pulled out a roll of scotch tape and a small, plastic container of chocolate powder. She carefully lifted the only clear fingerprint from the front window and placed it in another small brown container she kept in the glove box. She scribbled the words 'Possible Interloper' on it and the numbers 022192 and slid it under the driver's seat. A quick glance at the clock and she realized she was going to be late meeting her family for the picnic if she didn't hurry. It was going to be a rare outing because she had finally committed Mattie to a date and time that worked with Kash's schedule. It was exciting to think about all of them being together for a few hours and she was hoping that things would turn out different than she already knew they would. However, she couldn't risk changing the course of events because of what she knew, so off she went, forgetting about the broken window for the moment. As she drove into the driveway, she saw Kash out on the lawn, sitting on the picnic basket, flipping the tablecloth at the gnats that were hovering in the shade.

"Is everything OK?" Amber asked as she turned off the car. "Where's Mattie?

"She's not coming."

Amber knew all the answers to every question from this point forward, but had to carefully maintain the setting of what lay ahead to avoid altering the course of events that must take place. "What? After all we've done to coordinate this with her classes, work, dates and everything else under the sun that she does?"

Kash forced a smile, trying not to act disappointed. "It's just us chickens, I guess. It'll still be a rare pleasure to spend a leisurely afternoon with you; especially if it doesn't involve breaking and entering or a high speed chase somewhere."

Amber smiled at the description of their lives and said, "So, what's the reason this time?"

"Mattie finally got asked out by her heartthrob, Trevor Karington, and she couldn't see anything beyond his face. I've never seen her get ready that fast in her whole life."

"Oh, of course," Amber said sweetly. "She's been dying to go out with that Karington boy for months. I hope she has a good time. Did you check the weather report?

"No, but there's not a cloud in the sky."

"That's kind of careless don't you think?"

"Oh, we haven't had a storm in weeks," Kash said, shrugging his shoulders. "Don't get paranoid on me now. Let's go! We're losing daylight. Hey, what happened to the window?"

"Someone broke in when I was in the Post Office."

"Did you report it?" he asked.

"No. No time, no need."

"What do you mean by that?"

"Never mind…I'll report it when we get back," she reassured him. She caught herself staring at Kash in an effort to capture every detail of his face and each gesture he made before it was too late.

"What?" Why are you looking at me like that?"

"Like what?"

"Like you're going to say goodbye forever!"

"Don't be silly," Amber replied, trying to put the inevitable out of her mind.

Kash strolled around to the other side of the car. "Scoot over, would you, and I'll drive."

Amber cleared her voice and made an extra effort to appear excited. "Where're we going?"

"Just stick with me and you'll see," he said secretively.

Kash drove to a favorite picnic spot they had gone to several times when Mattie was a toddler. It was a secluded meadow near the edge of the forest, about a half hour drive from Benten. It was just as beautiful as it had been 15 years earlier. They spread the blanket beneath the only poplar tree that had grown out in the middle of the meadow, checked the skies again and settled down for a restful afternoon together.

Short breaks were usually few and far between since Amber had Inherited. It was such a pleasant, balmy afternoon. They sat down and ate lunch; Kash eating double, not wanting anything to go to waste since Mattie hadn't come along. He stretched out with a slightly painful, bulging stomach and Amber snuggled up close to him, laying her head on his chest. They reminisced about the old days before the Splitting had begun. It wasn't long before the shade of the tree and the cool grass beneath the blanket lulled them both to sleep.

1:00 P.M. – Downtown, Benten

The sidewalk café was the perfect place for Trevor to take Mattie. She loved the feelings it stirred up in her of various outdoor cafés she'd been to all over the world. Her parents always took her with them during her summer breaks from school as they traveled to distant places. It felt magical sitting there next to him. She'd been dreaming about this day for months. He knew exactly what would impress her and he didn't even know her yet. That alone was extraordinary to her.

"What would you like, Mattie?"

"Oh, surprise me," Mattie replied with a hint of school girl jitters. Mattie was so distracted by his almond shaped eyes and handsome face that she could hardly concentrate.

"Are you sure?" Trevor asked, tilting his head and winking at her as his meticulously cut brown hair reluctantly released a single, small lock onto his forehead.

Mattie was so nervous that her mouth was getting dryer by the second. Her head was spinning and she felt like her heart was fluttering a hundred miles an hour. She had a funny sensation in her knees that she had never felt before and was becoming short of breath!

"Course of…" she hesitated, shook her head and said, "I-I mean…of course! Surprise me." She smiled weakly. It was hard to act like she didn't care that much while her head was swimming with the many possibilities of what their future children would look like and what their names might be.

Trevor smiled, which only added to the problem. *"He's so cute!"* she thought to herself. Her knee started bumping up and down nervously under the table. Mattie let out a quiet sigh of amazement at how ridiculous she must appear. *"Gosh…get a grip!"* she thought to herself.

"Waitress!" Trevor called out as he lifted his hand, beckoning her with his fingers, "we're ready to order."

Suddenly Mattie felt a sharp pain behind her eyes. She dropped her head into her hands and before she knew it Trevor had put his arm around her shoulder. He gripped her wrist gently with his other hand.

"Are you OK, Mattie?" His voice was soft and filled with a genuine concern. She felt a mix of love and appreciation for his kindness, yet she felt sick and dizzy. Something else was going on inside of her that she liked even less than her silly school girl symptoms. With the pain flashed a scene where two people were running desperately through some trees in the darkness. She felt their fear, yet she had no idea what she had just seen.

"Oh…my goodness, I'm sorry. I don't know what's happening. I don't feel very good."

"Do you want me to take you home?" Trevor asked. "We can go right now."

"No…no, just give me a minute, I'll feel better in a minute. I'm really sorry."

"Don't think a thing of it," Trevor replied thoughtfully. "Would you rather go somewhere else?"

"No, let's go ahead and eat. Now I'm starving! I'm fine though; really. It's gone now." Mattie was so embarrassed she could hardly look him in the eyes. "*What a crazy bunch of sensations,*" she thought.

Trevor raised his hand again and called out to the waitress, ready to place their order.

Everyone was content except for the ones who were dressed in the clothes of their time. They acted restless and unsettled by comparison.

"Dad! It's me...Mattie!" Mattie ran to embrace her father. She wasn't sure she would ever see him again. "I'm so glad to see you, Dad."

"How'd you get here, Mattie? And how on earth did Trevor and...what's Lila doing here?"

"She was the key to bringing you back, Dad. We couldn't have done it without her."

"How'd you convince her to help you save me? She hates my guts!"

"No, she doesn't, Dad. She came happily to help bring you back."

"Thank you, Lila." Kash said softly as he came closer to her, peering directly into her eyes. He turned back to Mattie and asked, "How did you know what to do?"

Mattie continued describing the events that led up to their trip to the core. "We used the *Book of Ancestors* to decipher the code to move beyond the maps boundary. It made sense that the Interloper would bring you here; though I can't figure out how he did it. Have you seen Mom?"

"I haven't yet, but other people have that I've talked to. I've only been here for a few minutes and that's not nearly enough time to find her. There are countless people here, and there's no end to the open space as far as I've been able to detect."

"Dad," Mattie said, "you've been here for over 11 hours."

"Nah…really?" he said in disbelief. "How could that be?"

"We better try and figure out how to get back home. Apparently the time frame is different here. Going by what you just said, several hours may have already passed since we arrived. We don't want to risk missing the midnight deadline or we'll all be trapped here forever."

"I'm ready." Kash said. "What do I do?"

"I've got a lock of your hair that was set apart years ago. According to the *Book of Ancestors* all we have to do is link our hands together, say your full given name and the rings will do the rest."

"Let's get to it," said Trevor. He didn't like the thought of being stuck in the middle of time before he had the opportunity to do some hunting and fishing in Alaska and have a kid or two.

Lila stepped forward to start the process by reaching out her hand towards Kash.

"Place your hand in hers, Dad…" Mattie instructed. "Palm up." Then she placed the sample in her own fist and layered it on the stack. When Trevor closed the hand sandwich by placing his on the top of Mattie's the rings sent out the reliable whirlpool of mist and the return trip began. Mattie took a deep breath and said, "Kash Bott." Everything spun into a white downward vortex and within seconds it all stopped. The four of them stood facing each other in the basement of the library with their hands joined in the circle.

Lila's eyes widened and her face flushed with shock when she saw Kash appear out of nowhere. "Where'd you come from, Kash?"

"Me? Where'd you come from?" Kash fired back. "All of you?"

Collectively they dropped their hands to their sides and stood staring at each other, unaware of what had taken place beyond the maps boundary.

"Where'd you all come from and where's Rainey?" Kash questioned, "…and where are we?"

"Wow, I guess we already made the trip." Mattie responded.

"How'd I get here, Mattie and how on earth did Trevor and…what's Lila doing here?"

"She was the key to bringing you back, Dad. We couldn't have done it without her."

"Why would you do that for me, Lila? I thought you hated my guts!"

"No, I don't, Kash; I never have. I didn't know where I fit into the family after a while, that's all."

Kash was baffled. He felt like it had been only a second ago that he was being dragged from the Chamber by the Interloper. "Well…thank you, Lila. I appreciate your help, though I really don't know what's happened here." He wrinkled his forehead and shifted his eyes from side to side. "Does this conversation seem familiar to anyone else other than me?"

"Yes it does," Trevor agreed.

Trevor and Mattie looked at each other, back to Kash and over to Lila. They simultaneously stepped towards each other for a group hug except for Lila, who stepped back. She felt unsure of herself.

Mattie was more than relieved to see her father. She stood there hugging him for the longest time. To her, it was the first time she had seen him since that morning. The memories of what had taken place beyond the maps boundary were erased and it was as though they had never left the library at all.

Kash extended his hand towards Lila. "This is a family hug, Lila, and you are part of this family."

Lila's eyes began to water. She joined the rest of them in the circle, reaching her petite, plump arms around the family as far as they would go and held on tight. She laid her head against Mattie's shoulder and soaked in the feelings of love that she had nearly forgotten existed. She felt like she was finally home after being away for too many years and vowed to herself that she would never pull away from her family ever again—no matter what.

Chapter 27

The Trap

The tangled, thick foliage guarded the secret location of the battered mobile home making it virtually impossible to see from any angle. The dense setting held the light of the moon at bay, limiting its rays to a scanty few. Inside, Bayne tossed and turned on the couch trying to find a comfortable position to get *some* rest in the short time he had remaining. He knew Missy, his impatient, mean-spirited cohort would be returning soon, which kept him subconsciously on guard as he slept. He was unaware that Missy had already arrived and had crept quietly through the weeds until she stood in front of the torn screen door. Squeezing the handle between her thumb and first finger she pulled it open little by little to avoid the incessant squeak of the rusty springs. She stepped inside to find Bayne in the exact location she had left him. It made her angry that he was sleeping. On the other hand, in a twisted sort of way, she relished the idea of causing him further discomfort by shocking him awake. She carefully rummaged through a pile of dirty dishes in the sink where she discovered a greasy skillet and metal serving spoon that would work perfectly together to create a noise loud enough to wake the dead. She crept over to the side of the couch and lowered the pan within an inch of his ear.

With a smirk on her face she hit the pan sharply with the spoon, launching Bayne from the couch and driving his head into the overhanging cabinets. He fell at Missy's feet, covering his ear with one hand to protect it from further damage and rubbing his throbbing forehead with the other.

She reached down and yanked one of his hands away and yelled, "It's nearly time, Bayne. Get up off the floor and start the Divvy. I want those rings by midnight and you should, too. If we don't get them soon your body's going to be fried beyond repair from all of these illicit Divvies you've been doing."

Bayne used the side of the couch to help him stand. "If you don't stop treating me like crap you're going to kill me all by yourself! Then you'll never get the rings!" He sat back down on the edge and groaned, "I feel terrible."

"And whose fault is that?" she said, without a smidgen of compassion as she tossed the pan and spoon back on the pile of dishes, creating another noisy surprise. Bayne flinched again. "Jumpy, aren't you?" Missy laughed. She pushed a pile of clothes off the chair and sat down. "See if you can hold your attention for a few minutes while I review the plan before you start hunting for a foot print. It's nearly midnight and you've got to get out of here."

Mattie carefully placed her father's hair sample back in its box and handed it to Lila to be re-filed in the archives.

She glanced at her watch. "My gosh, it's 11:30. We were gone for nearly five hours. We've got to decide on a plan to catch the Interloper when he comes for the rings and get back to the beach house in Seaport."

"Did he actually give you a time he was going to return?" Kash asked.

"He gave us until midnight," Trevor replied.

"We've got to work fast." Kash was concerned for his daughter, knowing how dangerous the situation was and how inexperienced she was with her powers. "Lila and I obviously won't be able to go back with you and help. You're going to have to be extremely careful and really smart. You need to try and capture him rather than kill him so we can find out who he is and where he came from. There might be more like him and we need to learn as much as we can to protect ourselves in the future."

This concerned Mattie. She thought about the experience she and Trevor had had with him where he used the Half-Parallel to try and kill Lila. "How do you capture a ghost, Dad? He may have a few tricks that we don't even know about—not to mention the ones we do. If we were lucky enough to capture him, what's to say he's not going to pull another trick out of his hat and get away?"

"There's no guarantee of anything, Mattie. However, we do know that his hands have to be separated to prevent a Parallel of any kind and if he can't get back to a foot print, he can't Divvy. We can start there."

"I've got an idea," said Trevor. "I could bait him to come after me when he arrives and Mattie could do a Half-Parallel into his body to knock him off balance. He'd never know what hit him. Then I can pin him down. He's got to be pretty weak from being shot earlier today. I should have the strength advantage and Mattie will have the element of surprise."

Kash rested his hand on Trevor's shoulder. "That might work. It's simple and direct. Besides, he'll probably be overly confident, thinking I'm still his bartering tool. You'll have to act fast though, because he'll probably pull a gun on you like he did me."

"That doesn't feel like a solid plan to me at all," Mattie said warily. "It sounds way too simple. This guy is out to kill us—or at the very least, cut off our fingers."

"Well…I admit that it isn't the best plan I've ever made, but we've only got about 15 minutes to get into position before he arrives," Trevor replied. "If we don't beat him back to the house, we'll lose the element of surprise and then it could turn out really bad for all of us."

Mattie shook her head. "I don't know."

"You need to trust your abilities as a Trekker, Mattie and remember, I've got a few of my own as a Splitter now. We make a pretty good team."

Mattie smiled at how much Trevor had changed in the past few weeks. He had gotten more confident, much quicker, and definitely more clever. "What do you think, Dad?"

"I think Trevor's right. As a Trekker you'll be able to anticipate the Interloper's actions and as smart as you are, Mattie, I think you'll be able to outwit him right from the beginning. If you get into trouble, either one of you, get out of there. It isn't worth risking your lives. We'll face him another time."

"Yes, but not when we have the upper hand like we do this time," Trevor added.

"I can see we don't have a lot of choices right now. We'd better get going. I don't know if it's still raining outside or not, but we don't have time to find out. Trevor and I will try to do a Full-Double-Parallel underground to the house in Seaport. I hope it's not too far away for it to work. If you want to go back to Lila's house, we'll call you when it's all over."

"You mean Trevor can travel with you in a Full-Parallel?"

"We discovered it out of desperation, Dad, but it's only possible to do because of the rings."

"We'd better get out of here, Kash," Lila said. "There's some aftermath that comes with their departure. No one knows the extent of its effect on those remaining. My car is at the end of the tunnel. I'll wait for you there." She turned and scurried back down the passageway, anxious to put some distance between her and the after-shock of the Parallel.

Kash pulled Mattie under one of his arms and Trevor under the other. "You two be careful! You're everything to me and I want some grandkids to play with in my old age. Got it?"

Mattie blushed, "I'll call you as soon as I can; love you, Dad."

"Love you too, Mattie Pie." He squeezed them in close one last time and stepped away to see what a Full-Double Parallel looked like.

Trevor stepped behind Mattie, taking his position. Mattie set her Parallel on top of Trevor's arms. "You better go, Dad. We'll see you later."

Kash nodded his head and hurried down the tunnel to catch Lila.

"To the beach house…"

The mist whirled and they began the rapid movement back through the walls, rocks, pipes and wiring of the cities they passed through at a blinding speed. Within seconds they came to a standstill inside the front entry of the beach house.

"I'm glad we made it. I was afraid we'd get stuck in the middle of a rock formation or something because of the distance we traveled." Mattie straightened her hair.

"Did you notice that huge pocket of gold on our way here?" Trevor asked excitedly. "I sure wish I knew where that was in relationship to the house. We'd be rich!"

"Yeah!" Mattie chuckled. "We'll have to hunt for that later. That'd be fun." Mattie scanned the room for a good hiding place. "He'll probably materialize near the front door. If you'll hide behind the grandfather clock over there, I'll crouch down behind the loveseat with an open view of the entry. That way when you step out to draw his attention I can see him to do a Half-Parallel body block."

They both took their positions and waited. The storm had passed, the skies were clear and the moon lit the entryway through the tall, narrow windows that framed the front door.

"*If anything happens to me you get out of the house, Mattie. We can't risk him getting both of the rings,*" Trevor thought.

"*I was going to say the same thing to you Trevor,*" Mattie thought back. "S*o I guess that means that neither one of us is going to cut and run, huh?*"

"Mattie...this is no time to argue."

"I'm not arguing Trev, I'm just telling you what I intend to do!"

"You're such a strong headed woman!"

"...kind of like you Trevor, except you're not a woman."

"Ha-ha...very funny."

Suddenly Mattie saw a sequence of red footprints shoot across the entry way and the smell of decaying flesh saturated the air.

"Trevor...do you smell that?"

A scuffling sound broke the silence. *"Mattie…he's standing right behind me with a gun to my head."*

"Don't make a sound or it'll be the last thing you ever do!" the Interloper whispered in Trevor's ear. "Step back slowly." He glanced over his shoulder and started half-dragging Trevor with him down the hall towards the kitchen.

"*He's pulling me backwards into the kitchen, Mattie. Circle around the front of the house to the back door. Hurry! If you can come in from behind him maybe you can knock him out with something.*"

Mattie could see a small opening in the window and Half-Paralleled outside. She sprinted over to the shed to see if she could find something that would disarm him. Her eyes scanned the room searching for something useful. The wooden paddles that were lying inside the canoe caught her attention. She picked one up and started towards the back of the house when she heard Trevor thinking again.

"*He's backed up against the wall where he can see everything in the room and he's cocked the gun. He says I have ten seconds to get you in here or he's going to kill me.*"

Mattie felt a stabbing pain in her chest. She sensed a sudden rush of weakness flow through her arms and she dropped the paddle. She kicked open the screen door and stepped into the kitchen with her hands raised over head.

"Turn on the light, Mattie…" the Interloper commanded, "and set your ring on the table or I'm going to make Trevor into a wall decoration."

Mattie and Trevor were surprised to hear the Interloper's demands. First of all, how did he know their names? Second, and more importantly, it was quite obvious that he didn't know the rules of the rings. Mattie knew if she could lure him away from the wall she'd have a good shot at separating him from Trevor. She turned on the light and stepped towards the table as he had ordered, wiggling the ring as though she were having a hard time getting it off her finger.

"You know, of course…" Mattie said in a serious tone, staring directly into the eyes of the Interloper, "that if I remove this ring myself without having Trevor remove it from my finger at the exact same time I remove his, we'll all die from the explosion and the rings will melt from the heat and be gone forever."

She continued working on the ring as though it were stuck. The Interloper became uneasy.

"Wait!" He said sharply, pressing the barrel of the gun harder against Trevor's temple. He stood there for a minute to think. Then, pushing Trevor towards Mattie he shifted behind her, pointing the gun at her head while holding her by the back of the neck. "Take each other's rings off now! You've got to the count of three before I shoot you both and take my chances. One…"

Mattie rattled off an idea silently to Trevor as fast as she could think. "*On the count of three you run out the back door because I'm going to flatten this guy.*"

"Two…"

"I'll follow you out as soon as he's down."

"Three…

Trevor bolted for the back door and Mattie threw a reverse Half-Parallel body block into the Interloper, knocking the gun from his hand. He flew backwards, slamming his injured shoulder into the oven and crumpled to the floor in pain. Mattie set another Half-Parallel and scooted through the screen door before it bounced shut. The Interloper struggled to get up. His wound was bleeding again from the impact and throbbed with every pound of his racing heart. He pulled himself together, located the gun and stumbled outside in hopes of maybe hurting one of them before they could get away. But they had already disappeared.

Mattie and Trevor Boosted to the shelter of the rocks on the far end of the beach.

"Maybe we should get the police involved Mattie."

"No…we can't. They'd totally freak out if they saw some of the things that are sure to happen tonight. Besides, we want to try and capture him for questioning, remember? I noticed a faint trail of light particles that was left behind me when I did a Half-Parallel in the dark."

"I didn't see anything."

"It must be something only Trekkers can see. I'll bet that he can see it, too. I'll use it to side-track him with a bunch of Half-Parallels to different locations if you'll take the car out to Blue Cliff and set a trap for him. There's a wooden oar inside the boat in the shed. Pull the fishing net down off the wall and take it with you. I'll make my way over to the lower cliff where I did my first Half-Parallel next to the bushes at the bottom of the trail. I'll bait him to step left at the end of each Parallel until I reach you and then I'll step right instead. When he steps left he'll step into you and you can throw the net over him and knock him to the ground. Be sure and hold his arms away from each other."

"Gee, Mattie, that sounds really risky for you."

"We'll be several yards away from the edge of the cliff, and it shouldn't be a problem."

"That's not what I mean. What if he catches you before you get there?"

"I'll have to stay one step ahead of him. This kind of danger is going to be fairly commonplace in our lives from now on and we're going to have to get used to it. I'll be as careful as I can. Make sure you wait for me in case it takes longer than I think."

"OK. If you have anything unexpected come up, send me a thought and I'll do whatever you think I should do."

"Wait at least a minute after I leave you, until I can Parallel to the road at the end of the field with him behind me. I'll try and detour him for about 15 minutes, giving you time to get to the cliffs. Then I'll head back towards you. My watch says its ten minutes after midnight. Keep an eye out for me at around 12:25 and be ready!"

"I will. Don't go crazy out there."

They gave each other a hug and Mattie began the risky game. The Interloper had moved around to the side of the house to see if he could catch a glimpse of them somewhere. To his great pleasure he could see the vaguely illuminated ion trail from Mattie's Parallel and set his own in her path. He took the bait like she was hoping he would. Mattie Paralleled to the old highway and headed for town.

Trevor waited for a minute and proceeded to the shed. After he gathered everything he needed he drove towards the cliffs to take his position and wait for Mattie to return with the Interloper.

Chapter 28

The Chase

Mattie realized that with each Parallel she could feel the pressure from his body drawing closer to hers. Occupying the same stream created a magnetic force within it that increasingly compressed the space between them with each new run. By the fifth Parallel she had entered Main Street. It appeared to be completely deserted.

"Trevor, can you hear me?" she thought.

"Yes, where are you?"

"I'm in town and the Interloper is closing the distance on me faster than I thought he would. There's no way I'm going to make it back to you before he reaches me from within the Parallel stream. I've probably only got one or two more runs before he overtakes me."

"What are you going to do?"

Suddenly she noticed a young man was sitting alone on the bus stop bench in front of the real-estate office. Focusing in closer she could see a yellow, glowing footprint in front of him.

"Where'd he come from?" Mattie thought, flustered by the fact that she hadn't seen him there a split second before.

"Who? Where'd who come from?" Trevor was concerned that someone else had come to join the Interloper to help capture Mattie.

"There's a 15 or 16 year old kid here, sitting at the bus stop. Why would he be sitting alone out here at midnight?"

As Mattie sped past the boy she made a special effort to avoid the glowing print and then glanced back at the Interloper who had barely become visible to her within the ion stream. To her amazement she noticed the boy's head actually following her as she past in front of him.

"This kid acts like he can see me during the Parallel."

"What does that mean?"

"I don't know, but I'll have to get back to you later; I have to focus." She ended the Parallel under the light post at Reiger's Grocery Store near the end of the block and stepped left as planned. She glanced up at the boy and saw him motioning to her to make a run back by him again. He drew the path with his finger that he suggested she take and then pointed at the Interloper behind her.

"Trevor, this guy acts like he knows what I am and he's aware that I'm being followed. I don't know how he can see me doing this stuff, but I think he intends to buy me some more time somehow. I'm going to have to trust him; the Interloper will catch me on the next run."

"Mattie, this drives me crazy waiting around here. I should be with you!"

"Stay put, Trevor! I've gotta go!"

She started to set another Parallel, but had spent too much time communicating with Trevor. The Interloper anticipated her step to the left and adjusted for it in his landing. The impact from his body slamming into hers threw her several feet in the air. When she hit the pavement the rugged surface tore through her clothes and skin as she skidded to a painful stop. The collision left her with several patches of bloodied rash that stung in the early morning air. He lunged toward her, pointing the gun at her face and pinning one of her legs under his size twelve boot. Out of nowhere a young woman, with the exact same coloration as the boy on the bench, jumped on the Interloper from behind, knocking him to the ground and freeing Mattie. The girl smiled sweetly at Mattie, ran a Half-Parallel over to the boy and sat down beside him. Mattie jumped up and set another one of her own in their direction and disappeared before the Interloper could grab her again. He staggered to his feet and set his Parallel before the ion stream could dissolve. Both kids stood up and watched Mattie as she passed by. They stepped into the ion stream, facing the oncoming Interloper and locked their forearms together. The girl hovered her left foot over one of the yellow prints and the boy braced himself for contact. The moment they collided she stepped on one of the yellow prints and they both disappeared. The impact hurled the Interloper off path and robbed him of some of his energy, leaving him even weaker than he already was. He lay in the gutter groaning between uneven gasps for air. Mattie was grateful for a few moments to recuperate at the edge of town before resuming the chase. She hurt all over and felt the fatigue from so many back-to-back runs, but there was no time to relax.

"Those kids saved my life Trevor."

"Kids…as in more than one?"

"They looked like they could be twins and they were definitely Trekkers."

"Two trekkers; I don't get it!"

"They bought me some time to catch my breath; thank goodness. Are you ready?"

"I'm ready. I'm at the bottom of the path. Be careful that you don't land too far away from me. The cliff is closer than I remembered."

"I'm on my way."

Mattie could see the Interloper struggling to stand. When she was sure he could see her light trail she set another Parallel and headed towards the cliffs. He followed the stream, but was unstable on his landings and was beginning to overshoot every one of them.

"Trevor, he's really weak. You shouldn't have any trouble capturing him when I get there. He's overshooting his landings too, so I'm going to pull up short or I'm afraid he'll launch himself right over the cliff."

"Sounds good; you get out of the way when you land and leave the rest up to me."

"I'm on my last Parallel and should be there any second now."

Mattie landed ten feet in front of Trevor's hiding place. She immediately stepped to her right in case the Interloper had regained his bearings. She turned her head just in time to see him blur past her and land way beyond Trevor's location.

"He's gone by you," Mattie yelled as she ran to help, "quick…throw the net; he's too close to the edge!"

Trevor swung his head around to get a fix on where he had landed and saw him staggering towards the rim. He lunged at the Interloper and threw the net as high as he could in an attempt to cover him completely. He hoped he could draw him back away from danger, but he was too far away. The ledge began to crumble, easily pulling the Interloper further off balance. The Interloper reached out and barely grabbed the edge of the net with his wounded arm, but his momentum had already taken his upper body beyond the edge. The ground slid away beneath him. His weight and forward motion pulled Trevor to the ground, dragging him rapidly towards the rim. Trevor had to choose between trying to save the Interloper and being swept over the cliff himself. He reluctantly let go of the net. The terrible sound of the Interloper's guttural screams became more muffled as he fell further into the darkness. Within seconds the only audible sound was that of the waves crashing into the jagged rocks below. Trevor crawled back from the ledge to a safe distance. Mattie stooped down to rest her hand on his shoulder while he got his breath back.

"I'm sorry, Mattie. I really blew it."

"You did all you could, Trevor. We both did."

Trevor noticed her torn clothing and could see the blood that had seeped through the material from the road burns. "Wow, Mattie, you sure got beat up."

"It's OK. I can feel the wounds healing already. Everywhere I have a cut it feels like my skin is crawling. In fact, it feels kind of bubbly."

Mattie got up and walked over to the ledge to see if she could see the broken body below. It was so dark that she could scarcely see the white splash of the waves as they hit the craggy rocks.

"Do you think I ought to try and Parallel down to see if he's still alive?"

Trevor came up from behind her and slid his arms around her waist. "It's too dark to even see where to land, Mattie. Nobody could live through that fall anyway. We'll have to come back tomorrow and bring the police. Let's go home."

Trevor took Mattie by the hand and they started walking back to the car.

"Whoa…Trevor," Mattie stopped abruptly and knelt down on one knee, "something's wrong." She braced her elbow on her thigh and leaned her head on her hand. "I'm really dizzy and sick to my stomach."

"How's that possible? The rings were supposed to prevent that."

"I know," Mattie whispered. "I don't get it either. I feel terrible..." When she shut her eyes, she started swaying and fell against Trevor's leg.

"Mattie...!" He swept her up in his arms and carried her back up to the car as fast as could. He laid her down gently on the back seat and propped her head up with a blanket he found in the trunk.

"I'm taking you to the clinic, Mattie." There was no argument.

He turned the car around and drove to the emergency room entrance where the night attendant was wedged between a tipped chair and the building. He was half-asleep. Trevor yelled out his window to set him in motion as the car was rolling to a stop. "Hey!" The man rocked the chair back to the ground and jumped up. "Can you find me a wheelchair?"

Without acknowledgement the attendant instantly vanished through the automatic doors and by the time Trevor had lifted Mattie out of the car he had reappeared with a wheelchair.

"I feel like I'm going to throw up, Trev."

"Hang on, Mattie. This attendant will roll you inside while I get you admitted. It won't take me long. I'll come find you when I'm through."

Kash and Lila were sitting at the kitchen table catching up with each other's lives for the past ten years when the phone rang.

"Go ahead and get it, Kash. It'll be the kids."

"Hello…Mattie?"

"It's Trevor, Dad. We lost the Interloper over the edge at Blue Cliff. It was an accident. We'll have to go back in the morning with the police to extract his body from the rocks, but we've got another problem."

"What? Is Mattie alright?"

"That's the problem…we don't know what's wrong with her. She tangled with the Interloper and got banged up a bit, but the rings took care of that pretty fast. As we were leaving to go home, she got dizzy and sick to her stomach. She nearly passed out on me. We're at the clinic now. I just finished the paperwork and am going to go and look for her. The doctor should be here in a few minutes."

"The rings should have mended any kind of injury. I don't understand!"

"I don't either Dad, but she's definitely not responding to their healing properties."

Kash covered the phone and leaned towards Lila. "Mattie got hurt and Trevor's taken her to the emergency room.

Would you consider letting me take your car to Seaport? I'll bring it back tomorrow night, I promise."

"Absolutely not…" Lila said abruptly.

Kash was startled by her response. "But…"

"Not without me!"

Kash leaned his shoulder against Lila's as a silent sort of "thank you".

"Trevor…Lila and I are going to be there as soon as we can. We're leaving now."

"Thanks, Dad. Be careful. If you get too tired, be sure and pull over for a while. At this point, there's nothing any of us can do for Mattie and falling asleep at the wheel will only double our troubles."

"We'll be careful! See you in four or five hours." Kash hung up the phone and put his hand on Lila's shoulder. "Thanks, Lila. This means a lot to me and I know it'll mean a lot to the kids."

"What are families for?" she said warmly. It made her feel wonderful to be able to return the phrase. "Besides, I don't want to miss out on anything anymore, and it's the least I can do to help. I hope she'll be alright."

"Me, too." Kash pulled out Lila's chair and lifted his hand towards the garage. "I'll drive if you like."

Trevor went back in to be with Mattie until the doctor arrived.

Kash and Lila rolled into the clinic parking lot at about 5:30 A.M. There were plenty of parking spaces available so he pulled up next to the entrance and turned off the key. He reached over and nudged Lila gently to wake her up. He stepped out of the car and stretched his arms high above his head. Lila got out and shook herself all over; top to bottom and side to side. It felt good to stand up and move after riding in the car for five hours. They both inhaled a deep breath of clean, ocean air and wearily closed their doors. Kash was lost in thought as they walked up to the information desk. Lila could only imagine how worried he must be and assumed the lead.

"Could you tell us which room Mattie Karington is in please?"

A kind, elderly woman smiled warmly at Lila. Lowering her head she located a clip board with a short list of names that were hand written on a yellow piece of paper and ran her finger down it, stopping at Mattie's name.

"She's in room two across the hall."

"Thank you. Can we go in?"

"I think I'd check at the nurse's station first." She pointed to a counter that encircled a work station out in the middle of the room. Inside sat a sleepy, bored nurse who was hypnotically monitoring several electronic gadgets that bleeped and jumped sporadically in a variety of vibrant colors.

"Excuse me," Lila said quietly.

The nurse sat up, shaking her head to help her focus. "Yes?" she said pleasantly. "May I help you?"

"Would it be alright if Mattie Karington's father and I…I'm her aunt…went in to see her?"

"She's still asleep and her husband left about 20 minutes ago to go get someone. He said he'd be back in about an hour."

"Can you tell us anything about Mattie's condition?" Kash asked; his voice full of concern.

"I'm sorry, I don't know anything yet. Her tests came back before Mr. Karington left, but the doctor hasn't brought me the file yet."

Kash slumped and looked away. "I see; thank you." His tone was indifferent. "I'll wait over there then."

Disappointed, he and Lila slid some chairs together in the waiting room and stretched out in front of the TV. It wasn't long before they both fell asleep, exhausted from traveling through the night.

Trevor shook Kash's shoulder gently. "Dad, wake up; Mattie and I need to talk to you."

Kash, frowning from fatigue asked, "How long have we been asleep?"

"Maybe about an hour or an hour and a half, depending on when you got here."

Rainey sat down next to Lila. She didn't have the heart to disturb her sleep and was contented to watch her daughter for a while. She studied every new line in her face that had appeared since the last time she had seen her.

"Wake her up, Rainey. She won't want to miss this," Trevor encouraged.

Rainey timidly reached over and tapped Lila's hand with one finger. When Lila began to stir Rainey drew her fists back to her chin in anticipation. She took a sharp breath and opened her eyes wide with eagerness.

Lila blinked sleepily. She pulled her glasses from the collar of her blouse and placed them on the end of her nose. When Rainey came into a clear view Lila said, "Hello, mother," in a sweet, loving tone. Rainey burst into tears. Lila sat up and hugged her for the first time as her mother.

"Why didn't you tell me, Mom?" Lila whispered in her ear. "In many ways you felt like my mother all along. I'm happy to finally know the truth."

"There were reasons," Rainey replied; her voice quivering and cracking.

Trevor thoughtfully placed his hand on Rainey's back and said, "If you'd like to join us, Mattie and I need to talk to everyone." He tried to seem casual.

Kash's spirit dropped. That didn't look or sound like anything good to him. His eyes flickered to Rainey's and back to Trevor. He searched Trevor's eyes for some glimmer of hope.

Trevor solemnly stared at the floor; he was exhausted. Finally he stood up straight, took a deep breath and turned towards Mattie's room, motioning everyone to follow. He opened the door where Mattie was standing fully dressed and smiling.

Kash was confused. "What's going on?"

Mattie's eyes danced excitedly from person to person, settling on Kash. "Dad, do you remember telling us to be careful because you wanted grandkids someday?"

Kash nodded his head; a smile started growing.

"Well…today's the day!"

"What?" Kash felt a rush of excitement at the news and then a profound emptiness came over him. "Amber would be thrilled," he said thoughtfully. "I wish she were here."

Everyone started laughing and hugging each other.

Kash stepped over to Trevor to shake his hand. "A honeymoon baby, huh?" He smiled wryly. "I can't believe it—congratulations, son!"

"Thanks Dad. It really threw us for a loop at first. It sure does explain why the rings didn't take care of the sick feelings she was having though."

"Yes it does!"

"I should have guessed," Mattie said, shaking her head, "We weren't planning to start a family for at least two years." She gathered her things together and gave them to Kash to take back to the house with him. "Dad, we've got to locate the Interloper and then we probably ought to call the police."

"Come and get me before you call them, would you?"

"We will, Dad," Trevor promised. "Dad, would you mind driving the car back to the house? We'll use the rings to get around." He handed him the keys. "We'll be back soon."

Mattie and Trevor strolled to a secluded spot behind the clinic and boosted to Blue Cliff in an effort to finish the task of finding the Interloper's body. They approached the edge carefully so as to not crumble it further and began searching the rugged shoreline.

Mattie pointed to where the net sprawled across the rocks. "Over there! I see the net, but where's his body? I'm going down there to take a closer look."

"I'm going with you then," said Trevor.

They boosted to the flattest part of the rocks below and searched the crevasses and water inlets. Trevor gathered up the net and rolled it into a loose ball against his ribs.

"I don't see any sign of his body landing anywhere," Mattie observed. "There's not a single drop of blood on anything." She was unsettled by the lack of evidence needed to confirm that he had actually been killed.

"He was probably swept out to sea by the current and is fish bait by now."

"E-u-w-w, Trevor. That's an icky thought!"

"Yep!" Trevor grinned.

"I'm afraid we're going to face some future consequences for not finding out more about him before he died."

"Oh well, at least we won't have to try and explain anything to the police. I'm glad it's all over with, personally. Let's go home. This has been a long day already and it's barely 8:00 in the morning. Maybe we can go looking for that pocket of gold after breakfast…what do ya say?"

Mattie sighed. "We really ought to try and get settled into the house first, don't you think? Besides, I'm really tired. There'll be plenty of time to find the gold later. I'm sure it'll still be there."

Trevor raised his eyebrows in anticipation and his eyes sparkled; thinking of the possibilities. Mattie returned his excitement with a weary smile of her own. She slid next to Trevor, reaching for his hands. "Let's eat; I'm sure you're as starved as I am! *BOOST!"*

Words & Terms Dictionary

Book of Ancestors – An ancient book that contains a record of every Trekker, Splitter, and Sentinel throughout history, including all of their important missions, functions and actions they perform. It also spells out all of the rules that govern each of their destinies.

Boost – A rapid movement towards the Trekkers chosen mark that jerks both the Trekker and Splitter upward, forward and finally down to the target. The Rings of Prather Mendell are the source of power that makes the movement possible.

Divvy – A single trip (mission) back through time to correct a specific problem that was never addressed during the original time period it occurred in.

Double Down – Any shelter that has at least double depth protection from a storm, such as a two-story building or one story building with a basement; a deep cave or underground shelter.

Full-Double Parallel – A specific position formed by a Trekker and their Splitter that propels them both in a rapid movement through solid objects. It can only be performed by the rightful bearers of the Rings of Prather Mendell.

Full-Parallel – A specific position formed by a Trekkers hands and forearms that propels the Trekker in a rapid movement through solid objects. It is dangerous and life-threatening for the Trekker to perform this skill.

Half-Parallel – A specific position formed by a Trekkers hands and forearms that propels the Trekker in a rapid movement towards a stated target. There must be a clear path of air between the starting and ending point.

Interloper – An illicit time traveler that dies a little bit each time he performs a Divvy. The Rings of Prather Mendell are his only hope of surviving the Divvy's and restoring his health.

Sentinel – A relative of the Trekker that guards the historical artifacts and performs specific duties relating to his or her mission.

Soul Box – A small, brown box that contains an individual's specific DNA samples which could consist of saliva, hair or even a piece of their flesh. A fingerprint will also work since they are unique to the individual.

Splitter – A spouse or blood relative of the Trekker who possesses the ability to split time, bringing the Trekker back to the present. They possess unusual strength and stamina along with the same youthful qualities of their Trekker.

Stagma –A normal person; a human being that does not possess the ability to travel through time; non-time traveler.

Trekker – A time traveler that moves back through time using blue, glowing footprints as a portal. The footprints appear from an ancestor that is summoning the Trekker for help. This is an inheritance from a parent who passes the magical abilities and responsibilities along to only one child within each generation.

Chapter 2

The Lightning

5:00 P.M. – Back at the Picnic Meadow

C*rack!* Amber sat up with a start. She immediately glanced towards the sky. "Oh…my…gosh!" Her face distorted with panic as she dragged the picnic basket out of the way. "Wake up, Kash! Wake up! We've got to get out of here. Now! Move so I can fold the blanket. Thunderheads are forming!"

Kash rolled over, sat up and lazily glanced towards the sky. "Whoa! We'd better get going! You're not kidding! Where did they come from?"

"I don't know, just hurry!"

"How long were we asleep?"

"Only a couple of hours I thought," Amber said, panicking.

Kash glanced down at his watch. "It's 5:00! It's too dark for 5:00 in the afternoon. What happened to the clear, peaceful, pleasant day?"

"I don't know, just come on!"

An evil wind had abruptly kicked up, bringing with it massive dark clouds at an unearthly pace. By the time they reached the car the sky was almost black. Amber took the blanket and threw it in the back seat of the old Chevy. "What have we done? We're miles away from a Double-Down! What are we going to do? It'll blast right through the car and kill both of us!"

"Maybe we can find one in there?" Kash said hopefully, pointing towards the thick grouping of trees a short distance away. "Leave everything here. We'll get it later. Maybe the trees will divert the lightning until we can find one. Run for it! I'll be right behind you."

Amber immediately started running towards the forest, with the hope of finding something that might serve as a Double-Down. Before they could even reach the edge of the thicket, the clouds had transformed into indigo whirlpools that swirled towards the earth bringing with them a heavy rain, making it difficult to see.

Their two bodies darted hastily in and out of the trees at a reckless pace. "I've never seen it rain this hard—this fast," Amber yelled back towards Kash as she ran. The ground was rapidly becoming slippery, and the wind was getting stronger.

In the distance they heard another crack of thunder. The lightning was a forbidden stalker, but it did provide some illumination for the darkened, unfamiliar terrain. *Crack!* The earth shook with the sharp impact of energy. The lightning was picking up its pace and intensity as the legends had described. It was methodically marching forward; heightening the electricity in the air and was unmistakably moving towards them

in a relentless pursuit. Its mindless goal was to catch her and claim her for its own. It was her against nature and her time was running out.

In this dimension Kash was typically the one who kept her safe from these potential dangers, but he hadn't seen this one coming. After all, he was the Splitter, which gave him privileges and powers of insight, and anticipation and stamina beyond an average man. "This stinking mud is going to ruin my shoes!"

"What? Are you nuts?" Amber called back, "See if you can focus! I need your help to find me a Double-Down before it's too late."

"I'm looking, but it's hard to see through this rain," Kash yelled.

Amber's usual strong, graceful movements were becoming erratic and sloppy, as the ground grew more and more slippery. Amber was nearly 45 years old, though her bloodline would maintain her body around the age of a 25 year old for many years yet to come. Ever since she was 35 she began aging in reverse, which is typical for every Trekker until they hit 55; one of the bonuses of Inheriting.

"Can you see anything yet?" Kash called out as he recovered his balance from a misplaced step.

"Not yet," replied Amber in a raspy, breathless voice. "There's not much time left." Her wet, silky-black hair flipped from side to side, mirroring the quick sweeping movement of

her head. She anxiously scanned the densely wooded landscape for a burrow deep enough to block the lightning's attraction to her.

"What's that?" Amber whispered to herself. She squinted her eyes and strained her neck in the direction of a faint red glow that had flickered in the dark for a split second. All of a sudden there were several of them in a sequence, only a few feet apart that disappeared before she could really see what they were. "Is there someone there?" she called out.

"What?" answered Kash as he wrapped his arm around a nearby tree to help support himself during his next turn.

"Nothing…just…I just thought I saw…something," said Amber, wrinkling her brow and shaking her head with a hint of uncertainty.

The increasing wind carried less of the sound of their voices between them with each passing minute. Kash was yelling consistently now as he tried to communicate with his wife, who was running ahead of him.

"I can hardly see you, let alone a Double-Down!"

A few yards away Amber noticed a hollowed out log as she ran past it. "My only hope of survival is to find a print. You drop back. It's safer that way and at least I can move without worrying about you. Hide under that log and I'll see you when I re-enter!"

"I'm not deserting you like a coward," snapped Kash. He felt helpless about his inability to meet Amber half way in

her struggles. It wasn't that he didn't want to, he couldn't! She had to do this alone.

Kash resentfully turned his attention towards the log. When he changed direction, it was too fast for the stormy, wet conditions and he stumbled on a muddy clump of grass, losing his footing again. This time he was thrown forward, headfirst into an uncontrollable slide towards a steep drop to the jagged rocks in the deep ravine below. He started grabbing at everything he could reach, cutting his hands on the wet, sharp blades of grass and sticks as they slipped through his fingers. If he could only hang on to something solid it might stop him from being swept over the ledge. With any luck he could handle at least this situation by himself without drawing Amber's attention away from her search.

Amber was still in pursuit of the footprint that seemed less and less likely to appear. By now she had moved several yards ahead of him and was frantically scanning the ground to see if she could make the discovery before it was too late. She glanced back towards Kash and saw him sliding out of control, headed towards the cliff. She knew there might not be enough time to save him and save herself, but she couldn't stand the thought of him being hurt. Her love for him replaced her instincts for self preservation.

Kash saw that Amber had become aware of his situation.

"Don't worry about me," he yelled as he continued to slide towards the edge, "I'll be alright. You've got to find a print, before the..."

Another deafening bolt of lightning struck only a few feet away from them, muffling the rest of his words. The shock slammed Amber against an old oak tree that appeared to have been hit by lightning before. Kash's eyes grew wider as he anticipated his own impact on the rocks below at any moment.

Amber pushed herself away from the drenched, entangling shrubs and out of pure reflex she clenched her fist in a Half-Parallel, igniting a burst of energy so bright that the whole world seemed to disappear.

"To Kash," she blurted out.

Kash, having no warning, was temporarily blinded. He couldn't see anything except leftover silhouettes that created ghostly images in the darkness as his vision returned. Without any normal explanation, he came to a complete stop at his wife's feet, inches from the crumbling edge. She had appeared out of nowhere! Terror struck his heart because he knew she had wasted precious time to save him.

"Are you crazy?" Kash shouted. "Saving me could be the death of you. Go! You've got to go!"

Kash crawled back to a safe distance as Amber tried to see through the pouring rain. Out of the corner of her eye she finally spotted the familiar, bright, fluorescent-blue glow that was her ticket to safety. Her shortness of breath mirrored the shortness of time remaining and fear was beginning to raise its ugly head. The print was at least 30 feet away across a clearing, yet the ability to see one at all in the midst of the storm sparked a small glimmer of hope in her.

"I see one!" she shouted. "Maybe I can make it…"

"Hurry! The next bolt will hit you! Go!" He knew the likelihood of her reaching the print was slim if she ran for it, but maybe if she could lock in a transfer she could still make it! "Hurry Amber, hurry!"

Amber spun around and ran as fast as she could towards the footprint. She wiped the rain from her eyes so she wouldn't lose her bearings and miss the small, glowing target on the ground that was critical to hit. The wind was pushing her beyond her normal ability to run, making it very difficult to remain standing. She had positioned her arms for transfer when a blinding flash of red light filled her vision. Without warning she ran head-on into something that hadn't been there the moment before. She was knocked backward to the ground, completely out of breath with a stabbing realization that she must have only a few seconds left. As she laid there stunned in the muddy trail, she saw a pair of feet directly in front of her. Her eyes followed the long body upward until an angry, older man could be seen in full view. He had a mean laugh and was enjoying seeing her crumpled on the ground, struggling in the mud. His chiseled features had a familiar feel to her. His straight, graying hair was neatly trimmed; not a single hair out of place. When he turned his head there was a patch of pure white hair behind his left ear the shape and size of a nickel. He reminded her of her grandfather, though she couldn't recall ever really seeing him before. He was dressed in the most unusual clothing. The shimmering hue of the fabric adjusted itself to reflect his movements and the dancing light of the atmosphere that whirled and shifted around him. His countenance appeared

dark and radiated a cruel, gloomy feeling that carried the putrid odor of decaying flesh. It was as if his presence had sucked all of the oxygen out of the air, leaving nothing for her to breathe, except the stench that came from him. He appeared blurry, like he was half in her world and half in another, completely dry and untouched by the wind and rain. His arms were in a Half-Parallel, but how could that be? How would he know what a Half-Parallel was? She was the Trekker. Only she and Kash knew!

Amber heard the stranger call out, "To the print!" and another blaze of red light filled the air. Before she could sit up the stranger re-appeared over the blue, glowing footprint, threatening her only hope for survival.

"*He can see the print!*" she thought to herself, "*It's exactly as Mattie said!*"

He glared back over his shoulder one last time, positioned his arms in a different Parallel and without an ounce of regret or concern for her safety, said flippantly, "Second corridor Missy!" stepped on the print and was gone. In spite of the noise that surrounded them, both she and Kash could hear him laughing as he dissolved into the dark, swirling storm taking her last means of escape with him. There were no other prints in sight and the lightning would complete its morbid duty, striking her at any moment.

Kash began screaming, "Get up and run! Run!" though he knew it was too late.

Suddenly the storm stopped as if time stood still just for them; just for a moment. Simultaneously they rose to their feet as though they were performing a scene they had rehearsed over and over again. As they faced each other from across the clearing, the rain continued streaming down their faces. Their soaked, heavy clothing hung from their tired, torn frames. Their eyes locked on each other as a terrible silence fell over them, surrounding them in a bubble of calm. It was the "Dome of Silence" they had read about in her *Book of Ancestors*. They both thought it was a myth; a fairy tale passed down through the generations of time. It never crossed their minds that it could possibly be real!

They both knew this was the last time they would see each other and it felt like their spirits joined together in one last embrace from across the field. Kash could see the tears streaming down Amber's face, each one radiating a peculiar blue glow independent from the falling rain. He'd never seen her cry before; not once in all the years they had been married.

"I love you with all of my heart," she said in a gentle, strangely amplified voice that echoed in the still. She was oddly calm and seemingly unafraid. Her incandescent, blue eyes were on fire and Kash could see them clearly through the heavy precipitation. "Tell Mattie that I love her and I'll see her again. Teach her who she is and remember the book if you run into trouble. She is the only one left now and it must not die with her."

Kash gazed longingly at her, hoping for a miracle. "Amber…I…"

Amber interrupted him, sensing the time was short. "I'll find a way to…" Crack! A fatal bolt of yellow lightning struck Amber from behind and in a burst of green light she was gone. Gone forever!

Kash dropped to the ground. He could hardly breathe from the terror he felt inside. The storm instantly began to dissipate now that it had accomplished its deadly task. The rain slowed to a gentle, rhythmic pattern, tapping its own melody of regret on Kash's back. He felt dizzy, nauseated and completely alone as he buried his head in his hands and sobbed.

"What am I going to tell her?" he repeated to himself over and over again in a condemning mantra. "How can I explain how foolish we were to get caught in the thunderstorm? Why didn't I see it coming? This is going to kill Mattie!"

There had always been a deep bond between Mattie and her mother. They looked so much alike, and it was as though they had always shared the same consciousness in everything they ever thought or did since Mattie was old enough to walk and talk. He tortured himself with the thought that she may hate him for the rest of her life or worse, would refuse to learn who she was and what her heritage had bestowed upon her. He replayed everything in his head over and over again like a looped movie scene trying to change its horrifying outcome to a better ending, yet the reality was always the same. Amber was gone.

A throbbing pain filled his chest, his stomach knotted and his thoughts darted back and forth to a dozen questions he could hardly bare to entertain any longer. "How could this have happened? How could I have been so stupid? Why didn't she

flash to the footprint instead of running? Could she have bypassed the stranger if she had? Why was she crying? Am I dreaming? Please let this be a dream!" The reality of his living nightmare came rushing back to him. He knew it wasn't a dream. She *was* gone!

For a brief moment his thoughts returned to the deadly stranger and rage filled his heart. It was a welcome relief from the pain that engulfed him to feel the anger inside instead. Thinking of the unwelcome predator that destroyed his greatest treasure and the most amazing woman he had ever known brought a different range of emotions and strength that only comes with the distasteful desire for revenge.

Like Amber, Kash had also seen and heard the stranger and had detected a brief whiff of the sickening odor before he vanished. He would never be able to forget his face or the sound of his cold laugh as he mocked his sweet wife in her darkest hour. Disturbingly, the old man was familiar to him, too. He began searching his memory for clues as to who the deadly intruder was and how he could have appeared and disappeared so abruptly. He found nothing accessible within his experiences to answer the endless stream of haunting questions burning in his mind.

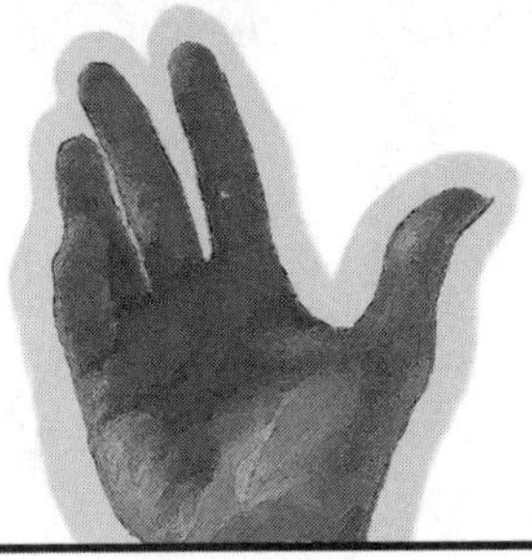

Chapter 3

The Inheritance

5:10 P.M. – Back at the Café in Benten

The last thing Mattie remembered was reaching over to place her hand on Trevor's during the best conversation she'd ever had with a guy. The hours felt like minutes as they talked about everything in their lives that had brought them together. It had even started raining, in fact, pouring as they sat under the awning, yet they were completely oblivious to the weather and everything around them. It felt as though they had always known each other. Now she was lying on the cool, hard ground, struggling to focus on what appeared to be a few people standing over her talking in hushed tones. She sensed that someone was holding her hand and supporting the back of her head. Everything was a bit blurry. As the light began to fill in the colors of clothing and people's faces again she saw the concern in Trevor's eyes as he watched her face for a sign of recovery.

"Don't move, Mattie," Trevor said kindly. "Take your time; there's no rush."

She began to realize that he was the one holding her hand and supporting her head as he knelt close to her. She felt warm inside and a sense of complete trust in him.

"What happened?"

"I don't know, Mattie. One second we were talking and the next you grabbed your head again and passed out. I laid you down on the ground so you wouldn't fall and hurt yourself. You've only been out for a few seconds."

"I dreamed something or saw something in my head like before."

"Before?" Trevor was confused.

"Yes. Something's happened to my parents. My father's alone somewhere in the forest. He's hurt and he needs my help."

"Do you feel like you can sit up, Mattie?"

"I think so." Mattie sat up and tried to remember if her parents had said where they were taking her on the picnic. It was going to be a surprise for her; somewhere that was special to them since they used to take her there when she was a little girl.

"Come on, Mattie. Let me take you home." Trevor helped her up to the chair, "I'll go get my car; stay here. Will you be alright?"

"Sure…sure," she stuttered. "Thank you." After Trevor left, Mattie noticed her fingers were beginning to tingle. When she looked down at her hands, they were surrounded with a glowing blue light. She glanced around to see if anyone else was watching. When it started raining everyone went inside, except one of the waitresses who remained to clear a table on

the other side of the patio. Mattie stuffed her hands into her pockets, shoved the chair back sharply with her legs and started running. The further she went the further the blue glow moved up her arms towards her head. She didn't know what was happening, but she knew she didn't want Trevor to see any more of the freak show than he'd already seen in one day.

It was strangely dark and had been raining unseasonably hard for such a mild afternoon so there was scarcely anyone in the streets, which helped her get back home without being noticed. By the time she walked into the house her whole body was surrounded by a fluorescent blue glow and her eyes were as bright as flood lights. She felt strong and powerful like she had never felt before. As she stared at herself in the mirror the glow that surrounded her body popped to a bright white light and then stopped instantly. It was gone!

"What on earth?" Mattie shook her head in disbelief as she slumped down in her favorite chair by the fireplace in her bedroom. "Well, I guess that'll be the last time I ever see him," she said to herself sadly, feeling stupid inside. She thought about how wonderful he was and how completely crazy she had been. If first impressions meant anything, she knew she'd never see him again.

8:00 P.M. – Somewhere Near the Forest

Kash lay in a heap where he had last seen Amber; soaked, bleeding and lost in a swirl of thoughts that were paralyzing him. He had lost all track of time. With great effort

he managed to stumble back to the car where he fell asleep in the front seat for several hours. Finally, he woke up still dazed, peering through the rain splattered windows to the stars that were now shining brightly through the clear night sky. He struggled to stay awake as he drove home to Benten. Kash drifted into the driveway, finally jerking to a stop.

Mattie saw the headlights through the living room window where she had been pacing all night, waiting for her parents to return. She threw the front door open and called out from the porch. "Dad! Where have you been? It's two in the morning!" Mattie hurried over to the car, "Where have you been? Dad?"

"Mattie…I…a-a-a-a…"

"What's wrong Dad? Where's Mom? Why are your clothes all muddy and torn?" She reached through the window to help support his head. "What happened, Dad?"

"She's gone."

Mattie wiped the dirt from her father's cheek with her sleeve. "Who's gone?"

"The lightning…"

"The lightning's gone?" said Mattie with a puzzled expression on her face.

Kash rolled his head towards Mattie and hung his arm out the window, "It took her!"

"You're not making any sense, Dad. Let's get you inside." She carefully opened the door and pulled him out of the car. He kept mumbling something about a red light and footprints. "Come on Dad, you've got to help me get you inside; I can't carry you by myself."

They stumbled into the house and up the stairs towards his bedroom before she collapsed under his weight on the rug at the foot of his bed.

"Get up, Dad! You have to help me!"

Kash was unconscious and there was no way she could get him into his bed alone. She did her best to remove most of his wet clothes, placed a pillow gently underneath his head and covered him with a quilt. Then, she went back out to the car to see if she could find any clues as to where her mother was. All she found was the smashed in window, a picnic basket, and the blanket in the back seat. She also noticed a faint odor of chocolate. She took the leftovers inside and went back out to pull the car into the garage before "old lady Schnettle" began her early morning snoop around the neighborhood. She had always been a source of trouble for the family and took every opportunity she could find to discredit Amber. She was such a jealous old bitty.

She paced the floor for another hour or so as her mind raced with concern for her mother. She didn't know where her mother was or what had happened to her father. Unexpectedly, a warm, peaceful feeling came over her as though someone was telling her that everything would be alright. She checked

on her father one more time and was finally able to lie down and fall asleep herself.

Her dreams carried her fretfully through the events of the day. Each time she reached the part at the café where she had felt a sharp pain in her eyes she would flash from her experiences to what appeared to be her parent's experiences during the same time frame. She was living everything through her mother's eyes until there was nothing left to see anymore. Each time she arrived at the abrupt end of the information she became upset and would wake up. She laid in bed trying in vain to figure out what it all meant until she fell back to sleep, only to start the dream sequence again. She saw the red footprint in town, the chocolate powder on the stick shift; the crumpled tape on the floor and the mean elderly man in the forest that disappeared over a blue footprint. This happened in three separate dreams; each becoming more detailed than the one before, painting a clearer picture of how all the pieces fit together.

Morning finally arrived and with it came an awful feeling of loss for Mattie as she awoke. All she wanted to do was ask her father a million questions. She remembered that she had left her father on the floor and immediately jumped out of bed to go check on him. She threw her robe on and ran into her parents' room. Her father was nowhere to be found.

"Dad," she called out. "Where are you? Dad?"

She ran from room to room, fearing that he had fallen somewhere and couldn't respond since he was so weak the last time she saw him. As she was leaving the kitchen she noticed

the refrigerator was angled slightly forward away from the wall. *"That's strange. Who'd pull out the refrigerator like that?"* she thought. As she drew closer she could see a small opening behind it and could faintly hear a muffled voice repeating something over and over again, but couldn't quite make it out. She wedged her body between the fridge and the wall, expecting that she would need a lot of leverage to push it open further. To her surprise it glided easily away from the wall, revealing a small doorway that led down a set of winding stairs. As she crept quietly down the steps the chant became clearer though a bit slurred.

"By bloodline you're destined, by marriage we're tied; let the strength of our love bring you back to my side. By bloodline you're destined...."

"Dad?" Mattie called out as she recognized her fathers' voice. "Dad...what are you doing? What...is...what is this place?"

She glanced around the dimly lit room while her eyes were adjusting to the light. What she saw was the strangest thing she had ever seen. The room was draped with beautiful, full, dark blue velvet curtains that covered every wall. The ceiling was painted in the same deep blue and was covered with jewels that resembled twinkling stars; smattered from edge to edge. In the center of the room there was a platform that was surrounded by a plush, burgundy rug. On the platform she could see her father wedged tightly inside of an elaborately carved, three-sided box where he stood, slumped and tired; repeating the chant over and over again. His bare feet were placed exactly

over a pair of metal footprints that were shaped perfectly to match them. The interior was lined with satin cushions that were sown in a diamond cut pattern. The open face of the box was bordered by two brass bars on either side and reinforced by heavy rubber sleeves that connected them to the floor and ceiling. Another thick rubber pad covered the top edge of the box itself where her father's forearms rested for support and acted as a buffer between surfaces. Mattie could see that her father had been holding onto the bars so tightly that the blood had been forced out of his knuckles, leaving them as white as powdered bone. Directly facing him was another such box with porcelain footprints and white satin cushions, except it was empty. Mattie could hear him quietly repeating the same phrase, "By bloodline you're destined, by marriage we're tied; let the strength of our love bring you back to my side."

She approached Kash slowly, quietly, and without hesitation she reached up to gently place one of her hands on top of his.

"No, Mattie!" Kash yelled out with what little strength he had left in him. "Don't touch me!" His warning came too late. The moment she touched him a burst of energy started from out of their hands, warping the air flow. Tiny, silver strands of light bound both of them tightly to the bar. The particles formed a beam that swirled outward, completely filling every crevice, every fabric, every inch of the previously dimly lit room. When it felt like it was impossible that it could get any brighter the light was drawn inward towards the empty box. It outlined the shape of a person that grew clearer and more formed with every passing second. The blue box began pulsing with a bluish

light that illuminated her father as he began to stand tall and strong. His face began to beam with its own energy and he appeared to be growing younger in years. Mattie tried to let go of the grip, but couldn't. Her hand felt like it had melted into her fathers' and the bar appeared to have turned to glass. She was terrified, but couldn't get away. When she looked back toward the white box she could see that it was her mother that was forming out of the white light. She was hovering within it as though she were made of extremely fine particles of light herself. The sight of her mother brought a sense of peace, reminding her of the feeling that had come over her during the night.

"Amber," Kash said excitedly. "Is that you?"

Amber smiled lovingly. She appeared to be happy and content. Her lips were forming words; still the room remained completely silent. She was repeating the same words over and over again, but neither Mattie nor Kash could make them out. Finally, she clasped her hands together over her heart as if to say, "I love you both" and immediately began to fade.

"Don't go…" he whispered. "Please don't go!"

Suddenly, Mattie got another sharp pain behind her eyes. "Dad…my gosh, Dad…what's happening?" Her mother's entire life started playing like a fast forwarded, three-dimensional movie that was being projected on the tiny particles that still remained. She saw cities and times of the world that had long since passed away. She felt the pain and joy of people she didn't even know. Curiously, her compassion for all those strangers and their struggles burrowed deeply within her soul.

She could see a thousand scenes that were all changing because of her mother's presence. She saw her grandfather, his mother and on and on as each generation of her ancestors produced a single representative to carry on the unusual inheritance. She felt the love, support and guidance they all had towards her mother in a whole host of unexplainable dangers that surrounded her on every journey. Her mother's knowledge, experiences, joys, fears, struggles and beliefs filled her up and blended with her own as each generation had done before her. Mattie felt as though she was connected to all of them and had a clear understanding of each person that was in her mother's line and it seemed like there was no beginning to them.

Then she knew! She was like them! Everything was clear to her and every event made sense. She had a full recollection of her mother's journeys for the past 10 years and felt every emotion her mother had experienced. An overwhelming feeling of appreciation and admiration welled up inside of her as she saw her father, at great physical cost, 'split' time for her mother to return to the present after each Divvy. They were a team! They did things that couldn't be explained to anyone; not even Mattie, until now.

The light began to dim and she felt her hand separate from her fathers. She noticed he was changing back to his old self except he was aging beyond his normal appearance. It was as though he was gaining a year for every second that passed. When the room finally became still, Kash reflected his true age of 45. He typified a weary, middle-aged gentleman rather than the vibrant, young man of 25 that Mattie was used to.

Mattie wasn't sure she could take any more. The experience left her feeling extremely weak herself as though she had lost two straight nights of sleep. She moved in close to her father and helped him out of the box.

"It's called a Time-Keeper, Mattie!"

"What is, Dad?"

"The box," Kash said as he moved sadly away from the footprints, "and I'll never enter it again. She's gone isn't she, Mattie?"

"I think so, Dad, but I'm not sure. I can't believe how amazing you are Dad and what wonderful things you and Mom did for thousands of people."

They stumbled up the staircase together. Mattie helped Kash sit down for a moment while she went to turn off the lights in the secret room. She slid the refrigerator snugly against the wall and went back to help Kash up.

"You shouldn't have Inherited yet, Mattie. You're way too young and you don't have your own Splitter yet. I don't know how much you learned through your transition. I don't even know if there will be a limit to your powers or not until you reach the proper age. You weren't supposed to Inherit for another 17 years."

"Come on, Dad. You need to lie down and we'll sort all of this out later. I've got to sleep, too… I'm so tired. Is this how it was for you and Mom every time she Divvied?"

"Yes. However the recovery time is quite short in comparison to what you would think. By the time we get upstairs you'll be completely recovered, or at least you should be. I don't know what will be different with you now."

"What about you," Mattie asked. "Won't you recover fast, too?"

"Not anymore," he said with a tone of regret in his voice, "not anymore!"

Chapter 4

The Unexpected Divvy

"I don't understand why we can't stay here anymore," Mattie said as she threw herself on top of the overstuffed suitcase; compressing it enough to zip it shut. "Nobody knows anything about what's happened here and we'll only look guilty if we leave now."

"You don't understand, Mattie. We won't be able to explain your mother's disappearance to our friends and her sister; not to mention Fran's nose for trouble. We'll be in over our heads," Kash tried to convince her.

"No one believes old lady Schnettle anymore. She's started so many rumors with so many people that she hasn't got a shred of credibility left. You know that, Dad!"

"I do know that, but we can't take any chances. If the police search our house, and you know they'll have to if your mother comes up missing, they'll find the time keeper. We can't allow that to happen."

"So what are we going to do…just disappear?"

"We have no choice, Mattie!"

"Are we going to burn down the house and everything in it?"

"No, of course not! I'm going to give the house to your Aunt Lila and we're going to move to the coast."

"Aunt Lila?"

"Yes, and we'll tell her that you've been accepted into Stanford and have to leave right away to get you into the next term or maybe... oh, I don't know what I'll say. I'll think of something."

"Why, Aunt Lila?" Mattie questioned.

"Because she always wanted this house after your grandparents disappeared ten years ago. She thought it should have been hers anyway, since she was the oldest. Lila was pretty bitter about the fact that the old house had been willed to your mother. She never understood why your grandparents would do that to her and she's never forgiven us for accepting it," her father explained.

Mattie pushed the suitcase aside and sat down on the edge of the bed. "So, that's why she stopped talking to us. I never could figure out why she disappeared from our lives. She was always my favorite aunt, too. Gosh, I haven't seen her since I was nine."

"She's never had a place of her own and since she's still working down at the library; it'll be perfect. I can't think of

anyone I'd rather have this house other than her. I'll seal up the wall behind the refrigerator and block off the tunnel. We'll leave tonight."

"Tunnel…what tunnel?" Mattie asked, but was side tracked by a knock on the door. Mattie's eyes became fixed on her dad. She stood breathlessly silent, not knowing what to do.

"I'll get it," whispered Kash. "You keep packing."

Kash crept quietly down the staircase hugging the wall, making a concerted effort not to be seen through the sheer curtains that covered the small glass panes of the front door. As he drew closer he could see a man on the porch pacing back and forth, nervously talking to himself as he marched. The man turned abruptly towards the door again and knocked. Kash jumped into the living room to get out of sight. He couldn't tell whether it was the police or not, but he didn't want to take any chances. To his surprise the man started calling out for Mattie.

"Mattie, answer the door! I know you're in there…answer the door! I'm not leaving until you talk to me! Mattie!"

Kash couldn't afford to have the neighbors become aware of the scene that was playing out on his front porch. He hurried over to the door, trying to collect his thoughts and gain some composure before opening it. He opened it at a slow, cautious pace as to not arouse suspicion.

"Can I help you, young man?" Kash said as calmly as he could. He didn't know who the man was, but he could see

that he had a kind face that revealed a few gentle character lines of concern.

"Yes sir. I'm Trevor Karington," the young man said politely. "I wonder if I could talk to your daughter." He shifted his weight nervously from side to side as if he could hardly bear standing still for even a moment.

"I'm sorry, Mr. Karington. Mattie isn't taking any visitors today. She's busy packing for school and doesn't have a lot of time to spare right now."

"Packing for school? What school? Where? What do you mean?" The frustration began to show on Trevor's face as he awaited an explanation. After all, he was in the same Ancient Civilizations class for students last term where he was sure she had given him the "come hither" look; the look that made his heart leap inside. Long before that, in their senior year of high school, he became intrigued with her when he saw her chew out a fellow classmate for trying to steal answers off of her paper during a test. To his surprise and delight, she fearlessly popped the guy on the side of his head with her opened hand and stared straight into his eyes until he turned and walked away. At that moment, he knew she was the girl for him. He'd never seen that much passion in a woman before and after such an incredible afternoon with her yesterday he couldn't lose her now!

Kash, sensing the young man's increasing frustration, moved back a couple of steps into the house. "Look, young man…this just isn't a good time! I'll tell her you came by. Good

day!" Being the gentleman he was, he courteously bowed his head and began to close the door.

Trevor stuttered a few "but...Sirs" and at the last second thrust his foot forward, stopping the door from closing.

Kash was torn between two camps of thought. His first inclination, though very short lived, was to admire the tenacity of this total stranger who was obviously smitten with his daughter. It was no mystery to him why this boy would be so taken with Mattie's spunk and beauty; all the boys were, though this one was obviously different because he had some spunk himself! Yet, as far as Kash was concerned, no man could ever really be worthy of what his precious daughter was destined to become which led him to his main reaction. His next thought was more of a feeling of outrage at the audacity this *kid* had to push his way inside his house. "What do you think you're doing, boy?" Kash snapped as he lowered his shoulder into the door to force it shut.

Trevor automatically lowered his shoulder into the door in response and started pushing back with all he had. Being young and strong, Trevor immediately had the strength advantage and Kash was starting to lose ground. However, Kash, being experienced with strategic moves through years of Splitting, released some of his pressure against the door, throwing Trevor completely off balance. Then, to Trevor's surprise, Kash threw his entire weight back into the door, jamming the edge into Trevor's forehead, opening a small cut above his eyebrow. Trevor fell back against the door frame and blood began flying all over the place. For some reason that

struck Kash as funny and, unable to resist, he blurted out a couple of hearty chuckles, which made Trevor absolutely determined that the *old guy* was not going to get the best of him. He groped backwards with his foot, trying to find a stronghold to push against for balance. Finally, he found the corner of the footboard, which gave him the leverage he needed to push back, and caught Kash off guard this time. The powerful response smacked the edge of the door squarely into Kash's knee. Kash let out a loud yelp, grabbed his knee, and lifted it towards his chest in pain while hopping up and down on his good leg. Without the opposing pressure on the door it flew open with the weight of Trevor still on it. Trevor's body angle continued to fling him forward, out of control, toppling them both to the floor. Trevor found himself face down on top of Kash who was still writhing in pain. Blood was pumping out of the minute cut over his eye, making it appear as though his whole head was split open. Kash also looked like he was bleeding from somewhere because there was so much blood on everything.

Kash tried to push Trevor off to the side, but was too tangled up with him. "Get…off…me…boy!" he grunted as he continue to try and free himself.

Hearing all of the commotion downstairs, Mattie came running from her room. She appeared at the top of the staircase with a boot in her hand. "What on earth is going on down there?" At first glance, all she could see was an entanglement of arms and legs everywhere, covered with splatters of blood. Her fight and flight instincts took over. She threw the boot at the man that was on top of her father, ran down the stairs until

she was within jumping distance and dove head first onto Trevor's back. The weight of her body knocked the wind out of both men whose priority turned immediately to gasping for air. Mattie started kicking her bare feet in hopes of landing a lucky hit anywhere that might count.

"Get your toe out of my ear!" Trevor yelled as he blocked Mattie's other foot from landing a stunning blow to his already damaged face, "Mattie…it's me…Trevor!"

Mattie stopped moving immediately. She was horrified by her behavior and thought she was going to die of embarrassment. Never before had she wished this hard for a hole close enough to climb into and disappear. It took some effort to untangle everyone from the knotted mess they had become in the confusion. One by one they sat back on the floor, facing each other in a daze. No one spoke for several seconds.

Finally Mattie broke the silence. "What are you doing here?"

Trevor spoke quickly, "What school is he talking about?"

Kash blurted out immediately, "You've got nerve, boy!" then dropped his head back and burst into laughter. He could see himself in this spirited young man and for a moment completely forgot about the predicament they were in. The unpredictable behavior of Kash started Mattie and Trevor laughing which continued until all three of them were rolling on the floor, wiping away the tears.

"Dad," Mattie sputtered between laughs, "this is Trevor Karington. Trevor, this is my father, Kash Bott."

"Yes," both Kash and Trevor said simultaneously, "we've met."

Mattie sat up again with renewed composure. "Now what?"

"Go get something to clean up this mess and our messy guest, too." Kash pointed to the living room and offered Trevor a chair. "See if you can keep from bleeding all over my couch until Mattie can get you cleaned up."

Trevor pressed the palm of his hand tightly over the cut, crawled over to the staircase and sat down on the steps. "This will be fine, sir."

"You've come at a bad time son."

"I can see that, sir, but I…something happened to Mattie yesterday and I care for your daughter, sir."

"Yes, I can see you do and that's unfortunate. You're just going to have to get over her; because we're moving!"

"Where? Why?" Trevor was visibly upset at the news.

Kash stood up and casually brushed off his slacks with the back of his hand. "I don't see that it's any of your business, young man."

Trevor immediately stood up to face Kash, "I'm making it my business, sir, whether you like it or not! I can't help

myself!" He threw his hands up and said, "She's all I can think about. I can't get her off of my mind!"

Kash squinted in a sudden rush of irritation and grabbed Trevor by the collar with the intention of throwing him out of his house, again. When he yanked him in close, almost nose to nose, he could see Trevor's puzzled face which brought back a flood of memories about his own experiences when he was dating Amber. The signs and symptoms were obvious and Kash's instincts revealed to him that Trevor was destined to be Mattie's Splitter. He released his grip. "My boy…you're in for quite a ride."

"Sir?" Trevor's face was displaying fluctuating signs of bewilderment, frustration, confusion and love sickness, all rolled into one.

"Never mind," Kash said, dangling a new tone in his voice that carried the sound of compassion and humor. "If you want to go with us, you need to go pack your bags; we leave tonight. I hope you're ready for 'Mr. Toad's wild ride!'"

"Do you really mean that, sir?"

"Well…do you want to go with us or not?"

Trevor stammered excitedly, "Yah…yes…I do."

"Then go get your things. We have to hurry!"

Mattie entered the room in time to see Trevor trip over his own feet as he ran out the front door. She dropped the tray

on the coffee table and snapped, "What did you say to him, Dad?"

"I told him that…"

"You had no right to drive him away…"

"…that he should…"

"I love him, Dad, and you just ruined my life…"

"…that he should go and get packed…"

"I don't know if I can ever forgive you for…"

"…because he's going with us."

Mattie froze with astonishment. "What?"

"Close your mouth, Mattie, there's a fly in the house." Kash chuckled softly to himself. "We don't have a lot of time to prepare ourselves for the trip. Let's get back to work, OK?" He went into the garage to get the plaster and paint while Mattie stood by herself in the living room in disbelief.

"Hey, Mattie!" Kash called to her from inside the garage. "Don't just stand there; you've got to finish packing!"

Mattie shook her head side-to-side gently as a smile slowly widened across her face. She darted towards the staircase, springing up three steps at a time in excitement to get back to her room. "Pack, pack, pack…" she said happily, anxious to return to the task that was utterly depressing only ten minutes earlier. The split second before her foot planted

itself on the top step, a blue, glowing footprint appeared out of nowhere. Mattie wouldn't know what it meant even if she had seen it. Her foot touched down squarely on the print and she disappeared.

Kash was unaware that Mattie had been swept into a divvy and continued to the kitchen to close the opening to the chamber. He worked diligently all morning to fill in the passageway. By early afternoon he was ready to paint. It was time to take a break and go visit with Lila before she left the library. If he could catch her at the library she would have to talk to him in a calm, rational manner because of her surroundings. If he waited until she got off work she would never talk to him no matter what he had to say.

Kash slipped his overalls down to his ankles and kicked them off in a pile near the front door. "Mattie," Kash yelled up to her, "I'm going to go and talk to Lila. I'll be back in an hour. I'll grab us something to eat on the way back." He picked up the deed to the house and left, without waiting for an answer.

Chapter 5

The Library

Kash stood at the bottom of the curved cement staircase, rehearsing the speech he had sketched out in his mind on the way over. As he faced the oversized double doors that had welcomed its curious visitors for over 100 years he remembered Amber telling him what a strange, magnetic lure those same doors had for her all of her life. The red brick, two-story building boasted its time in existence through the original colonial design and proudly displayed the name of its benefactor etched in a granite plaque posted over the doors: Davis L. Graham Public Library.

He felt a twinge of anxiety when he thought about facing Lila again after all these years; especially in her own territory. Lila was adopted by Amber's parents three months after they became pregnant with Amber. She had a naturally kind disposition and a love for beautiful things. The weight of a good ring on every single one of her fingers was essential for her to live a happy life. She and Amber were best friends as they grew up. Seldom did anyone see the one without the other. She had lived with her parents until they vanished ten years ago. When Lila heard that Amber got the house in the Will, she refused to live within a mile of either of them. Kash and Amber had even offered to build her a brand new home of her own

at the far end of the property, but, the angry feelings of resentment were already in place.

Kash timidly started up the stairs, trying to remember what Lila looked like so he wouldn't appear unsure of himself when he met her again. The last time he saw her she had auburn hair, large, gentle eyes (one blue and one green) that always appeared to be half closed; and a perpetual smile that never left her face. She was what Amber used to call "a sweet petite!" She was smart and clever which always intimidated the suitors that came calling over the years and by Ambers' recollection, there were plenty of them. Some had become quite prominent citizens in the community and state, like Judge Whipple. He'd still marry her to this day, but a good book had always been her lover and she had been content to read in her solitude as the years slipped by. She was highly educated and had accumulated three different advanced degrees by the age of thirty. Her uncanny knack for details was phenomenal. Many of the professors in the history department at Benten College considered her a genius and would often request her insight into various events throughout history that were unclear. The locals affectionately referred to her as "Professor Graham" though she had never officially earned the title.

He swung open one of the big double doors and stepped into the lobby where his eyes lifted towards the small domed ceiling inside. He had forgotten how exquisite the gold leaf core of the dome was and how richly carved the dark rosewood walls were. The library was filled with the sweet hint of orange oil that glistened on the walls and mixed lusciously with the smell of a fresh pot of licorice tea steeping in the office. The

round room offered four doorways to choose from. The door to his left led into a children's book section with colorful pictures, large letters and simple inspirational sayings thoughtfully placed on the walls to stimulate the imagination of children. The next door opened into the main part of the library, which was a magnificent two story room. The wall on the far end was mostly covered by full length windows that rippled with numerous flaws in the handmade panes of glass. The windows were framed by large wooden staircases on either side that lead to the open balcony above. A plush, red runner flowed up through the middle of the winding stairs and seemed to call out "come and see." The balcony was supported by large, wooden pillars and lined by a beautifully hand carved railing that guarded its patrons as they perused through the many colorful books of all shapes and sizes. On the main floor there were free standing bookshelves placed strategically through the middle of the great room with tables, couches and a few standing plants scattered amongst them. The room was well lit by chandeliers and the dark green carpet gave an earthy quality to the room, creating a warm, inviting atmosphere. The third door was more like a vault and had a locking bolt on it the size of Kash's arm. It appeared as though it was part of the original construction that was present the day the building was dedicated over a century ago. It gave the impression that it was built to keep out giants. Kash briefly wondered what could possibly be behind a door that would warrant such a huge bolt, and then finally turned his attention to the last door which lead into the librarian's office where he was sure Lila would be.

His throat was dry and scratchy. He moved hesitantly into the office and stepped up to the counter. An older, heavy set woman, gnawing on a donut, approached him with her nose still in her book. Her mousy-grey hair was peppered with strands of auburn remnants of years gone by and her glasses sat on the end of her nose reflecting the reverse image of the words in the book she was reading.

"May I help you?" she said in a hushed, pleasant voice; her face still in her book.

"Yes…thank you. I'm looking for Lila Graham. Is…is she here?" Kash stammered.

"You're looking at her. What do you need?"

Kash lost all train of thought and stood silent. He didn't even recognize her. Lila briefly glanced at him over the top of her glasses and returned to her book. "Well…what do you…" Her face lost its kindly expression. She became silent, too. Slowly lowering her book to the counter, she drew her eyebrows down over the top of her large blue and green eyes like a great, dark wall. With her head still down, she lifted her gaze directly into Kash's and said firmly, "Get—out!"

"Lila, I just need a minute of your time." Kash whispered, rushing his words. He could see Lila's face turning a brighter shade of red by the second.

"You've got nerve coming in here after all these years," she said in a low, growling tone. "If I weren't trapped here behind this desk with witnesses floating around in the library,

I'd be throwing everything I could get my hands on at you right now."

"Lila, I…"

"Get out, Kash. We have nothing to say to each other." Lila dropped her donut and picked up the biggest book she could lift. She raised it above her shoulder as if she actually considered risking her position as head librarian to have the pleasure of striking her brother-in-law over the head.

Kash pulled the deed out of his pocket and slammed it down on the counter top. "The house is yours!" he blurted out as he shielded himself with his other arm in anticipation of being hit.

Lila lowered the book to the counter and reached for the deed. "Oh, shoot!" She had accidentally set it on what was left of her donut, making her even more irritable. She picked up the book, pealed the donut away from the cover and flung it in the garbage. While she wiped the book off with a tissue she glanced through the document, searching for indications of authenticity. "Is this real, or just another one of your underhanded lies and what do you want?"

"Yes…no…and nothing," Kash responded. "You can move in tonight if you like. We'll be gone." He realized he was talking without any forethought. He also realized he was about to miss a golden opportunity to get something out of this rather than just giving up the house. He lowered his arm, straightened himself up and said softly, "Amber and I have always felt bad about how things turned out with the Will. We

wanted to share the estate with you and now feel like we have a way to do that. We'll take the old house on the coast and fix it up for us and you can take the house here in Benten."

Lila's body language began to soften and her eyes started to water. She was overwhelmed at such an offer.

"Lila, I…a-a-a…" Kash didn't know what to say. Crying women had always made him feel awkward. He never did know what to do in the presence of a weeping woman. Unfortunately, he had never had an occasion to practice his 'sobbing female chit-chat" technique since neither of the women in his life ever cried. Obviously the house meant more to her than he had realized. He felt uncomfortable and out of place.

She reached into her pocket and pulled out a lacy, white linen handkerchief and blotted her eyes. She cleared her throat and asked crisply, "Where's Amber? Why isn't she here to do this?"

"Oh…a…," Kash was caught off guard by the question and stumbled through his words. "She…uh…uh…is…had to meet with a…a contractor about fixing up the beach house and um….had to leave unexpectedly this morning."

He could hear for himself how ridiculous he sounded, yet it was the best he could do since he was making it up as he went and had never liked lying anyway.

Lila raised an eyebrow suspiciously. Her eyes dropped back down at the deed. "How can I move in tonight if you haven't even moved out yet?"

Kash swallowed hard as he stalled for time to think. "Um-m…Amber said you deserved everything in the house that Mom and Dad owned since you never claimed anything when your parents disappeared. After we get the structure secured on the beach house, we'll find some furniture up there for…and…um…" He shook his head in frustration. "We'll be fine. We'll pack our clothes and personal belongings and get out of your hair."

Lila was smart and instinctively knew something wasn't right, but her desire for the old house was overriding her reason. "Fine, but this doesn't mean we're friends again. Do you have the keys with you?"

"*Oh-h-h, no-o-o…*" Kash thought, "*This story is getting me into trouble.*" He fumbled through his pockets as if he was trying to find them. "I guess I left them on the table in my excitement to bring you the news."

"Likely story," remarked Lila. "You're not telling me the whole truth are you?"

"I assure you that the house is yours, Lila. If we're not there when you're able to come over, I'll…we'll leave the keys under the pot on the front porch for you."

"Alright—I'll be over later on tonight after I close up the library," Lila said forcefully. "Tell Amber I want her to come and see me before she goes. The library closes at eight."

Kash was flustered by her final words. "I …will" he said hesitantly. "Take care, Lila." Kash turned to leave when

he heard Lila sniffling quietly behind him as he walked towards the exit.

"Thank you," she said under her breath, barely loud enough for Kash to catch it.

Kash turned around and caught Lila's eye. He smiled, nodded his head as if to say "you're welcome" and left.

"What an idiot!" he mumbled to himself as he bounded out the door and down the front steps. "That was pathetic!"

Kash shoved the car door closed with his foot since both hands were occupied with lunch bags. When he got to the porch a squeak from the far end drew his attention. Trevor was stretched out on the swing, leisurely rocking himself. One foot was propped up on the seat and the other rhythmically pushed away from a tattered travel trunk that sat on the floor in front of him. It was covered with stickers that represented different countries from all over the world.

"Wow, apparently you've traveled a bit." Kash said before stuffing the edge of one of the bags between his teeth, freeing up one hand to open the door.

"Yeah! My dad was in the Air Force. I grew up all over the world. I love to travel."

"Good thing. You're going to be doing a lot of that from now on!" Trevor was puzzled by his comment. Kash

hurried and changed the subject. "What are you doing out here anyway? You should be inside helping Mattie!"

"She wouldn't answer the door, sir. I rang the bell and called several times. I thought maybe you both had stepped out to grab a bite to eat or something."

"Huh…wonder why she didn't answer the door?" Kash motioned to Trevor to come in. He tossed the bags on the coffee table in the living room. "What do your parents think about you coming with us?" he called back, straight arming the swinging door to the kitchen; holding it open while he listened for Trevor's answer.

"They were transferred to Germany last year. I've been on my own ever since."

"That'll be convenient!"

"Pardon me, sir?"

"Nothing! Never mind!" He stretched his neck towards the ceiling, calling out for Mattie to come down for lunch. He didn't hear a response so he called out again, "Mattie! Come and eat!"

"With your permission, Mr. Bott, would it be alright if I check to see if Mattie's up there?"

"Have you had anything to eat, son?"

"Yes. Thank you, sir."

"Her room's at the top of the stairs. Tell her I have lunch waiting for her."

Trevor rushed up the stairs, excited to see her again. After checking every room on the top floor he returned without her. "She must be out back. I'll check out there."

"Good idea," Kash responded as he went back into the kitchen to get some drinks and was reminded of the wall he had left unfinished. He poured some paint in the pan and thought he'd try to roll a quick coat over the patched area before Trevor came back in. He could hear Trevor calling for Mattie as he stepped out the back door and moved around the yard. Trevor headed towards the old shed in the far corner of the property. Within a few minutes Kash had finished rolling a hasty coat of paint across the new portion of the wall when Trevor burst through the kitchen door.

"I can't find her anywhere, Mr. Bott. Could something have happened to her? She passed out on me yesterday and was disoriented when she came to. Could she have…" The expression on Kash's face stopped Trevor short in mid-sentence. "What?" Trevor reacted; his level of panic increasing. Kash turned pale and plopped down into a chair by the table. Trevor's voice grew louder, "What?"

"Oh…my…gosh; she won't have any idea what happened to her or what to do to get back to us. How on earth am I ever going to fix this one?" Kash covered his face with his hands. He was sickened by the realization that Mattie had divvied without an understanding about how it all worked. She would be caught in a different time frame, within the space of

the house, completely at a loss as to what had taken place and what she needed to do to return. "If I had only taken five minutes to prepare her for this type of catastrophe this would never have happened. Now I've lost them both!"

Trevor was completely confused, which was beginning to be somewhat of a routine for him. "What do you mean…lost them both?"

Kash could hear the rising alarm in Trevor's' voice. "Think, Kash, think…" he said to himself as he began tapping his forehead with his index fingers.

"What's going on? Where's Mattie?" Trevor questioned anxiously.

"Give me a minute boy, and I'll tell you what I can. Please sit down and be quiet for a while. I need to think!"

Chapter 6

The Jingle

Mattie had no idea what had taken place as she continued her dance on into her bedroom. She was ecstatic that Trevor was coming along. When she entered her bedroom what she saw stopped her cold. The smile that stretched ear to ear disappeared from her face instantly. Every bit of the luggage was gone and in fact, the entire room had been rearranged. Her favorite dolls covered the foot of her bed like they used to when she was a little girl. There were pictures hanging on the mirror that appeared to be painted by a child. She walked over to the closet and threw back the doors to find it full of children's clothing, shoes, and toys. Someone in the hall began humming the tune to a song that her mother always used to sing as she busily cleaned the house. Her heart started pounding harder and faster.

"Mom?" she called out expectantly.

"Mattie Pie…is that you in there? What are you doing home so soon? Where's your Dad?"

Mattie couldn't believe her ears. It was her mother! Only her parents called her Mattie Pie. In her excitement she leapt into the hallway outside to see if it was true. Amber stood up at the same time Mattie appeared and they both let out a scream.

Amber reached for the broom that was leaning against the banister and her face turned fierce as though she were a mother in battle to protect her child. "I don't know who you are, young lady, but you better get your fanny out of my house before I get close enough to use this on it."

Now Mattie was really perplexed. She blinked her eyes several times in disbelief. Why would her own mother talk to her like that?

"Mom? It's me…Mattie!"

Amber's head twisted in thought, though still ready for a fight. She locked her eyes sternly on the stranger who stared back at her from her daughter's room. Mattie could see that her mother's mind was racing through the possibilities, but wasn't going to take any chances.

"Where did you come from, Mom? You died yesterday!"

Amber lowered the broom and searched Mattie's face. Her fluorescent blue eyes were a dead giveaway once her mother took the time to reason, not to mention how much Mattie looked like her. "If you are my Mattie, tell me what we got you on your eighth birthday and why you cried about it."

"I lost the locket that you and Dad had given me when we went water skiing that afternoon."

Amber smiled warmly and opened her arms to her grown daughter. Mattie rushed towards her mother and hugged her firmly, "I thought I'd never see you again."

Amber turned, wrapped her arm around Mattie's waist and walked her towards her bedroom. "Apparently we have a lot to talk about dear, but first you need to know that you've moved backwards in time." Mattie's head snapped quickly towards her mother in shock. "Sit down dear, and I'll see if I can help you sort this all out."

Mattie spent the next hour telling her mother all that had transpired the day before. She told her about the picnic, the red footprints and how the lightning had struck her in the open field. She described what happened in the room behind the refrigerator and how she saw so many wonderful things her mother had done. She told her about the dreams; shared her feelings about Trevor; and expressed her concerns about the predicament she and her dad were in with having to leave the house and relocate. Amber sat patiently listening. Mattie hadn't detected any signs of concern in her mother as she continued to paint a verbal picture of the strange events that had taken place.

"Wait here, dear." Amber sauntered into the next room and returned with a large, leather-bound book under her arm. She removed the lid from the pen, opened the book and asked calmly, "What year is it in your present time?"

"It's February 22nd, 1992."

"Let's see, that would make you about 18 years old wouldn't it?"

"Uh-huh." Mattie was curious about where this was all headed.

"My, you've grown into a beautiful young woman. I would like nothing more than to sit and talk with you further about this young man you seem to be interested in, but I've got a lot to teach you in less than 24 hours. We've got until 10:30 tomorrow morning to figure out a way to get a message to your father—eight years into the future—so you won't be stuck in this time frame."

"Why don't you just tell him when he gets home this afternoon…while I'm here?"

"If I do that, our entire future will change and that could be devastating. The first rule of the Divvy is that you can't talk to any Stagmas about what you do or who you are while in venue." All kinds of questions began to whirl around in Mattie's head.

"What's a Stagma?"

"Non-time travelers, dear; people who are limited to a single time frame. There's only one Trekker alive with full powers in 'present tense' on the earth from each generation of our family. Apparently you are the current one since I was killed in the field. You can only travel backwards in time on your own through the glowing, blue footprints and when it's time to return to the future, you'll see yellow footprints in the same location

the blue ones had appeared. You only have two minutes to connect with them. After that, you can never return. If you have to return early, the prints will appear when you get within a few feet of them. However, you won't actually be able to materialize in the Time Keeper until your Splitter calls you back home."

"If I have to return early, where do I go until I'm summoned?"

"I really don't know. I guess you're suspended in time somewhere. My memory of what takes place in between time frames is always wiped clean before I re-enter." Amber raised her finger in point. "Oh…also, it's especially important that you never step on a print that is any other color than yellow or blue."

"What if I do?"

"It'll transport you to an entirely different time corridor without a direct route back to your own realm. Your Splitter won't be able to locate you through an alternate passageway and you may be lost in time forever. There are specific rules for safe Divvying and you must obey them with precision."

Mattie's mind started racing with the possibilities and began to worry about whether she could remember everything. "How many rules are there, Mom? How will I remember them all?"

Amber placed the large leather book on Mattie's lap and opened it to the first page which read:

The rules of the Divvy are clearly set,

If you break a rule you'll pay the debt.

Mark these words and learn them well,

Or pay the price that time will tell...

Mattie turned the page where the list of rules began. To her dismay each rule was fairly detailed and they went on for many pages. "There are dozens of rules Mother. I'll never be able to learn them fast enough to get home."

Amber chuckled and said softly, "You don't have to learn them all right now, dear. The *Book of Ancestors* is kept in a secret drawer at the base of the fireplace in the guest room. Push on the face of the clock that's carved in the mantle and it'll open for you. I'll show you later. If we can manage to get you back to your realm, you'll be able to learn the rules at your own pace. You're much too young to have received your Inheritance and probably won't be able to access all of your powers for several years yet. I think you'll have plenty of time to study."

Mattie felt relieved. A gradual sense of excitement grew as she perused through the heavy, yellowed pages of the book. "Who are these people and what do the dates mean that are listed under them?"

"Those are the names of your ancestors who were Trekkers before you. Each date beneath their name represents each Divvy they performed. There is a box of remnants for each Divvy that has DNA ties to each individual that had

summoned them back in time for help. These boxes are kept in a special locked chamber in the city library. Your aunt Lila is the current keeper of the artifacts, although she doesn't understand the significance of the content of the boxes. She simply receives them in the mail and files them away in the underground corridors that run to the outskirts of town. You'll learn more about these later." Amber turned the book to the back where there were several blank sheets. "Now we need to spend some time creating a message for your father. Tell me what it is."

"Me? Tell you? How would I know?" Mattie said with a baffled look on her face.

Amber smiled and placed her hand gently on the top of Mattie's. "...because you've heard me sing it for the past eight years." She paused to let Mattie gather her thoughts. "Think about it Mattie...you know what it is."

Mattie sat quietly; her eyes shifting about the room as she thought. She sat up straight and started laughing. "Oh Mom, you're so clever! You sent a message to Dad through the words you made up using the tune you were humming in the hall a few minutes ago."

"I did?" Amber asked, smiling, "How does it go?"

Mattie hummed the tune and then began singing:

"Two, two, two of ninety two, Daddy
knows just what to do,

To bring his baby home again he'll call for her bout' half past ten...

He'll speak the words that Mommy wrote amongst the family's many notes,

The final page to catch his eye will help him find his Mattie Pie."

They looked at each other and began to chuckle. "Two, two, two is tomorrow's date in my realm. It's the twenty-second of February, 1992. I was transported at about half past ten or 10:30 this morning. I remember Dad used to whistle the tune all the time and sometimes we'd even sing the words together before I went to bed."

"Yes, I would have especially made sure your father knew the jingle. I hope it comes back to him." Amber began writing down the words to the tune in the *Book of Ancestors*. She jotted down notes for Kash in hopes that he would remember the jingle and think to check in the book before the time limit was up. "He's very smart you know...your father. If he's not too distracted, he'll figure it out—no need to worry. Now...have you had anything to eat recently, dear?"

"No. Dad didn't get back with lunch before I divvied."

"Well then, let's go get you something to eat. I'll bet you're starving!"

Chapter 7

The Shed

"Got any ideas, sir?" Trevor asked. He was getting impatient and couldn't stand sitting quietly any longer, waiting for who knew what.

"If somehow I could get a message to her to stay put she might have a chance of figuring things out; though it's highly unlikely."

"Why's that?"

"Because she's only seen things in dreams without any explanation as to what they might mean." Kash paced the floor slowly while verbalizing fragments of different ideas, trying to remember something that might help him solve the problem. He began to imagine what might happen if he couldn't get her back in time.

"I can't sit here any longer, Mr. Bott. I'm going to search the property some more. Maybe I missed something that would tell me where she's gone." Trevor set out to make a more thorough search of the yard. Kash wasn't paying much attention to him and didn't notice that he had left the room.

"Miss Graham?" one of the librarians whispered. "Miss Graham?"

Lila sat unresponsive, staring at the deed to the house. She was lost in her own thoughts, trying to figure out why Amber would unexpectedly and so willingly give up the house that she had chosen over the love of her only sister.

"Lila!" Her assistant finally spoke out in a volume that was unacceptably loud for the library, forcing her attention. "Another small package arrived in the mail. Do you want me to put it in the room for you?"

Lila's lips tightened into a thin line as she shook her head rigidly from side to side. "You know the answer to that, Marlene. Why do you keep asking?"

Marlene rudely tossed the box on the desk and said, "I don't know what the big deal is. It's only a box and I'm simply trying to save you the effort of unlocking that hideous bolt. You ought to cut a 4-inch hole in the wall and just drop them in. It'd be easier than bothering with that nasty lock!"

"Yes, and give you an opportunity to see what's inside!"

"Oh you're such a control freak, Lila!" Marlene snapped.

"And you're on thin ice, Marlene," retorted Lila. "Best you get back to work!"

"When are you going to trust me? They're only little

brown boxes. I would never open one."

"It has nothing to do with trust Marlene. This is something that I've been charged with since I took this position from my grandmother. I don't understand why there has to be such strict rules, but there are. I made her a promise before she died and I have no intention of breaking it to suit your overly zealous curiosity."

Marlene let out a huff of disgust, shoved the chair out of her path and stomped away.

Trevor had searched the grounds several times until all that was left to search was the old shed in the far corner. The only problem was the padlock that held a two-by-four firmly in place across the only door. The windows had been boarded shut many years earlier and the shutters were both hanging crooked from weather worn hinges that had finally rusted through. He went around back to see if there was another way in and discovered that the old shed was built snugly up against the tall wooden fence that bordered the yard. There was barely enough room to squeeze a head between them and it would have to be a fairly small one at that. However, he could see there was one window that hadn't been boarded up and it was only about six inches from where he stood. He suspected it would be a risky undertaking for his head, but maybe, if he kept it pointed straight ahead he could move in far enough to see what was inside. He placed one hand against the fence and the other on the side of the old shed and inched his head in

carefully. He stretched his neck out as far as he could and peered into the window from out of the corner of his eye. All he could see was some tattered furniture, scattered yard tools and a few pots that were stacked without any organized thought. The rug was crumpled and filthy from years of dirt. It was pretty obvious Mattie wasn't inside. On his last glance around the interior he noticed an opening in the floor that the wrinkled rug revealed. "*H-m-m-m-m*" he thought to himself, "*that's interesting*; *I wonder where that leads to.*" As he started to pull his head back, his ears began folding over, wedging them tighter against the frame with each tug. The more he yanked, the tighter it got. The tighter it got, the more nervous he became. Claustrophobia set in, creating anxiety and an urgent need to hurry and get free. The more he hurried, the greater number of slivers found a home in the tender flesh on the edges of his ears.

"Crap! OUCH!" he yelped. Panic set in and he started kicking the shed with his foot and banging on it with his hand. To his surprise the deteriorated structure crumbled easily. He was able to pull the rest apart and within seconds his head was free. After he shook the splinters out of his hair, he realized he had opened up a pretty good sized hole in the wall that was just big enough to crawl through. It would be an awkward squeeze, but once he was in he figured he could push the chairs and tools to the edges of the room to clear a path to lift the rug. His curiosity peaked. He could hardly contain his excitement. He worked as fast as he could and sure enough, to his delight, when the center of the room was cleared he could see there was a trap door in the floor. He threw back the rug; choking a bit on the dust it kicked up. He reached down, stuck his fingers into the

latch and lifted the lid. "Man, that stinks down there!" he mumbled. "I probably shouldn't be doing this."

"Trevor!" Kash called from the back door. "Where are you?"

Trevor, startled by Kash's voice, stood up quickly, banging his head into some rusty pans that were dangling from the hooks in the ceiling. He let out a yelp as the pans clanked together several times before he could reach up to quiet them.

Kash, hearing the pans, darted out the door towards the shed. "Trevor.....what are you doing in there?" He yelled as he ran. He stuck his head through the newly broken hole and glared at Trevor. "What's the matter with you, boy? How dare you break into my property? Don't you know that when something is locked it means you're not welcome?"

"I'm sorry sir, I was looking for Mattie when my head got stuck between the fence and the shed and…"

"And so you caved…in…the wall? Did you think Mattie locked herself inside somehow from the outside? You come out of there right now!" Kash demanded. "We've got work to do." Kash hoped to distract him from the tunnel he had recently discovered by nudging him impatiently all the way across the lawn to the house.

"We've got to make sure we write these instructions clearly for your father and hope your young man loves you enough to take the leap of faith we're suggesting."

"I don't follow you, Mom."

"Every Trekker has to have their own Splitter in order to move them forward in time; back to their original location. The Splitter is typically a spouse, but can be a blood relative in a pinch. Your dad won't be able to bring you back because he is…was my Splitter and if I really am dead in your realm, he's lost his powers; and…you're not married yet, dear."

"I think I would have been in a couple of months if all this crazy stuff hadn't happened. I'm sure he loves me, too."

Amber sighed. "Let's hope that's the case because love will be the major factor in what I'm about to propose. We'll create a marriage vow that is sealed by time and your love for each other. If you're both willing to do this, it just might work!" Amber turned her attention to the book and began writing. After several minutes she wrapped her arm around Mattie's shoulder. "Is there anything you want to say to Trevor before I end the instructions?"

Mattie's eyes circled the room as she thought. "Tell him… that I love him. Put down that I've had a crush on him since the beginning of our senior year in high school and that I know we are made for each other. Tell him if he doesn't know in his heart that I'm the girl for him, I'll find him somehow and wring his neck!" Mattie started to get emotional.

Amber chuckled softly. "I'm sure he'll feel your love when he reads your words, dear." She wrote the words that Mattie had said, basically, with a touch of discretion, placed it in an envelope and sealed it.

Outside the window Amber heard the car pulling into the driveway. "Here they come," Amber said, "we should be in the living room when they first see you. Let me do the talking."

They hurried down the stairs to take their positions. Amber sat down on the couch and waved Mattie to sit on the love seat on the other side of the room. They both fluffed their hair briefly and took a deep breath in an attempt to calm down.

The front door swung open and Kash strolled into the room. "We're home!" he called out happily in search for a response.

"We're in here," Amber replied.

Kash continued over to the stairwell with an 11 year old Mattie following close behind him. "Who's this?"

"This is Mat…Madeline…Madeline Graham, a cousin of mine from back east." Amber turned to Mattie and said, "Madeline, this is my husband Kash and my daughter Mattison."

"How do you do?" said Mattie. "It's a pleasure to meet you both."

Kash patted his young daughter on the back of her head and said, "Here, Mattie, I'll take the poles and you take the fish into the kitchen. Fill the sink with some cold water and dump 'em in. I'll be in to help in just a minute."

Little Mattie nodded her head courteously to her eight year older self and forced a simple smile. She said, "Excuse

me please," and headed for the kitchen to carry out her father's instructions.

Kash tossed the poles and his fishing vest on the steps and walked into the living room to shake Mattie's hand. "My goodness, Amber, she could be your twin. How'd you say she's related to us?"

"Please don't leave those there," said Amber, pointing towards the fishing equipment, trying to distract him from continuing the conversation.

"I won't…I'll put everything away after I get the fish cleaned. Tell me again how she fits into the family?" If anything, Kash was a persistent man, not easily distracted.

"Well… she's from my grandmother's sister's son's daughter who stayed back east when the family moved west."

"What?" Kash laughed. He turned towards Mattie and said pleasantly, "I'm not sure what my wife just said, but welcome! Any relative of Amber's is a relative of mine. Will you be staying with us for a while?"

Mattie blushed and said, "Only over night. I have to be on my way tomorrow morning." She glanced over at Amber for help, hoping she'd reroute the conversation before her father asked her any more questions.

"That's hardly enough time to get to know you at all." Kash said.

Amber stood up and started walking over to the pile of equipment on the steps. "We can talk more at dinner, dear. Perhaps you could do us all a favor and take all of your smelly, fishy things into the kitchen." She smiled sweetly at Kash, as she always did, when she wanted something done immediately. He could never resist and she knew it.

"I'll get those, dear. You tend to our guest." Kash snatched up the smelly gear and headed for the kitchen.

Lila could see the lights on in several rooms of the old house as she pulled up to the curb. "I knew it was too good to be true," she said angrily to herself as she turned off the car. She could see someone in the living room pacing the floor. "*They're not going to make a fool of me this time*," she thought and restarted her car. "*I'll show them that I'm not going to put up with their lies any more. We'll see what they say when I come back with a policeman and a court order from Judge Whipple to vacate*." She cranked the car in gear and hastily pressed on the gas pedal, causing the tires to squeal a bit as she pulled out.

The squealing noise reminded Kash that Lila was supposed to come over to check out the house after work. "Oops, I'll bet that was Lila. I was planning to be gone by now. She's probably ticked that Amber didn't show up to talk to her like she asked her to this afternoon. I hope she hasn't gone to get the police, though that would be just like her to do that."

Trevor was nervous. Kash could see he was turning pale and was at a loss as to what to do.

"We've got to grab what we can and get out of here before she gets back. You go upstairs and start dragging down the suitcases Mattie packed and I'll pull the car closer to the house."

Kash grabbed the keys and flew out the door. Trevor ran up the stairs and started hauling the bags down to the porch as fast as he could. Kash opened the trunk and all of the doors to make it as easy as possible to throw the items in faster. He took off for the house, trying to think if he was forgetting anything. As he ran through the door, Trevor was running out with two pieces of luggage. They hit head on in the doorway, knocking both of them to the ground unconscious. Kash began to stir first. He crawled over to Trevor and tried to wake him up. Trevor was out cold! Kash pulled him up over his back as best he could and staggered towards the car.

"What's going on over there?" called out Mrs. Schnettle, after hearing the commotion from her front patio.

Kash could barely see her beady little eyes peering over the hedge. Her head was bobbing up and down from standing on her tip toes and her nose was pointed almost straight up in the air…as usual.

"Oh, a-a-a…. This young man is Amber's...um... nephew and he wanted to spend a few days of his break with us. He slipped on a puddle of water in the kitchen and knocked himself out. I've got to get him to the hospital…NOW!"

Kash resented the feeling of being required to explain anything to his nosy, meddling neighbor. She was such a pain!

"Are you going to put him in the trunk?" she said in her high, critical voice.

"No, of course not!" Kash snapped, "I was bringing in his luggage when I heard him fall. I've got to go." Kash laid Trevor carefully in the back seat, closed everything that was open and pulled out into the road. He could see her in his rearview mirror, watching him drive away.

"Oh-h-h-h-h…what happened?" Trevor said in long slurred words as he woke up."

"Are you alright?"

"Yeah; my head aches, but I'll be fine. Where am I?"

"You're in the car and I'm sorry I ran into you." Kash rolled to a stop and turned off the key. "We're on the other side of the block from the house. We'll have to sit here for a few minutes until my nosy neighbor leaves for her evening prowl of the neighborhood. She always takes the same route at the same time every night and early in the morning. She goes the opposite direction from where we are; the route she calls the "juicy" side of the town. We'll be safe where we are. She always coincidentally runs into her only friend two blocks down and around the corner. From there they start making the rounds together, sharing rumors and creating some of their own about the people that live in each home they pass."

"Wow, what an exciting life. To think I wasted all those years and my parents wasted all that money for school when I could have apprenticed under this extraordinary woman for a thrilling career in neighborhood watch!" Trevor exclaimed, sarcastically.

"This isn't funny, Trevor. She saw me putting you in the car. She could cause us a lot of trouble. We'll have to wait here a few more minutes and then it'll be safe to go home. I'll get the rest of my stuff and you go out back. See if you can nail some boards over the hole you smashed in on the side of the shed. Be sure and close the trap door and cover it with the rug first. I'll explain later."

Chapter 8

The Judge

Knock, knock, knock! Lila stood impatiently at the door waiting for the judge to answer it. *Knock, knock, knock, knock, knock, knock....*

"I'm coming! I'm coming!" the judge yelled from behind the door. "Don't get your pantyhose in such a knot!" He opened the door to find his old high school sweetheart still knocking in the air. "Oh, sorry, Lila." The Judge chuckled. "To what do I owe this privilege?"

If he wasn't known for being the Justice of the Peace he could easily be mistaken for Santa himself. His soft, curly, white beard and mustache framed a kindly face with big blue eyes. Two bushy, white eyebrows added to his animated character. His head was smooth and shiny for the lack of hair, and he even had a Santa Claus belly that bumped up and down as he laughed.

"I need an eviction notice right now, David."

"Good to see you too, Lila. Won't you come in?" The judge opened the door and lifted his hand towards the study. "Have a chair and tell me who you're evicting and why!"

"I'm evicting my sister and that no-good-liar-of-a-husband of hers from my home." Lila stuck out her lower lip and threw the deed on the desk. "As you can see…I have every right to kick them out."

"Don't you think you're being a bit harsh, my old friend? Kash and Amber are fine people."

"Don't pretend to understand our family situation, Judge. Just give me the eviction notice."

"To the point as ever, aren't you, Lila?" He studied the document for a few seconds and reached into his desk, pulling out a black folder and a pen. "It's too bad that it's come to this." He thumbed through several different forms, finally finding the one he needed and set it out to be signed. "Are you sure you want to do this, Lila? It could damage your relationship with your sister beyond repair."

"Just drop it, Judge, and sign the notice." Lila was fuming and all she could think about was seeing the shock on her sisters' face when she had the policeman serve the notice.

"You have no reason to be rude to me, Lila, because you're mad at your sister," the judge said patiently. He closed the book, moved around to Lila's side and sat on the corner of the desk. "You know I've only wanted the best for you all these years, don't you?"

Lila visibly softened as the judge touched her arm. "I know, David," she said in a calmer tone. "I'm sorry. You've always been good to me and I do appreciate your help."

They both got up and walked to the door arm in arm. "Let me know if there's anything else you need, Lila. I'm always here."

"Thank you, David. I'll talk with you soon." Lila headed directly to the police station. She didn't want to waste a minute more. By the time she got there she had already worked herself back into a frenzy.

Kash drove into the driveway cautiously, glancing around to see if there was anyone in sight. The front door of the house was still opened and the lights were still on. It appeared as though the coast was clear.

"OK, Trevor—you do your thing and I'll do mine. I'll meet you at the car in five minutes max! Do the best you can on the shed to secure it. You'll find some wood in the garage and the tools are inside the shed." Kash ran into the house and started throwing clothes, pictures and any personal papers he could find in garbage bags and tossed them into the back seat of the car. He went back into the living room and stood in the middle to think. Mentally he moved from room to room trying to remember anything he may have forgotten that was important. Trevor burst in the back door and scared Kash out of wits. He jumped to the side, knocking the vase off the coffee table.

"You're trying to give me a heart attack, aren't you?" Kash reached over to pick up the vase. It was a heavy piece of pottery that Mattie had made for him and Amber when she was in high school. "Oh…I nearly forgot this." It reminded him of easier times and he slowly lowered himself down on the couch in a melancholy state of mind, reminiscing as he stared at the vase.

After a few seconds Trevor interrupted his stroll down memory lane. "Sir, we'd better go. The shed is finished, though it's not the best repair job I've ever done."

Kash remembered that Lila would be on her way back and could arrive at any moment. He tucked the vase under his arm and said, "You're right…let's go!" Trevor ran out while Kash turned off all of the lights and stood in the doorway for one last goodbye to the old house. "Good bye," he said softly. "I'll be back for you, Mattie... somehow!" He flipped the lock and slowly pulled the door shut behind him. As he started down the steps he remembered he still had the key and returned it to its hiding place under the flower pot by the door.

Lila stormed into the police station, stomping up to the front desk.

"May I help you, Ms. Graham," said the sergeant, who had recently come on duty and was in a pleasant mood.

"Yes," snapped Lila. "I need an officer to serve a notice right now!" She slammed the eviction papers on the counter for him to see.

"I'm afraid we don't have an officer available in the precinct right now. How about tomorrow morning? Would that be alright?" He smiled kindly as he handed the paper back to her.

Lila snatched the notice out of the sergeant's hand and replied sharply, "No, it won't be alright. I have to do this tonight! RIGHT…NOW!"

The smile on the officer's face melted into a frown. "OK, Ms. Graham," he said quietly, trying to calm her down. "I'll see if I can find a policeman that could meet you over at the house. Would that be satisfactory to you?"

Lila curtly thanked the officer and left. She was so angry she could hardly see to drive. When she arrived, the policeman was standing on the porch waiting for her. She got out of the car, slamming the door and met the officer half way up the steps.

"Evenin', Ms. Graham." The officer tipped his hat courteously. "The sergeant said you needed some help over here to serve an eviction notice right away. It looks to me like you're too late. No one's here."

If anger could glow in the dark, Lila could have been mistaken for an enormous fire fly. She took four unusually large steps towards the flower pot by the door and tipped it on its' side. To her surprise, the key was exactly where Kash said it would be. "Well…what do ya know? He actually kept his

word and left me the key." She turned to the policeman, thanked him for his prompt attention and sent him on his way. Lila stood in front of the door for several minutes before unlocking it. Her hands shook as she inserted the key. When she pushed the door open and stepped through the frame she felt the familiar sense of finally being home again. It had been eight lonely years since she'd been inside. When she flipped on the light she expected to see a mess from the hasty departure of her sister. As her eyes wandered affectionately around the room she could see that everything was in perfect order. A flood of rich memories rushed in from the many happy years with her parents and sister in the old house. Seeing the family portraits and the familiar trinkets that were displayed lovingly throughout the room started the tears flowing again. The carpet was new and some of the decorations were different, but there was the same deep feeling of joy she had always experienced when she came home from being away.

Unexpectedly she felt a stabbing pain of regret for her actions and mean spirited comments towards Kash, the Judge, Marlene and everyone else she had verbally spit at throughout the day. She closed the door and began a tour of the house savoring every step as though each was a delicious morsel of food. She started with her old bedroom that Amber had made into a guest room after Lila had left. It was nothing less than lovely and she could see that her sister took excellent care of the place since their parents had disappeared. She opened the closet door and it was empty as though they had anticipated her return. She felt guilty about the way she had treated her sister and her family for all those lost years.

Kash paced the floor in front of the window trying to think of a solution to get Mattie back. His eyes were locked on the flickering light from the sign that was diffused through the sheer curtains. They had gotten the last available motel room and had sort of settled in for the night. Trevor was lying in the middle of his sagging, narrow bed with his bare feet dangling over the bottom edge. He was taller than the bed was long. His head was propped up by the pillow, facing the TV, though he appeared to be in sort of a trance.

"Oh, crap!" bellowed Kash. Trevor popped his head up off the pillow to see what was wrong. "I forgot the *Book of Ancestors*." He threw his hands up in the air, slapped them down to his side and started walking in a tight circle, mumbling to himself. "I've got to get it tonight! How can I sneak past Lila? I'll bet she plans to stay in her old room, too! Oh my goodness; oh… my…" Kash stopped still in his footsteps. "That's it!" he shouted. There's got to be something in the book of Ancestors that'll tell me how to get Mattie back." Kash turned to Trevor and announced, "We've got to go back when she's asleep!"

Trevor dropped his jaw, plopped his head back on the pillow and rolled his eyes. "Not again! Is there no end to this nightmare?"

Chapter 9

The Break In

"Sh-sh-sh…don't be so noisy; you could wake the dead!" Kash waved for Trevor to get behind him, "Follow me and be QUIET," he whispered fervently. "And watch where you step." They moved around the outside of the house as discreetly as possible, checking each window to see if they had forgotten to latch one without success. They had even checked all of the two story windows using a ladder from the garage!

"What about the key you left under the pot?" Trevor suggested, "Maybe it's still there?"

"Don't be ridiculous," Kash scoffed. "That's how she got in to begin with. She'd have to be a moron to put it back in the same place I put it and you don't know Lila like I do." After an hour of trying to find a way to get into the house they sat down on the porch, frustrated and discouraged.

"Maybe you could call the fire department and when they get her out of the house you could sneak in and get the book." There was a smug look on Trevor's face. He liked contributing ideas to the predicaments they got into.

"Oh…that's a brilliant idea," Kash said facetiously, "I'm sure no one would ever see me go in through the front door with all the other firemen and come out with a large book. If I wore camouflage I'd probably blend in with the workers and it would be like I was the invisible man!"

Trevor wrinkled up one side of his face and slumped back down to think some more. They remained silent for several minutes.

"Hey, what about using a credit card to unlock the door like they do on TV?" Trevor spoke out with renewed enthusiasm.

"That's perfect except I have no experience breaking and entering with a credit card. Do you?"

Trevor shook his head and wrinkled the other side of his face. Sitting there doing nothing made him nervous and was driving him crazy. He started poking around on the front porch for something to do. For the heck of it he lifted up the flower pot by the door. "Look…look," he whispered in a throaty sort of way. "Look what I found!"

Kash crawled over to the pot and picked up the key. "Who'd of guessed she'd do that?" he said in amazement.

"Well…I did!" Trevor instantly reminded him. "So is this Lila really a moron?"

Kash snorted trying to hold back a laugh and quickly slapped his hands over his mouth to muffle any further outbursts. "You wait here and stay out of sight. I'll be back in a minute."

Kash slowly opened the front door and crept up the stairs. "*Gosh it's dark in here. Thank goodness there's nothing in the halls to trip over,*" he thought to himself, right before he stumbled over a pair of shoes Lila had kicked off earlier on her tour around the house. For the most part he did an extraordinary job of concealing the noise from his fall. However, on the last motion required for a full recovery his knuckles bumped into the wall of Lila's bedroom with a thud. Kash froze where he was to see if he could hear Lila waking up. His forehead was beginning to form beads of sweat from the anxiety that was building within him. He heard the rustle of satin sheets and Lila making some sounds like she was chewing with her mouth opened. Then there was silence.

He crept forward peeking around the corner of the door towards the bed expecting to see Lila still asleep. To his astonishment and horror, the sheets had been tossed back and the bed was empty. Before he could pull his head back he found himself face to face with Lila. Shocks ran up and down his spine. It scared him to the point of silence! He stood petrified until he realized that her eyes were still closed. He pulled back around the door and flattened himself against the wall, holding his breath as she walked right by him towards the bathroom at the end of the hall.

As soon as she disappeared into the bathroom, he hurried over to the fireplace and pushed on the face of the clock carving in the mantle. The secret drawer popped open and he gently lifted the ancient book out of its hiding place. He slowly ran his hand around the bottom of the drawer until he felt the key and stuffed it in his pocket. He felt the drawer latch when he

slid it closed and stood up to leave when he heard Lila shuffling back down the hallway. He quickly sidestepped to get back over to the door where he could hide behind it. When he passed the vanity he bumped into the chair and a letter popped out of the old book. There was no time to pick it up before Lila would be back in the room. He left it lying there, hoping her eyes were still closed.

Luckily she was still half asleep and didn't notice the letter. She climbed back into bed and after several minutes Kash could hear her breathing get heavier and knew she had fallen back asleep. He crept back over to the vanity and snatched up the letter from off the floor. Hastily stuffing it in his back pocket he slipped out the door and into the hall to freedom. He stumbled over the shoes one more time for good measure, double stepped down the stairs and locked the door before carefully closing it behind him. He placed the key back under the pot and they both ran down the street towards the car, laughing hysterically as they went.

"What a rush!" said Trevor as he opened the car door and slid in. "You sure don't live a boring life, Mr. Bott."

Kash shook his head, "Oh, you have no idea, no…idea!"

It didn't take long for Trevor to fall asleep once they got back to the motel. Even though it was late, Kash sat up to search the book for ideas or clues of any kind that could help him get Mattie back. He started humming to keep himself awake

while he continued to turn page after useless page, without success.

"Two, two, two of 92…hmm-hmm-hmm-hmm-hmm-hmm…"

Kash continued to hum the familiar tune, singing a word here and there. His eyes were beginning to feel like there was sand in them as he fought to keep them open. Finally, after searching about half of the book, he gave up and decided he'd probably do much better in the morning if he could get a little bit of sleep. He kicked off his shoes, pulled the pillow out from under the quilt and sprawled himself face down across the top of the bed. He was almost asleep before his face even touched the sheets.

The next morning Kash was awakened by the sound of Trevor taking a shower. He glanced at his watch to see what time it was. "Oh-h-h, it's only 6:00," he muttered to himself and rolled over on his side, tucking his pillow in under his head. Seconds later he sat up with a jerk as the words to the tune he had hummed during the night came to life inside his head. He jumped up and began dancing around the room, laughing in a high pitched tone. Trevor opened the door to see what all the noise was about.

"I've got it, my boy! I've got it! I know how to bring Mattie back!" Kash's arms and legs were flying all over the place in rhythm with the jingle he began singing:

"Two, two, two of ninety two, Daddy knows just what to do,

To bring his baby home again he'll call for her bout' half past ten...

He'll speak the words that Mommy wrote amongst the family's many notes,

The final page to catch his eye will help him find his Mattie Pie."

Trevor stood in the doorway with a blank stare on his face, brushing his teeth. "I don't understand. How does that help us?" Trevor said in a juicy, toothpaste-in-his-mouth sort of way.

"Mattie must have gone back to her mother. Amber taught us the words to this jingle that I've been singing about seven or eight years ago. She wanted to make sure I knew how to get Mattie back home from the unexpected Divvy."

"Divvy...what's a Divvy?" Trevor asked.

"You'd better get dressed and then sit down before I explain the way things are."

Kash hurried back to the desk to open the *Book of Ancestors* and flipped to the last page. "Here it is," he shouted with excitement, "she wrote me the instructions for Mattie's return. Hey...here's the jingle, too."

Kash ran his finger down through the words that were written. The more he read the more serious he became.

"What's wrong?" Trevor asked, after pulling his shirt over his head.

"Something's missing!" Kash replied.

"What?"

"The instructions! I don't understand what to do!"

Kash began to retrace his steps. He couldn't help thinking that he had forgotten something, somewhere. All of a sudden he remembered the letter that had fallen out of the book in Lila's bedroom. "Maybe that's the missing piece." He reached into his back pocket and pulled out the crumpled envelope, opened the letter and began reading it. His face brightened up as he read. "This is it. It makes sense!"

Trevor ran a quick comb through his hair and pulled up a chair next to Kash. "OK, I'm ready" he said, stretching his legs out to get comfortable for the lengthy story he expected to get.

Kash turned his chair around to face Trevor. "I know you don't know me well, Trevor, and I know you probably have never met Mattie's mother, but I also know that you love Mattie. Am I right?"

"Yes sir, that's all true."

Kash placed his hand on Trevor's shoulder and looked him straight in the eye. "This is going to be a bit of a shock to you, but you need to be open-minded and trust me. Do you think you can do that? Mattie's life is at stake."

"I'll try, Mr. Bott. I'd do anything for Mattie."

"Call me Dad!"

Chapter 10

The Plan

Kash spent the next hour and a half explaining to Trevor everything that had happened during the past two days in as much detail as time allowed. Next, he read the letter out loud that Amber had written him 8 years prior.

February 22, 1984

My Darling Kash,

Mattie told me what happened yesterday and I'm sorry I couldn't prepare you in advance for my demise. You understand the rules of the Divvy and so I hope you will forgive me for keeping this secret from you for all these years. Please know that I love you and long for the day we can be together again.

Now you have the unprecedented task of bringing Mattie home without any evidence that what I'm about to suggest will even work. We haven't got a lot of time before this must take

place in your realm so please read this carefully, then make haste slowly.

On the back, inside cover of this book you'll find a blood document which must be completed in your time before it can be valid in either. It must be written within the book itself if it is to have any binding power for what you need to do. As you can see, Mattie has written her own wedding vows for Trevor. She has printed her full, given and married name, Mattison Amber Bott Karington and has placed her thumbprint on top of her signature using her own blood. Trevor must do the same to the side of Mattie's. It cannot be below or above her entry. He must first write his vow, then print his full, given name and sign it in his own handwriting. Be sure to use his left thumbprint, in his own blood and press it directly over his signature. This must be completed before 10:00 A.M. on February 22nd, 1992 to make sure we have enough time to Split dimensions before it's too late... if it's even possible at all. You must teach him the Splitting Words, too. Don't delay! Time is of the essence.

We hope and pray that Trevor will open his heart and mind to such a plan. If he does not, our family line will end today and there can be no more time travelers to help the people of the world undo their mistakes.

Tell Trevor that Mattie loves him and wants to share her life with him more than anything. Tell him that there has never been anyone else for her and never could be.

Hurry now, my love, and be of good cheer. If all goes well I'll see you again soon.

My heart is always yours,

Amber

P.S. – If this works and Mattie gets back to you, it is crucial that you get them legally married by sunset. It must take place before dark or the seal will be broken and I don't know what will happen then. I think she'll be pulled back in time piece by piece.

When he had finished reading, they both sniffled and tried to inconspicuously wipe the tears from their eyes as they sat facing each other. Kash handed the book to Trevor and said, "Now it's your turn. You understand what's at stake and it's your choice. We can't force you to do this." Kash moved back over to the bed to give Trevor some space. His heart pounded with the anticipation of Trevor's response.

Trevor opened the book to the back cover and began reading Mattie's inscription silently to himself.

I Mattison Amber Bott Karington, choose Trevor William Karington to be my best friend and husband for the rest of my life. He

and he alone will be the one that I love, cherish and cling to through the good times as well as through the storms we will face together. I will honor him; trust him; prize his companionship and pledge my whole heart and soul to him forever. I dedicate all that I am to his happiness and well being. I will always strive to bring a light to his darkest hour; comfort in his sorrow; relief through any sickness; humor to his everyday existence and give him children to honor his name. Therefore, I promise and covenant this day before God, in the presence of my mother, Amber Elizabeth Graham Bott, and by the ancestors that preceded me, that I will be faithful and true to this covenant forever.

Date: Saturday, February 22, 1992

Mattison Amber Bott Karington

Trevor closed the book and laid it on the edge of the bed. He stood up and wandered towards the door. "This is all too overwhelming for me, Mr. Bott. I feel like my head's going to explode. I've got to get out of here. I'm really sorry." His face was filled with sadness as he slowly, but surely, pulled the door closed behind him.

Kash's heart sank inside when he heard the latch click shut. He folded his arms over his chest and sat back, staring into space. As far as he knew, this was the end of his family, everything he had ever worked for and everyone he had ever cared about. He had lost his wife, his home, and now his only child in less than 48 hours. There was nothing left in his life that had any meaning without them in it. He felt empty and totally alone in a cheap motel room that only grew lonelier and more silent by the moment.

Chapter 11

The Cut and Run

By 7:30, Lila was in the yard working in the flowerbeds, enjoying the early morning sun. She and Amber used to plant flowers around the house that were so thick with color that the dirt was virtually undetectable. The sweet fragrance filled the air to the point that it was almost intoxicating to swing in the rocker on the porch, which their parents did often. Amber had been as meticulous with the yard and garden as she was with the inside of the house. Lila was thrilled to be home and to actually have a place she could call her own. As she sat on the grass, trimming one of the boxwoods that bordered the stairs, she saw a shadow of a woman fall over her and grow larger as she drew nearer.

Mrs. Schnettle, who had noticed Lila in the yard upon returning from her morning snoop, had come over to find out who the new gardener was at the Bott's. "What are you doing here?" she inquired curtly. "Who are you?" Her posture was rigid and offensive.

Lila twisted her head up and back to get a peek at her visitor. “Good morning,” she said, standing and slapping her hands together to get the dirt off before greeting her new neighbor. “I’m Lila Graham, the new owner.” She smiled and reached her hand out in friendship. “Do you live next door?”

“That’s right. I’m Fran Schnettle,” she said curtly, “and nothing gets by me in this neighborhood. Where are the Botts?”

“Well, apparently something got by you if you didn’t know the Botts were moving!” Lila reached down to pick up her tools. “May I offer you some lemonade?”

“Who drinks lemonade this early in the morning?” Fran replied rudely. “You’d better watch yourself in this neighborhood. We don’t put up with any shenanigans here.”

“My goodness; you don’t even know me and yet you’re threatening me on my own property? Some welcome!” Lila crossed back over to the other side of the walk and sat down to trim the other bush. “I can see we are going to be good friends, Mrs. Schnettle. Now if you’ll excuse me, I need to get back to work.”

Mrs. Schnettle turned abruptly to make a dramatic exit when she remembered she had one more question. “What happened to that young man that knocked himself out last night and had to go to the hospital?”

Lila turned and glared at her, irritated by the nerve of her new neighbor. “I have no idea what you’re talking about, Mrs. Schnettle.” Lila wasn’t sure if her neighbor was mentally

deficient and she wasn't about to put up with her pushy attitude for one more second. "I didn't see anyone or anything last night when I moved in and you'd do well to mind your own business from now on. Good day!"

Lila went back to trimming the bush again. Fran didn't quite know how to respond to someone who could be as forward as she was.

"Well," she puffed, "I never...." When she turned to leave she had forgotten about the bucket of tools behind her. She stumbled over it and tumbled to the ground face down. Her dress flew up over her head revealing more than Lila cared to see. The dress had wrapped itself around her head and arms, making it quite difficult for her to get free of all of the material.

"My goodness...are you alright, Ms. Schnettle?" Lila jumped up to help untangle her.

"Don't touch me," she said rolling around on the ground, spitting as she talked. "I'm going to sue you for damages."

"What damages?" blurted out Lila in disbelief. "You're not hurt!"

"We'll see about that." Fran pushed the bucket out of the way, staggered to her feet and marched home at a brisk pace.

Trevor walked down to the sidewalk café where he and Mattie had their first and only date two days earlier. He pulled up a chair at the same table where they had sat at together, talking for hours. In his mind he recalled the details of their time together and the more he thought, the more he realized how instant their connection had been. "*How weird is this?*" he thought to himself. "*I hardly know these people and yet I'm supposed to marry their daughter after one date? It's insane!*"

He ordered an orange juice and some pancakes. He figured there was no need going hungry, just because he was supposed to marry a woman in a completely different dimension of time in less than three hours. He didn't know what to do. Yes, he loved Mattie, which was really nothing new to him; he'd known that for quite some time. He watched other women that were there for breakfast with friends or dates or family and even took the time to observe several of the waitresses as he shoveled down his pancakes. He had to admit that none of the women he had seen since noticing Mattie in their senior year of high school could hold his interest at all when compared to her, including everyone at the café.

He sat talking to himself for over an hour, trying to justify a decision to run away and not look back. The more he tried to defend his reasoning the worse he felt. He kept returning to the same conclusion. He knew Mattie was the one for him and loved everything about her. He knew he intended to pursue marriage down the road with her anyway, and he'd be lucky if she said yes to his proposal whenever he was finally

able to work up the courage to ask. He began to see how easy this all was in comparison to going through the long, drawn out process of trying to convince Mattie that he was the one for her, too. He checked his watch to see how much time was left before it was too late. It was almost 9:00. *"Oh, my gosh! I've only got an hour and a half to get married and save my wife from oblivion. In 90 minutes she's going to be 8 years older than I am if I don't try to get her back now."* With that astonishing thought he jumped up, pulled a $10 bill out of his pocket, threw it on the table and ran back to the motel, hoping Kash hadn't left yet.

As he approached the door to the room he started yelling, "Dad! Dad, it's after nine! We've got to hurry!"

Kash was in the shower trying to wash away his sorrows in the steaming water. His hands were up against the wall and the shower was beating steadily on his sadly bowed head. He was deep in thought and couldn't hear anything that was going on outside the closed door.

Trevor burst into the room still calling out. "Dad, we've got to do this thing! Where are you?" When he stopped yelling he could hear the shower running in the other room. He ran to the bathroom door and started knocking on it as he opened it. "Dad!"

Kash jerked upward, flinging his hands out to the side in total surprise, ripping the shower curtain from the rod on one side and smashing his knuckles against the wall on the other. Trevor realized what he had done and reached out to break Kash's fall. He pushed Kash back into the tub, wrapping the

curtain around his head and pinning his falling body against the back wall. Kash let out an "ugh" on impact.

"What…what!" yelled Kash. "For heaven's sakes, you've got to stop scaring the life out of me. One of us is going to eventually get killed by the other!" Kash wrapped the curtain around him and stepped over the edge of the tub. "Do you think I could have a little privacy to get dressed?"

Trevor stepped out of the bathroom and pulled the door mostly closed. "Dad, I'm going to do it! I know it's the right thing to do and there isn't a lot of time left."

Kash's heart leapt inside. He felt that hope was alive again. "Are you sure?" he said with renewed enthusiasm.

"I've never been so certain about anything in my whole life. What's next…D-a-a-a-d?"

"You need to sit down and write a vow of your own on a piece of the motel stationary. Afterwards we'll transfer it to the book and head for the tunnel."

"The one I found in the shed?"

"The one and only! Now, get to it while I finish getting dressed."

Trevor spent half an hour drafting what he considered to be the perfect vow for Mattie. After all, it was the most important thing he'd ever written and he wanted it to be just right for his future wife and their posterity. Then, as instructed, he wrote the final draft to the side of Mattie's and signed it.

I Trevor William Karington, take Mattison Amber Bott as my one and only companion in this life and the next. She is the light in my darkness, the peace to my soul and the one I choose to ride the rivers of life with. My love for her runs deeper than the clear night sky and I promise to honor and cherish her always. I will happily pay tribute to her heritage as I stand by her through her trials and responsibilities that she is called upon to bear. I promise to understand and support Mattie in her destiny as she serves others throughout history to make a better world. I pledge to provide for her and our family physically, mentally and spiritually in such a way that she need never be concerned about the welfare of her parents, husband or children for as long as we live.

This I covenant before the witness of my soon to be father-in-law, Kash Bott and my own heritage given to me by goodly parents, whose name I have always tried to honor.

Date: Saturday, February 22, 1992
Trevor William Karington

He pulled a pocket knife from his jeans and poked a tiny hole in his left thumb to draw the blood. He pressed it carefully over his signature and sealed the vow with his thumbprint. “There,” he said in a muffled, thumb-in-mouth fashion, “it’s done!”

Chapter 12

The Rescue

"It's nearly 10:00, Trevor. We're running out of time. Grab the book and let's go." Kash snatched the keys off of the desk, Trevor grabbed the book, and they both headed out to the car. "Get in and I'll teach you the Splitting Words on the way." Kash started the car and pulled out of the motel parking lot. "Open the book to page seven. Start memorizing the words that you see."

Trevor opened the old book and read:

> *The summoning words of the Splitters Creed must be repeated accurately. Do not be mistaken in believing that the simplicity of the rhyme will allow room for error. One misplaced word or even a single unsaid syllable will render the entire directive powerless. Therefore it is crucial that the Splitter be meticulous and articulate in delivering the command. Preceding the mantra the password must be said ONLY ONCE, but the mantra may be repeated as often as the Splitter desires. The command goes as follows:*

Splitters Creed

The Password

I am a Splitter by destiny. (Spouse's first name) is a Trekker by Inheritance. (Spouse's first name) and I combine together to split time.

The Mantra

By bloodline you're destined, by marriage we're tied; let the strength of our love bring you back to my side.

"Holy cow, as nervous as I am right now I'll never be able to remember all of that in time to call Mattie back." Trevor said. "I should have started working on this hours ago!"

"Well," Kash responded thoughtfully, "you did the best you could. You've had some pretty big decisions to make in the last day or so. If it's any consolation, I admire you a great deal and appreciate you more than I can possibly express in words. Don't worry; it's not as hard as you think. You'll do fine. You'll actually have a two minute span of time to get it right."

"Oh, wow…a whole two minutes. That's makes me feel a *lot* better!"

"You only have to get it right once. For the next five minutes why don't you work on the password while I drive us back to the house? Think about what you're saying. It really makes a lot of sense if you try to see the bigger picture."

"OK, I'll try." Trevor began to mouth the words silently, working on memorizing one line at a time. "*I am a Splitter by destiny. I am a Splitter by destiny. I...am a Splitter...by destiny...*"

As they neared the house Kash could see Lila out working in the yard. He continued driving around to the opposite side of the block. He reluctantly pulled over to the curb and turned off the car. "That's what I was afraid of. Lila doesn't work on Saturday until noon. We'll have to jump the neighbor's fence to get to the shed and hope she doesn't come into the back yard until we're out of sight."

Trevor let out a sigh and said, "Oh, great, more pressure."

Kash tapped Trevor on his arm. "Come on. Bring the book; we're going to need it." They walked around the side of the house where they could see the shed over the top of the fence. By sheer luck, the neighbors were out of town for the weekend, but by dumb luck, they had left the dog chained up in the back yard. As Kash rounded the corner of the house into the back yard he faced a black, airborne Rottweiler with teeth the size of a lion. His drool was flying everywhere as he snarled through his sticky, wet nose. Instinctively, Kash reared back and as it turned out, it was barely enough to allow the dog to reach the end of his chain. The dog let out a yelp when he was jerked to the ground, landing flat on his back. His stubby, fat legs kicked frantically in mid-air as he tried to right himself. He twisted and turned until he was able to get back on his feet and run to the end of his chain again, barking incessantly.

Trevor had stumbled a few feet back, allowing Kash some room to retreat. "I'll handle this," he said as he inched slowly forward towards the dog. He started making a strange humming sound as he crept closer, pointing his fingers at the dog's face and rolling his wrist in a slow, clock-wise motion. Trevor, seeking Kash's admiration said, "I saw a guy do this in the movies once and it worked great!" The dog started whining, then to their surprise, the dog lowered his head and chest to the ground and started moving backwards on his hind legs. When the dog had retreated several feet and Trevor had advanced a couple, Trevor looked back at Kash with a cheesy grin on his face. Meanwhile the dogs' nose started to wrinkle, revealing a wet, toothy grin himself. When Trevor returned his attention to the dog all he could see were chomping teeth traveling towards him at a vicious rate. Trevor dove backwards as quickly as he could to avoid being chewed on by the aggressive predator. Once again the dog was held at bay by his chain, but his bark was enough to arouse suspicion for at least eight square blocks.

"Good try," Kash said as he laughed boldly. "Get ready to run!" He picked up a big stick, baited the dog with a couple of passes in front of his face and threw it to the other side of the yard. To Trevor's amazement the dog took off after the stick and Kash started running for the fence. "You better get up or you're going to be his next bone!" he called back.

Trevor jumped up and ran to catch him. He arrived at the fence just in time to help boost Kash over the top. The dog, however, had become aware of their escape and headed for the kill at an intense speed. This time the chain would have no hold on the dog and it was apparent that the dog knew it. Trevor

tossed the book over the fence. He jumped up to grab the edge at the same time the dog left the ground at the level of his seat pockets. Trevor's legs were sliding up and down on the smooth surface desperately trying to snag something rough enough to help lift him over the barrier. The moment the dog's huge, opened mouth was within snapping distance he felt Kash grab his arms and yank him up from the other side. To his discomfort the dogs' teeth sunk into the seat of his pants. As Trevor cleared the fence, the dog was jerked back into his own yard with a piece of fabric as his trophy. Trevor plummeted to the ground, safe on the other side and more flustered than ever. The dog had torn one of the back pockets off of his pants and the surrounding material with it.

"Good job son," Kash said, smacking Trevor on his back. "You're certainly no sissy-la-la. That'll be a valuable trait for the future that lies ahead of you." He smiled and gave him a nod of approval.

Meanwhile, Lila, who was pulling a few weeds near the front side walk, had paused to listen when the dog became strangely silent. She thought she heard voices coming from the back yard and got up to investigate.

Kash stood in front of the shed, glancing around to see if Lila was anywhere in sight. He dug into his front pocket to get the key that would unlock the padlock, but it wasn't there! He tried the other one. It wasn't there, either. He tried his back, left pocket only to find it empty as well. His heart began to pound harder, worrying that he had left it on the desk in the motel room and there wouldn't be enough time to retrieve it.

He sheepishly reached into the last pocket. It was like a bottomless pit as he pushed his hand in deeper, sweeping his finger anxiously. Finally, he felt the jagged edge of the key and let out a sigh of relief.

Lila peaked around the corner of the house to see if anyone was in the back yard. The bushes blocked the view of the shed from where she was standing. She continued to walk briskly around the shrubs and hesitated only when she heard a creaking sound in the direction of the tool shed.

Kash and Trevor slipped through the door and locked it from the inside moments before the structure came into Lila's view. Trevor immediately reached down to pull back the dust filled rug, revealing the trap door. Kash lifted its lid and laid it back against the old couch. They stepped down into the tunnel when they heard some shuffling outside the door. Lila stood hesitantly out front observing the bolt and the two-by-four lying on the ground. She reached out tentatively to open the door. Since it was locked from the inside, her hand spun around the slick, unyielding knob. Grabbing it with both hands she started tugging on it forcefully, cranking the door back and forth. After it became apparent that the door wasn't going to budge, she heatedly went from window to window to see if she could catch a glimpse of who was inside.

"Sh-sh-sh, don't move," Kash whispered

. "Who's in there?" Lila bellowed. "I know someone's in there!"

Amber sat on the edge of Mattie's bed and gently shook her shoulder. "It's time to get up dear. I'm afraid I let you oversleep. We stayed up far too late last night talking; it was selfish of me." Amber ran her fingers down Mattie's arm in a tickling motion.

"Gosh, I miss that, Mom."

"What, dear?"

"You tickling me in the morning when it was time to get up for school. You haven't done that for years."

"You're all grown up now and you probably get yourself up before I ever have the chance."

"Well, that's true. Still…I miss it."

"And I'll miss the grown up you! I'll love sharing that time with you in a few years, but for now, I'm enjoying the little girl you."

Amber pulled back the covers for Mattie to get up and walked over to the vanity to pull a hair brush out of the drawer.

"Where're Dad and…little Mattie?"

Mattie sat down at the vanity and began brushing her hair.

"You're playing in the championship game today. By the way, your Dad said to tell you goodbye for him. He wanted me to tell you that he enjoyed having you here and to come

back soon. I wonder if he'll ever make the connection as to who you are when you grow into adulthood. Anyway, I was wondering…who wins the game today?"

"We did. That was the game that I smashed the cartilage in my middle finger when I slid into home. You can still see how crooked it is." Mattie held up her right hand and sure enough, her middle finger bent slightly to the right in the last joint.

"Didn't I take you to the doctor to get that fixed?"

"Sure, but there was nothing they could do for it unless they fused the last two bones together. If you had allowed them to do that I would have never been able to bend the end of my finger again. It would have stuck straight out when the others were in a fist. You decided that wouldn't be good at all, so you had them wrap it for protection until it healed." Mattie snickered at the thought of how that would have appeared.

"Oh…I see what you mean." Amber laughed, too. "Well, it's getting close to the time you need to Divvy, Mattie. We need to get you ready. You said that you thought you Divvied somewhere between the bottom of the stairs and your bedroom; is that right?" Amber took the brush from Mattie and ran it down the back of her silky, black hair.

"Yes, as I recall, Dad and I were in the living room when he reminded me that I hadn't finished packing yet and needed to get back to work. I ran up the stairs to pack the rest of my things and here I am!"

"Well... it's nearly 10:00. We have a half hour to get you some breakfast and somewhere near the footprints before 10:30."

Kash caught Trevor's eye and beckoned for him to follow. "Pull the trap door behind you as you come," he whispered, "and try to bring the rug over the top of it if you can."

Trevor grabbed the rug and slung it up over the top of the trap door. He pulled the lid with him as he continued into the dark cellar below. As he felt his way down he heard scratching sounds in the dark that made his skin crawl. "Did you bring a flashlight, Dad… and what's that sound?"

Kash ran his hand down the railing at the bottom of the stair well until he felt the cold metal object on the floor. He continued to feel around until he discovered a box he had placed next to it. "I always leave a lantern down here with some matches and that sound is rats." Kash lit the lantern and started into the tunnel.

"R-r-r-a-a-ats," Trevor stammered uneasily. "Did you say rats?"

"Yep! Stay close. Do you have the book?"

Trevor had a terrible fear of rodents, especially rats. When he was about four years old he was at his grandparents' house for a swimming party when a baby mouse shot out into the middle of the kitchen from under the refrigerator. Trevor was snatched up by his aunt who proceeded to heroically jump

on top of a chair to save them both. Though his mother chastised her for doing such a thing to a 'boy child,' he'd never gotten over the fear of gerbils, Guinea pigs, hamsters or anything that walked like, smelled like or reminded him of a mouse. And these were rats!

"Oh-no-no-no, I can't go in there." There was a trembling sound in Trevor's voice as he stood back up on the last step. "I can't do it…I can't!"

"Don't turn chicken on me now, boy, we've only got twenty minutes to make this happen. Besides, they're as scared of you as you are of them. The light will frighten them into the cracks as we move through the tunnel." Kash swung the lantern to give Trevor a feeling of security and continued on down the passageway. Sure enough the critters scattered as the light came into range and they were able to walk through the channel relatively unmolested.

At last, to Trevor's relief, they reached a big, blue, wooden door; the type that would be used for the meat locker at the grocery store. It had a large round disc welded to a long metal bar that Kash pushed into the door to release the bolt. He grabbed the thick handle with his other hand and leaned back to pull the heavy door open. When he got it opened enough to slide in between it and the frame he turned to face the door from the inside to get more leverage to finish opening it up. It was as dark on the other side of the door as it was on the side they were coming from.

"How much further is it?" Trevor asked anxiously.

"This is it!"

"I don't see anything in here except another black hole."

Kash reached out, grabbing something in front of him and flung it aside. The soft lamplight poured into the chamber revealing several mysterious objects that had no meaning to Trevor at all.

"Whoa, this is too weird. Is that the contraption I'm supposed to squeeze into?" Trevor walked over to the porcelain Time Keeper and slowly ran his fingers over every inch of the beautiful carvings.

"No, that's where Mattie will be entering, you get the other one." Kash pointed to the dark blue box. "Take off your shoes and socks." He dragged an exquisite mahogany table out from behind the curtain where he laid the book. "Have you got the mantra memorized yet? We only have ten minutes."

"I-I-I think so," stuttered Trevor. "Do you want to hear it?"

"Let me show you how to get in position first and then you can try it out on me." Kash moved Trevor out of the way and backed into the Splitter's box. It was a tight squeeze, yet it seemed to fit him just fine. "You can never let yourself get fat, Trevor, or you'll never be able to fit in the time keeper."

Trevor chuckled nervously. Kash placed his feet exactly over the metal footprint in the floor and remembered that these prints were made for his feet, not Trevor's.

"Oh, by the way, Trevor, what size feet do you have? I hope a size ten and a half!"

"Pretty close. I buy ten and a half shoes, but I don't quite fill them up."

"That'll have to do. I know if your toes were hanging over the edge we'd be doomed." Kash rested his forearms on the rubber pads and griped the shiny brass bars on either side in front of him. "This is the Splitters Mark, Trevor. When the chime sounds in the Epoch Chronometer you say the password followed by the mantra. You must not move off the mark until Mattie can be displaced from the past to the present, undergoing the harmonic motion, materializing completely. If you slip off the mark at all she'll be caught between dimensions and we'll lose her forever. Do you understand?"

"I understand," Trevor said solemnly. "Let me repeat the creed to you." Trevor began to recite the creed as he'd memorized it. "I am a Splitter by destiny. Mattie is the Trekker by birth."

"No," Kash interrupted, "that's not right! It should be Mattie is <u>a</u> Trekker by <u>inheritance</u>, not <u>the</u> Trekker by <u>birth</u>. Try again."

Trevor went through it again. "I am a Splitter by destiny. Mattie is a Trekker by inheritance. Mattie and I combine together to split time. By bloodline you're destined, by marriage we're tied; let the strength of our love bring you back to my side."

"Perfect!" Kash said with enthusiasm. "Let's get you into the box. We've only got a couple minutes left. Remember, it's not how fast you say it. The important thing is that you

say it perfectly. Got it?"

Trevor nodded his head timidly. "I hope so. I'll do my best."

Trevor pulled off his shoes and socks, backed into the box, placing his feet directly over the footprint comparable to what he saw Kash do.

"Now grip the bar and rest your forearms on the arm-rest. It's easier if you lean back against the box for support. We can adjust the portable time keeper to your height and weight later," Kash coached.

"There's a portable version of this thing?" Trevor asked as he settled into the box.

"Of course, how do think we do this when we're somewhere else in the world? We'd never make it back here in time from the other side of the planet with only a 24 hour period to make connections."

"Well, that makes sense," Trevor agreed.

Kash backed away from the platform and leaned on the edge of the table. "Remember, you have two minutes to get it perfect. Say the password only one time and then you can repeat the mantra as much as you feel you need to. That should be plenty of time, so relax. Don't begin before you hear the end of the chime."

"What does the chime sound like? Is it just a 'dong' or does it play a tune?"

"It chimes a tune that lasts for about 10 seconds; wait until it ends. The Splitters two minute time frame doesn't start until it finishes. Oh, I forgot to tell you that once the chimes end, I can't say a word to help you. You're on your own."

"Great…that's just great! What if I can't remember the words perfectly?" Trevor was getting more concerned as the seconds passed.

"I can mouth the words silently, which probably won't help much unless you are good at reading lips. Don't worry; you're not going to have any trouble. You'll do fine. Relax!"

"Yeah…right," Trevor said sarcastically. "Relax!"

Kash and Trevor sat quietly for a few seconds before the Epoch Chronometer began to strike. 'Ding-g-g-g; ding-g-g-g; ding, dong, ding-g-g-g; dong, ding, ding, dong, ding-g-g-g-g.' Trevor glanced over at Kash for reassurance. Kash smiled and nodded his head for Trevor to begin.

"I'm a Splitter by destiny." Trevor had barely gotten out the first sentence of the password when Kash jumped up off the edge of the table shaking his head aggressively from side to side. He mouthed the words, "start over" and then stared at Trevor intently.

Trevor had no idea what he had said wrong. Never-the-less he immediately started over.

"I'm a Splitter…" was all he got out this time before Kash started throwing a silent fit. Once again, Kash mouthed something that looked like "am"…"am" which he repeated several times.

Trevor tried again, this time the only word he got out was “I’m” before Kash started squirming all over the place. A light went on in his head and he understood. The first word was really two words. He started over, saying the words carefully and more distinctly so he wouldn’t make another mistake. There wasn’t any time remaining for error now. “I *am* a Splitter by destiny. Mattie is a Trekker by inheritance. Mattie and I combine together to split time. By bloodline you’re destined, by marriage we’re tied; let the strength of our love bring you back to my side.”

A beautiful white light began to swirl within the chamber. The jewels on the ceiling began to glisten against the deep, blue background. Thousands of minute particles began to sparkle in the air as they migrated towards the white Time Keeper. The house began to rumble as the particles gathered closer together. Trevor continued to repeat the mantra, captivated by the sequence of electrical events that brought the room to life.

Lila screamed and ran to the center of the lawn when she felt the earth trembling. Her body teetered like a baby elephant standing on a beach ball as she tried to balance herself on the shaking ground. She thought it must be ‘the big one’ everyone had been talking about for years. After the quaking stopped she waddled as fast as she could around the house to see what the damages were. The second time around she was practically hysterical and her small energy supply was gone. She rested her hands on her knees, trying to catch her breath when she heard a voice calling out to her through the hedge

that bordered the driveway. "What's going on over there?" It was her nosy neighbor that she now mistakenly assumed was concerned for her welfare.

"Are you alright over there?" Lila replied. "Did you sustain any damage?"

"What are you talking about? Why would I have sustained any damage?"

Fran was baffled. She hadn't felt anything unusual at her house and honestly didn't know what Lila was having such a fit over.

"...from the earthquake, Fran, what else?"

"What earthquake?" Fran said mockingly. "You are certifiably crazy!"

"Oh, go soak your head, woman! You obviously live in another dimension or nut house, which ever comes closest to the truth!"

Lila left her neighbor alone with her attitude and ran into the house to call the city office. She thought maybe someone could tell her the size and epicenter of the earthquake. After it rang for quite some time she remembered that it was Saturday and no one was there to answer the phone.

"You need to get ready dear...it's almost time." Amber stood up and reached her hand out towards Mattie. "How are you feeling, Mattie?"

"I'm a little bit scared, Mom. What if this doesn't work?"

"Have some faith, dear. You know it doesn't hurt, since you've already done it once. The only difference between coming and going is that you'll be a bit tired when you return to your time. It won't last long though."

"If it wasn't for Trevor, I'd stay here with you. I miss you, Mom."

"I'll miss you too, Mattie, but everything will work out; you'll see." Amber gave Mattie a hug and a kiss on the cheek. "You're going to be a great Trekker, Mattie. I have complete confidence in you."

They walked up the steps together. As they got closer to where the print had originally appeared, a new one formed in a warm yellow color.

"Look Mattie…there it is."

Mattie stared at the print for a moment and turned back to look at her mother one last time. She wanted to hold a detailed picture of her in her mind; since this would the last time she would see her mother alive. This memory would have to last for the rest of her life. "I love you, Mom," Mattie said solemnly.

"I love you too, Mattie Pie," Amber responded tenderly. "Give your dad a hug for me when you get back."

"I will, Mom." Mattie stepped away from her towards the glowing print, until their fingers separated. She set her focus on the print, placed her foot squarely on top and was gone.

The particles moved in a rhythm that created a delicate musical sound that bounced off of the curtains and intermingled within themselves as it rebounded to the center of the room. The effect it produced was hypnotic. To his utter amazement, Trevor could see a figure forming out of the tiny particles of light within the other Time Keeper. It was Mattie. He was so excited to see her that he could hardly contain his emotions. It had worked! Kash was down on his knees with his head bowed as though he was praying. The Epoch Chronometer began to chime again. 'Ding-g-g-g; ding-g-g-g; ding, dong, ding-g-g-g; dong, ding, ding, dong, ding-g-g-g-g.' On the last ring Mattie's form filled in completely solid and the house became still. She dropped to the arm rests within the Time Keeper, her body weak from the transfer. Trevor's strength was also gone and he slumped down in his box. Kash ran over to Mattie and lifted her into his arms where he held her tight. Tears were streaming down his face. He tenderly removed her from the box and sat her down on a velvet couch over by the winding staircase. He hurried back to help Trevor out of the Time Keeper and carefully sat him next to Mattie. They were both incredibly weak from the Divvy. Trevor gently reached over and took Mattie's hand in his and gave it a gentle squeeze. They had a deep appreciation for each other now. They understood each other completely.

"You did it, son. Thank you," Kash whispered. "Thank you for bringing my…our Mattie home."

Everyone was exhausted and there were no words to express what each was feeling so they sat silently for several minutes.

Mattie sat up straighter. Her energy was beginning to return.

"Dad?" Mattie said, breaking the silence. "Is it possible that Mom may still be alive?"

Kash's eyes strayed towards the white Time-Keeper. "I don't see how. I saw her evaporate myself when the lightning struck. Why do you ask?"

Mattie's eyes wandered about the room. "I thought I saw her for a moment, before I could see the chamber forming. It was kind of like she was between here and there."

"I think you must have been mistaken, Mattie. I'm sure you want her back as much as I do. You probably imagined it."

"Maybe so," said Mattie. "It has been a long, tiring experience the last couple of days."

Kash stood up and walked over to the book. "There are two important things we have to do now."

"What's that?" Trevor asked.

"We need to find a way to get out of here without Lila seeing us and you two need to get married…legally!"

Chapter 13

The Escape

"Listen, Mrs. Schnettle. You're asking me to arrest one of the most revered women in this community," the officer said as he stepped out of the house onto the porch. I've got to have some evidence before I can make any decisions here."

Fran stepped towards the officer, until she was standing right under his nose. Her bony, long face turned to a splotchy, burgundy color and her eyes opened wide enough to see the whites all the way around the brown middle. In a controlled, agitated way she said, "I don't care who she thinks she is or for that matter who anybody thinks she is, she tried to kill me! Now, you better do something about it immediately before she gets away!"

"Gets away?" said the policeman. "Lila…I mean, Ms. Graham, I hardly consider her a big flight risk." The officer grinned at such a thought and sat down on the edge of the porch. He pulled his pen and note pad out of his back pocket to jot down a few notes. He took a slow, deep breath and said, "OK…go ahead and tell me exactly what happened and we'll see what I can do."

Fran began to explain how Lila had placed a bucket of tools directly behind her, while she wasn't paying attention, so she would trip over it and break her neck. According to her, Lila did it while she was distracted by a bee that was buzzing around her head. She finished the story by saying, "The bucket was full of sharp knives and tools that were pointed straight up and it was a miracle that I didn't get skewered when I fell."

"Is that it?" the policeman asked impatiently.

"What do you mean, is that it?" Fran retorted. "I nearly died! Isn't that enough? Now, get over there and arrest her!"

"Oh, brother!" The officer mumbled under his breath. He pushed himself up off the porch and called over his shoulder, "Let's walk over and see what's in the bucket and how the crime scene lays out." He tucked the pen and pad back into his pocket and motioned for Fran to come with him. "Ladies first," he said, turning his head away from her so she couldn't see him roll his eyes.

Lila was walking back around to the front of the house to take her gardening supplies in with her. She intended to call the police herself when she heard people talking in the front yard.

"Is this the deadly bucket of sharp objects you tripped over?" the policeman said, pushing the brim of his hat up off of his forehead.

Fran's mouth was in quite a pucker. She could see that the bucket contained a few tulip bulbs, a rag and a couple of hand tools with rubber handles rather than the sharp knives she'd

reported. "She must have dumped out the bucket and replaced the sharp objects with this other stuff," she snapped.

Lila appeared from around the corner where she had overheard the conversation as she approached. "I did no such thing, you bone headed old goat, and you'd be wise to leave well enough alone before I take you to court for defamation of character."

"You tried to kill me and you know it."

"I don't even know you. What would I stand to gain from killing you, other than freeing the neighborhood of one of the rudest, nosiest people in the community?"

Fran lunged at Lila. The policeman stepped in between them with outstretched arms to hold them apart and said, "Ladies, ladies, let's not blow this thing out of proportion any further than it already is. Obviously, Mrs. Schnettle, you were mistaken. Accidents happen and it's unfortunate that you scraped your ankle, but there are no grounds for an investigation as far as I can see."

"Of course not," Lila said, "however, there is something I'd like you to check out in my back yard since you're already here. I think someone broke into my shed and locked it from the inside. They're still in there, I'm sure. Follow me."

Mattie turned her head abruptly and said, "We've got to get out of here…NOW! In 3 minutes, Lila, Mrs. Schnettle and a policeman will be coming back to check on the

shed you came through. We've got to replace the lock and get around to the other side before they can get there."

"How could you possibly know all that?" Trevor asked, amazed.

"I don't know…somehow I can see it all in my head. What do we need to take with us, Dad?"

Kash jumped up and pulled back one of the curtains, exposing two metal containers. "It's part of being a Trekker. They get all kinds of promptings and can see things within a five minute span that helps them escape danger. Apparently Mattie has enough of her powers to help us get away. You can bet your life she's accurate. We have no time to waste. Mattie, you grab the book. Trevor, you get the white case and I'll carry the blue one; hurry!"

They each picked up their assigned items and scurried out of the chamber. Mattie and Trevor ran ahead. Kash pulled the door closed and ran to catch up. The rats were scrambling everywhere to get out of the way; making it sound like a Texas hail storm inside the tunnel. After they had all gotten out, Trevor bent over to close the trap door and pull the rug back over the top.

Mattie laughed at what she saw. "Nice polka-dot shorts, Trev. What happened to your pants?"

Trevor blushed, covered his seat with his hands and turned his back to the wall. "I risked body and limb to save you, Mattie…you owe me!"

"Knock it off, you two!" Kash interrupted. "Pull the chairs and some of the junk over the top of the entrance. With any luck, Lila won't try to clean this mess up for a long time. She doesn't have the key anyway." He opened the door boldly and stepped out. "Let's go!" When they were all outside, Kash replaced the board and padlock as it had originally been. Mattie led the way, sprinting across the yard. They barely turned the corner of the house on the opposite side when Lila appeared.

Lila marched towards the shed, followed closely by the policeman and Fran. "I know I heard someone in the shed and whoever it was knew that I was outside the door, too. The board and the lock are both on the ground and they had locked it from the inside. You'll see what I'm talking about when you get back there."

They marched closely behind Lila until she stopped abruptly in front of the old shed. The policeman stumbled into Lila and Fran stumbled into the policeman.

"A little warning would be nice if you're planning to stop," Fran said curtly.

"I…I….don't understand," Lila stuttered. She was puzzled and flushed with embarrassment about what she saw.

"I thought you said the lock and board were on the ground?" the policeman reminded her.

"They were. I wasn't gone for more than five minutes and no one has been in the yard except for me, which, by the way, I'd appreciate it if you'd get off of my property Mrs. Schnettle and mind your own business from now on."

Kash opened the trunk of the car and everyone set their items inside carefully. "Get in. We've got to get out of town and find someone to marry you two before nightfall. I don't want to take any chances that the Split could unravel and send Mattie back."

"Is that possible?" Trevor said, concerned for his new bride of sorts.

"I don't know," replied Kash, "but you two are meant to be together and I intend to reduce the risks of that not happening."

Mattie saw the excitement in Trevor's face. They smiled at each other and wedged their bodies tightly into the overly packed car and headed out of town.

"Now what?" asked Trevor. "Where do we go from here?"

"Mom said we needed to head for the beach house; do you know where that is, Dad?" Mattie inquired.

"Boy, I sure do. That's where I was heading myself. It's like your mother and I share the same brain sometimes; even if it is eight years apart!"

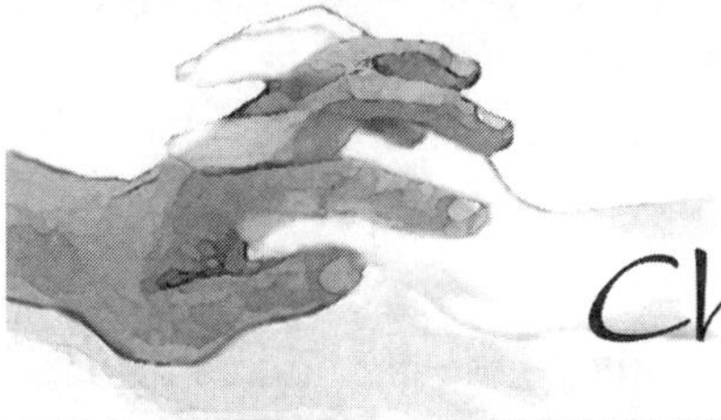

Chapter 14

The Kidnapping

"It's nearly 5:30. We've been driving for hours," Trevor complained, squirming uncomfortably in the back seat. After all, he shared it with an overstuffed piece of luggage, a large garbage bag full of shoes, a stack of books in the back window that kept falling down on his head and one wilting potted plant with sprawling branches of leaves that pressured him against his door. "We must be 500 miles from civilization out here."

"We're almost there," Kash replied. "I'm going to go to the old house first. We need to dump some of this stuff and then we'll go back into town to see if we can find someone to marry you two before time unravels everything."

The small road that they had pulled onto was bordered by thick, plush foliage. There were no buildings or ocean views to indicate they were anywhere close to a beach house, just tall pine trees and brush that filled in the gaps. The road was bumpy, tossing the car and its passengers around a bit as the tires moved over numerous small holes and loose gravel that the coastal weather had broken down. It appeared to them that no one had traveled over the road for decades. Trevor tried to imagine what

the old beach house must look like, considering the poor condition of the access road, and wondered what he had gotten himself into.

Finally Kash slowed down and pulled through an opening in the thick brush onto a narrow dirt road. As he rounded the bend, the ocean opened up into full view about fifty yards ahead. There was a sprawling, open field of grass to the left of the road and the thick foliage continued on the right side, towards an old, two story house that was nestled cozily into the edge of the forest, facing the beach. Most of it was hidden within the wild thicket and tall grass that surrounded it. The landscape was pristine and beautiful.

Trevor was in awe. "Wow, this is beautiful in here," he said. "It feels like we're in a world of our own."

"It is beautiful," Kash replied. "Amber loved it here, though we haven't been here for nearly 10 years."

Kash allowed the car to roll to a stop in front of the old house where they all sat for a few minutes taking it all in. The house was visibly run down to the point that the paint was nearly all gone on the outside and the lacy trellis work was broken apart and dangling here, there and everywhere it was not supposed to be.

"Oh my," Mattie said sadly. "It looks like it's going to fall down. Do we dare open the door?"

Kash spoke up with an unexpected tone of excitement in his voice. "Things aren't always as they seem Mattie Pie...be patient." He threw open the car door and jumped out with the same enthusiasm as a child that was surrounded by a pile of chocolate covered donuts.

"We're home!" he exclaimed as he threw his arms up, taking in a deep breath of fresh country air. "We're finally home!"

"Yeah, if you say so!" Trevor said skeptically.

Mattie turned to Trevor and whispered, "I guess beauty really is in the eyes of the beholder."

Trevor grunted and started pulling things out of the back seat to take inside. "Here Mattie, let me hand you some of this stuff. I hope the front porch will hold our weight."

Kash chuckled softly as he pranced towards the front door, beckoning them to follow him.

Trevor and Mattie slowly started walking towards the house together. He leaned in next to her ear and said softly, "Do you get the feeling he knows something we don't?"

"Boy, I sure do," said Mattie, "He seems too happy to see this beat up old place."

"Come on," Kash said. "Pick up your pace! I can hardly wait to see what you think."

Mattie and Trevor smiled at each other. They picked up their pace and arrived at the front door as Kash started to open it. What they saw took their breath away. They expected to see cob webs everywhere; holes in the floor; a broken down staircase; mice and bugs running freely throughout the house, and lots of dilapidated old furniture with caked on dirt and water damage from a leaking roof. They stood in the open doorway with their jaws and eyes wide open. They would have never guessed that it would be this way inside, especially with how rundown it was from the outside.

"Rainey!" Kash called out, "Are you here?"

"Who's Rainey, Dad?"

"Rainey, we're home!" Kash set his things on the floor and continued to call out as he walked from room to room.

"Hmmm, I wonder where she is?" Kash said as he came back into the entry.

"Dad," Mattie insisted, "who…is…Rainey?"

"She's the house keeper, grounds keeper, maid, cook and chief bottle washer. Rainey is your mother's favorite aunt. She's a little bit crazy, but wonderful!"

Mattie set her things down and said, "How come I've never heard of Great-aunt Rainey? I can't believe how many big surprises I've had during the past few days…and look at this place! It's incredible! It looks like a palace in here."

Kash swung open the screen door, calling out as he walked back to the car, "Let's get everything moved inside and I'll show you around later. We've only got about 3 hours left to find us a preacher and that's not going to be easy on a weekend."

They spent the next half hour bringing things in from the car, filling up the entry way. "We've got to go find a preacher; we're getting short on time and it'll take us 10 minutes to get into town," Kash reminded them.

They drove into town and parked in front of the only gas station they could find. Kash left Mattie and Trevor in the car and went in to talk to the attendant. He returned a few minutes later.

Kash leaned against the car and said, "I don't know what I was thinking. It's Saturday. The judge won't be around today." His face showed some stress from the pressure of finding someone to marry them before the sun set.

"I'd like to be married in the church, Dad, not the courthouse!" Mattie interrupted. "Can't we find a local preacher that could marry us instead?"

"I hope so, but we've got to get the marriage license first or the preacher won't be able to marry you anyway. The only way we can get a license on a weekend is to get it through a judge. Why don't you two see if you can find a phone book and locate a church nearby while I see if I can find out where the judge lives?"

Trevor and Mattie walked over to a phone booth and started thumbing through the phonebook. A few seconds later Trevor started slapping his pockets for a pen.

"There's only one church in town," Trevor said. He turned to Mattie and asked if she had a pen to write down the address.

"I don't!" she said, "Maybe there's one in the car. " Mattie ran back to the car and started rummaging through the glove box. After a thorough, unfruitful search there, she tried groping around underneath the seat. As she reached back farther her finger tips bumped into something hard. She got out of the car and knelt down on the ground to see if she could dig it out of its hiding place. It appeared to be an old ring box. Most of the brass finish was tarnished with age and handling and it was wedged in snuggly against the metal frame. She wiggled it

until it came loose and pulled it from its hiding place. As she dug into the edges with her fingernails to open the lid Trevor called out to remind her that he still needed a pen.

"I can't find one…" she called back, "I'll go in the gas station and see if they'll loan me one in there." Mattie stuffed the box in her pocket and hurried inside. A minute later she and Kash came out, irritated about something.

"Don't bother writing down any preachers address, the only preacher in town isn't." Kash said sarcastically.

"What do you mean?" Trevor asked.

"There's a save-the-world type clergyman's convention in L.A. and he won't be back until late tonight. We're way too far away from the next town to find another authorized official before it's too late. The only shot we have is to find the judge and get him to marry you within the next two hours. I'm sorry about the church wedding Mattie."

"We can do that later, Dad. The important thing is to find the Judge. Did the attendant know where he lives?"

"Yes, but it's his wife's birthday and he doesn't think he'll be at home. They suggested we check around town in some of the restaurants. He was going to take her out to dinner."

Trevor interrupted them, "How hard can that be?"

Kash shrugged his shoulders! "Does anyone know what the judge looks like?"

"Oh," Mattie exclaimed, "we'll ask the people at the restaurants. Certainly everyone would know the judge in such

a small town. Besides that, how many restaurants can there be on one street?"

"You're right!" Kash said, "Let's split up and see if we can find him. We'll meet back here in thirty minutes."

They each ran off to a different diner to see if they could find the judge. A half hour later they all returned without any news.

"Did we cover all of the food places?" Trevor asked as he sat down on the curb next to Mattie.

"I think we did," replied Mattie.

There were no other restaurants in town and they only had about an hour left before dusk. As they sat on the curb, wondering what to do or what they could do they saw an older man waving as he hurried down Main Street towards them.

A slightly bent, scruffy bearded man approached them out of breath; one hand placed over his chest. "Did I overhear you say you were trying to find Judge Linden?"

"That's right," Kash said.

"He took his wife to Blue Cliff Lodge for her birthday." He pointed north and said, "The lodge is about two miles out of town heading in that direction, along the old highway. It's hidden a bit by the trees. Watch for a brick wall that stands at the drive entrance and you won't miss it. It's almost completely covered with ivy."

Mattie jumped up and gave the man a hug. "Thank you," she said. "I don't even know your name."

"Brinley…Dale Brinley." The man blushed and smiled as he turned to walk away. "…and you're welcome."

They piled back into the car and headed for the restaurant.

"There it is!" Trevor called out. "See it?"

"I see it!" Kash replied, turning the car into the driveway that wound down towards the cliffs. A large, gable building stood firmly on the flat of the land overlooking the ocean. He pulled up to the door where a young man in a nice suit opened his door to greet him.

"Good evening sir. If you'll leave the keys in the car, I'll park it for you."

"No, thank you," said Kash. "I'm only going to be a minute. They're dropping me off and then they'll move the car out of your way."

"Very good, sir," the young man responded and returned to his station by the door.

Kash turned to Mattie and Trevor to tell them where to meet him and his eyes opened wide in shock. "Mattie, where's your hand?"

"What?"

"Your hand!"

Mattie glanced down at her hands to find her left hand was completely invisible. Mattie's face pinched together in horror.

"It's beginning." Kash exclaimed, "I've got to find the judge." He hurried into the restaurant, where he was stopped by the doorman before he could get two feet inside the lobby.

"Sorry, sir…you must have a tie to go any further," the doorman informed him.

"A tie? You want me to find a tie while my daughter is dying in the car?" Kash snapped.

"This is a formal dining room sir and a tie is required."

"You've got to be kidding me!" Kash pushed the door man aside and started towards the reservation desk. "I need help to find Judge Linden immediately…" he said in a loud voice. "It's a matter of life and death!"

The doorman rushed up behind him and grabbed him by the collar with one hand and his arm with the other. He pulled him back towards the door, creating quite a scuffle. Kash began struggling to get free and started yelling for the judge in hopes that he would hear him and come to his rescue. This brought several large men running from various areas of the room to help muscle Kash out of the building. Everyone in the dining room stopped what they were doing and those who were close enough to see into the lobby stood to watch the show. Kash was stronger than they thought. He managed to throw several to the ground before they could wrestle him to the exit.

Before they were about to toss him out the door, a voice interrupted them.

"Wait…gentlemen…let me see if I can help this man. Everyone calm down. Now…what's going on out here?"

The men released Kash and stood back to let the judge move closer. Kash stood up, straightened his clothes and said, "Are you Judge Linden?"

"That's right. What seems to be your problem?"

"My daughter needs to get married within the hour and the only clergyman that can do it is out of town. You're her only hope."

"You make it sound as if she were going to die if she doesn't get married by sundown!"

The men chuckled and spoke quietly amongst themselves; laughing at how ridiculous they thought Kash was acting.

"Well…er…a…it's extremely important, Judge." Kash sputtered. "I'll pay you anything you want!"

That offer shut the men up instantly. They remained silent as they awaited the Judge's response.

"Money isn't the issue; I'm sorry. I can't help you tonight for two reasons. First, it's my wife's birthday and second, I still have to drag her with me to perform another wedding in less than an hour that I can't miss for anything. It's impossible for me to perform a marriage for your daughter until later tonight."

"That'll be too late judge; it has to be right now!"

"Well, I can't possibly do it right now. I was getting up, ready to leave when you came bursting in." He turned to the men and said, "Gentlemen, kindly escort this man to his car." The judge went back to the dining room to gather his things and get his wife. The men escorted Kash out to the parking lot where Trevor and Mattie were still waiting.

When Kash got back inside the car he could see that they were even more upset than when he had gone in only a few minutes earlier. "What's the matter?"

"Mattie's left ear and top of her head keeps appearing and disappearing." Trevor blurted out.

"I don't know what to do," said Kash solemnly. "Maybe there's something in the chamber that can help us back at the house."

"There's a chamber at this house, too?" Trevor asked.

"It's the oldest chamber left in the world. That's why I said we were home!"

"Let's try, Dad. We have nothing left to lose except more of my body parts." Mattie said. "The sun sets within the hour."

Kash sat up straight and gazed out the front window. "Wait…I've got an idea. Mattie, I need to see if your powers are present to do a Half-Parallel."

"A what?" Mattie said curiously.

"A Half-Parallel! Just a minute and I'll explain." Kash drove away from the restaurant, over to the edge of the cliff to the lookout point. "Get out and follow me."

Mattie and Trevor got out and followed him down the path out to the edge of the cliff. It was a clear evening and the sun was drawing low over the horizon. The fresh, salty air was exhilarating and the view was spectacular of the waves crashing against the jagged shoreline a couple hundred feet below.

Kash stopped and pointed to the small patch of sandy beach to the side of the great boulders that dotted the ocean front. "Do you see that small spot of sand down there Mattie."

"You mean that little space on the far end of the shore?"

"Yep…that's the one."

Mattie scratched her disappearing ear. She was confused about what her dad was getting at.

Kash pulled Mattie over close to him and said, "I want you to make a fist with your left hand and lift your left arm in front of your body in an "L" shape, parallel to the ground at your chest level like this." He demonstrated for Mattie as he explained the procedure. "Now, bring your right palm up facing your left fist and connect them together; fingers close together and pointing upward. Keep your right elbow close to your body. Then say, 'to the sand patch' while you are looking right at it." Kash searched her face for signs of fear. He placed both of his hands on her shoulders and said, "Do you think you can do that, Mattie?"

"Why couldn't I, Dad?" Mattie was stumped by his overly concerned behavior.

"Take a deep breath. Your mother said that there's no air during the trip. Don't be afraid."

"I'm not afraid, Dad…I just don't understand why I'm doing this."

"You'll see. In fact, we'll all see if you have enough of your powers to do it."

"OK," Mattie agreed. "I don't get it, but I'll do what you ask."

Mattie placed her hands in the Half-Parallel position that her father had demonstrated for her. She focused her eyes on the suggested target and said, "To the sand!" Her body started to fade in and out of a transparent state, yet she didn't move an inch.

"What was I supposed to do, Dad? Is that all there is? I don't see how that's going to help us get married."

"Try again Mattie. Concentrate on the sandy area and don't let anything else come into your mind. We want you to move to that small patch of sand within our present time frame." Kash patted her on the back and said, "Try again. You can do it…" and stepped away from her.

Mattie took her position again and stared at the slight spot of brown sand nestled amongst the rocks at the bottom of the cliff. Then, stretching her neck forward said quickly, "To the sand." She disappeared instantly and reappeared in the plot of sand she was focusing on several hundred feet away.

Trevor shook his head in disbelief. "Holy cow, that was incredible. Does she get back the same way and do I need to move?"

Kash started backing away from the cliff. "I think it's a good idea to give her some space, since she's such a rookie at this stuff."

Trevor hurried over to stand near Kash where he could still see Mattie. Once again she disappeared instantly and reappeared out of nowhere, standing right in front of them. Mattie was so excited she could hardly stand still.

"Wow, Dad. That was amazing!" Mattie said as she danced sideways to stand by Trevor. "Tell me what you're thinking, Dad. How can we use this to solve our problem? I noticed my left foot disappeared following the first shift to the sand."

Kash pushed them ahead of him to go back up the trail to the car. "The Judge and his wife are going to be coming out of the restaurant in a few minutes. He's supposed to marry another couple at 6:30, but we're going to side track him to our house first. You're going to have to kidnap both of them Mattie, by transporting yourself to the back seat of their car as soon as they open it to get in."

"But, Dad, that'll make me a criminal! Besides, why would they want to go with me? I could never hurt them or anything like that!" Mattie hesitated for a moment, weighing the situation in her mind. "OK…" she said undecidedly. How do we do it?"

"Here's what we need to do…get in."

Mattie and Trevor got in the back. Kash got in the driver's seat and leaned over back towards them, pointing to the floor. "Do you see that small, empty, burlap sack that's stuffed under the seat?"

"Yeah," Mattie said.

"Hand that to me would you please?" Kash pulled out his pocket knife and cut a couple of holes in the sack. "Put this on your head Mattie and let's see if the holes are where they need to be for your eyes."

"Are you suggesting that I wear this when I kidnap them? You're joking, right?"

"Think about it, Mattie. The sack will serve two purposes. Number one, it'll hide your disappearing head and number two, they won't see who you are. Neither of them have ever seen you before and they won't have any idea how you got in their car. You can use the end of your lipstick tube as a gun. They won't know the difference and you can order them to drive you out to the house. I'll straighten it out when you get there."

"Isn't there another way, Dad?"

"This is the only way I can think of, and unless either of you have a better idea I think we better go with this plan right now." Kash sat patiently waiting for either of them to come up with something better. "Besides, Mattie, if you run into any trouble, you know how to shift to another location in an instance. All you need is a clear path of air to your target."

"Wait a minute," Mattie interrupted. "What do you mean by a clear path of air?"

"In order to do the Half-Parallel, you have to have a straight shot to the target. You can't have any solid objects between you and your final destination. Come on…we're running out of time, Mattie. You can do this."

Mattie sat quietly staring at the space where her left hand used to be and said, "I guess I don't have much choice, do I?"

Kash pulled up next to one of the big pillars near the front of the restaurant to let Mattie out. He described the judge to her and drove off to get things ready at the house. With the bag in one hand and her lipstick in the other Mattie huddled up against the rock base and watched for the judge to come out to his car. Mattie tied her long black hair into a knotted pony tail and tucked it inside her collar so it wouldn't get in the way or be seen underneath the sack. Several minutes passed before she heard the doorman say goodnight to the judge and his wife. The valet handed him the keys to his car and opened the door for his wife. Mattie slipped the sack over her head and waited for the judge to get in the car himself. When he reached to pull the door shut Mattie set her Half-Parallel, stared at the back seat of the car and said softly, "To the back seat of the car…" and disappeared. She stayed scrunched down on the floor, trembling. Mattie couldn't believe she was doing this, but knew there was no other choice. It was either do this or die! What was surprising was that she actually kind of liked the excitement of it all in a contradictory sort of way.

She waited until she thought the car was well out of sight from the restaurant personnel before making her move; giving her some time to work up her courage. When she shifted her weight to push herself up off the floor she miscalculated the location of her invisible hand and jammed it into her knee. The lipstick popped out of her fingers and rolled under her body. Her ability to search was restricted by the tight squeeze between the seats. She tried and tried to find the small, round tube without success. The lipstick was nowhere to be found. Mattie felt sick inside. She had only been working the plan for three minutes and had already blown it. She didn't know what to do; her mind was blank. She laid there on the floor racking her brain for an alternative plan. She was trapped with solid objects all around her. There was no way she could Half-Parallel anywhere.

To her relief, the Judge rolled down his window a couple of inches to let in some fresh air, which quickly circulated over Mattie. It awakened her senses and calmed her down, allowing her to think again. With the window open she thought that maybe she could Half-Parallel out of the car, transport out in front of the judge by a few hundred feet and lay down in the road like she'd been hit by another car. Surely they would stop to help her and she could ask them to take her to the house. The only problem was that she couldn't see anything other than the tops of the trees since she was down on the floor and couldn't sit up. The judge wasn't driving fast, yet it was still difficult to focus on a single tree long enough to make the transfer. She thought it might be possible to sit on one of the larger limbs until she could shift to a different location. She set the Half-Parallel and tried several times to lock in a focus. The trees

were passing too quickly. Finally she saw a thick patch of oak trees that were strung together. She decided to give it a shot whether she had a perfect line of sight or not, because she had everything to lose now and the judge could close the window at any moment. "To the branch…" she said quickly and the next thing she knew she was sitting 25 feet in the air on a small limb that was rocking up and down with her weight on it. The Judge drove on without a hitch. Mattie sniggered to herself at how easy that was to get out of the car, lost her balance and fell backwards out of the tree. As she was breaking through the tree branches she managed to hold her focus on a soft patch of grass near the side of the road. She locked in a Half-Parallel and said, "to the grass" and disappeared. She safely reappeared on the grass lying on her back, though the pull of the gravity during her fall still had some affect. It knocked some of the wind out of her, but not enough to slow her down.

The front door to the old house flew open as Kash turned off the key to the car. Out came a fidgety, elderly woman with gray hair that was tied in a tidy knot on the top of her head. She had on a clean white pair of mechanics coveralls with an apron tied around her waist. Blaring, white tennis shoes poked out from underneath the extra long cuffs that dragged on the ground. She was a sight to behold as she scurried out to the car, waving her hands uncontrollably.

"Kash," she called out "He smelled like burning flesh!" The woman threw herself into Kash's arms the moment he got out of the car. "He was going to kill me!"

"Rainey, my goodness Rainey…who tried to kill you?"

"The man in the shimmering clothes! He grabbed me from behind and forced me into the cellar where he tied me up." Her voice became harsh in tone. "He didn't do a very good job of it though; must have been a city boy." Returning to her sympathetic pitch she continued. "Anyway, when he turned around to pick up the hatchet near the wood stack I got one of my hands free. I grabbed the coal scoop and smacked him in the head as hard as I could. I thought I knocked him out because he was just lying there bleeding all over the floor. After I untied myself, I headed for the stairs. He must have grabbed my ankle and pulled me off my feet because I hit my head on the bottom step. When I woke up about an hour later I had a nasty cut over my eyebrow and he was gone. After I saw all of your things in the entry way I thought I had missed you and had failed Amber. I'd rather die than fail Amber."

Kash wrapped his arms around Rainey and patted her on the back to comfort her. "Everything will be fine, Rainey, we're here now. You did good…really good."

Rainey turned her head towards Trevor. "Who's he?" she said suspiciously.

"This is Trevor Karington, Rainey. He's going to be my son-in-law soon."

"Oh!" she said to Trevor crisply. "Welcome!"

Her face went serious again when she remembered the message she was supposed to deliver to Kash. "Amber left a

letter for me to give you the moment you arrived." She pushed herself away from Kash, grabbed his arm and pulled him towards the house. "Come with me quickly. You were supposed to get this around 4:00 this afternoon and it's almost 6:30."

Mattie stood up immediately to see how far away the Judge had gone. The car had moved out of sight. As she studied the area it began to feel familiar to her. She noticed a wider gap in the foliage on the left side of the road and figured that the Judge had probably turned there. She transported up to the area and recognized it as the road they had taken earlier to get to the beach house. After a series of Half-Parallels she found herself positioned strategically behind the tool shed with the Judge's car parked out front in full view.

Chapter 15

The Wedding

Kash and Trevor followed Rainey up the winding staircase to the second level. They passed several rooms before stopping in front of the door at the end of the hall. Rainey reached above the door frame and pulled down what appeared to be an ancient key. She slid it into the lock and pounded the door with her foot 3 times before turning the knob.

"Amber said it would be safe to bring anyone that was with you into the Chamber," Rainey said. "She said I could trust them."

"What else did she say?" Kash asked.

"She said she was going away for a while and not to worry—she'll be back, although it could take some time. I'm not sure what she meant by that, but that's what she said."

"*I'm not sure either,*" thought Kash. "*I wish I was.*"

Rainey turned and stepped into the dark room. She knew, by habit, where everything was and walked straight over to a small, round table towards the back. She picked something up and returned with it in her hand. "Here…" she said, handing it to Kash. "She wanted me to give you this letter."

Kash reached out to take it when the front doorbell rang and someone knocked on the back door simultaneously.

Rainey yanked the letter back, holding it tightly against her chest with both hands. She jerked her head up and stretched her eyes wide open; appearing a bit insane. "Who could that be?" she said with pursed lips. Her eyes flickering from side to side as if she were trying to remember the last time anyone had come to visit her. "I'll go see who it is," she whispered loudly. "You stay here."

Rainey stuffed the envelope into Kash's hand and scurried quickly out of the room. Kash tore the end of it off, blew inside and slid the note out. He read it silently at first and then, with a smile, he started at the beginning and read it out loud to Trevor.

My Dearest Kash,

I have another small surprise for you that will probably relieve your troubled mind. Since Mattie returned from her first Divvy this morning by way of a prayer and a promise, she has to get married by sundown tonight or I think she may start disappearing piece by piece into the core of time.

I've taken the liberty of setting up Mattie and Trevor's marriage arrangements in advance. They are simple, but it's the best I could do under the circumstances. The only qualified clergy in town wasn't available so I had to book

the Judge. Tell Mattie that I'm sorry it isn't in a church like she always dreamed of. I promise when I get back we'll do things right and throw a wonderful reception for her.

Kash stopped reading for a moment. "I wonder what she means when she says we'll do things right when she gets back. She keeps dropping hints and I don't know what to do with them." He lifted one eyebrow at Trevor and continued reading.

You should expect to see the Judge at the front door by 6:30 tonight with a marriage license in his hand and his wife as a witness. I understand they had some other special plans this evening and were good enough to take the time to do this for us as a favor to my parents who were good friends with his parents. The most important thing right now is to get them legally married to stop her from being pulled into the void bit by bit.

Tell Mattie there is a wedding dress in the closet for her to wear tonight and a tuxedo for Trevor. I hope I got him the right size. All I had to go on was a description of him from Mattie over eight years ago. You have a new black suit in our closet, white shirt and all the trimmings, too. I even had Rainey get herself a new dress and shoes for the occasion. She doesn't know exactly why, but she will in a few hours. Give her a hug for me and thank her for being such a wonderful aunt. I've booked the wedding suite for Mattie and Trevor at the Inn at San Salto, just up the beach. I worked

out a deal with the manager and they can stay as long as they want to. A limo will be out to pick them up around 8:00 tonight. Gosh, I feel like a fairy godmother! It's been really fun and I wish I could be there in person, wearing a new dress myself.

Have a wonderful time, my darlings. I love you all. Please tell Trevor I said welcome to the family. I look forward to meeting him in person some day.

All my love,
Amber

"She did it again!" Kash said, bewildered by her letter. "It's like she's simply out of town or something."

Rainey shouted out from the bottom of the staircase. "Kash! There's someone here to see you. Trevor…there's someone here to see you, too!" Rainey took off her shoe and pounded it on the railing. "Hey you guys, did you hear me?"

"We hear you, Rainey. Ask our guests at the front door to please come in and have a chair and Trevor will be right there. You need to go and get your new dress and shoes on right away."

Rainey rocked her head loosely from shoulder to shoulder and stopped abruptly, locking her eyes on the ceiling. "How did you know about my new dress?" She called back.

"I'll tell you later." Kash turned to Trevor and said, "That's got to be Mattie at the back door. If you'll go and fill

her in it would be helpful. I'm going to go to the attic and see if I can find some of Nana's old formal gloves to cover Mattie's invisible hand."

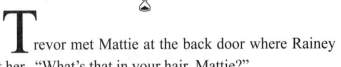

Trevor met Mattie at the back door where Rainey had left her. "What's that in your hair, Mattie?"

"I don't know…what?"

"Sticks and leaves? Huh! What a mess…"

"I love you, too," Mattie said sarcastically. She told him what happened in the car and how she Paralleled into the top of the tree and lost her balance. Trevor started pulling the debris out of Mattie's hair as he summarized Amber's letter to Kash.

"I can't believe Mom did all of this, knowing she was going to die before it all took place," Mattie said quietly.

"You have an amazing mother, Mattie, and your Dad tells me you're a lot like her." Trevor gave her a kiss on her cheek and said, "Come on…we need to hurry and get ready."

Mattie came out into the hall to join Kash and Trevor as they were helping each other with their ties. "I don't think I've ever gotten ready this fast for anything in my life." She was dressed from head to toe in white and was visibly nervous.

"Wow, you look beautiful…what's left to see of you!" Trevor said teasingly.

Mattie tilted her head, exhaling heavily. "Yeah, yeah; very funny. How am I going to keep them from noticing my missing hand and foot, not to mention the whole left side of my head fading in and out?"

Kash picked up the long, white gloves he had found in the old trunk up in the attic and handed them to Mattie. "These will cover your hand; your dress will cover your foot and the veil will help cover your missing ear. We'll steer you to the left of the Judge and make sure his wife is on the other side of the room with Rainey. As soon as you say 'I do,' your missing parts should reappear."

"Oh, my goodness," Mattie sighed. "Nothing is ever simple, is it?" She pulled on the gloves and picked up the train of her dress.

"It'll be fun…" Trevor said, trying to comfort Mattie and lighten the tension he himself was feeling. "Who in this world could ever lay claim to so many fantastic things happening at their wedding? We'll remember our special day forever with total clarity!"

Mattie forced a one-sided smile, since the other half of her face was sputtering out of sight at the moment and no one could see it anyway.

"We'd better get this show on the road," Kash said. "I'll go down first and get everyone in position." Kash went down to greet the Judge wondering how he would respond to seeing him again. When he entered the room, he tried to act surprised at seeing the Judge.

"Judge Linden. I thought you had another wedding to perform tonight," Kash said.

"Well, well," the judge said. "It's you!"

Kash walked towards the judge, hoping he didn't appear phony. "I hope you'll give me a second chance after giving you such an unruly first impression, sir?"

The judge laughed softly and stood up to shake Kash's hand. He then turned to his wife and said in a humorous tone, "This is the gentleman from the restaurant tonight dear, the man that made your birthday a memorable one. This is Amber's husband, Kash Bott. Kash…this is my wife, Lois."

Kash reached out to shake her hand. "Pleased to meet you, Mrs. Linden. I hope I didn't ruin your birthday celebration."

Lois smiled and said, "Are you kidding? You were the best part of the evening! At our age there's not much we can think of to do that's exciting anymore and you were exhilarating to everyone there. That was more excitement than we've seen for twenty years around here."

Kash blushed and bowed graciously. "You're very kind, Mrs. Linden."

"Call me Lois, you cute thing."

"That reminds me," the judge interrupted. "Where is Amber?"

"It's a long story, Judge. She wanted me to express her deepest gratitude to you and your wife for performing this

wedding for us tonight. You have no idea how important this marriage is."

The Judge sat back down and stretched his arm comfortably across the back of the couch. "I'm sorry she couldn't be here. I would have enjoyed seeing her again. Amber made arrangements with me over the phone several weeks ago. The way you acted at the restaurant tonight I can see that it must be important. Regardless, I'd do anything for the family of Dane and Marion Graham…anything! They treated me like their own son when my dad died. It hit me pretty hard when they disappeared. We spent the last ten years trying to find out what happened to them. That's one mystery we never did solve and it haunts me to this day."

"I know what you mean. It was an awful shock to Amber," said Kash, "and it still haunts us, too.

Out in the hallway the floor began squeaking every few seconds, like someone was sneaking around. Unexpectedly, Rainey stuck her head around the edge of the door with the silliest grin on her face. To everyone's surprise she jumped into the room giggling like a little child. She was showing off her new dress and shoes that Amber had her buy for the occasion. It looked like she had shaken her head upside down in a wind storm and sprayed her hair stiff. Kash fought back a smile as he went over to take Rainey's hand to usher her into the room. He regained his composure and said, "You look lovely, Rainey; picture perfect for a wedding. You picked out the perfect dress and matching shoes, too...you look like an angel!"

Rainey cocked her head, keeping Kash in sight out of the corner of her eyes. She was convinced that he was psychic and she wasn't sure how she felt about that. Kash led her over to the right side of the room and set her down next to Judge Linden's wife. He proceeded to set up the room and its occupants so that when Mattie came in she would be off to the left side of everyone. He lit several candles that he placed thoughtfully around the room, pulled all the curtains closed and turned out all of the lights. "Mattie loves candlelight," Kash declared, "and she has always dreamed of having a candlelight ceremony."

"Really?" said Trevor as he strolled into the room. "She never mentioned that to me!"

Kash turned his head towards Trevor and frowned. He couldn't believe Trevor didn't have enough sense to play along under the circumstances. Trevor tipped his head slightly, frowning back. Then he realized what Kash meant and tried to fix the problem.

"Oh, yeah…I do seem to remember her saying something about candles on our first date."

Kash shook his head discreetly and changed the subject. "Judge and Lois, this is Trevor Karington—the groom. Trevor, this is Judge and Mrs. Linden. They have graciously come out tonight to marry you two."

"I'm happy to make your acquaintance and thank you for coming." Trevor fidgeted for a moment and then excused himself to go get Mattie.

"Ya ready, Mattie? Your dad turned off all of the lights and lit a few candles to help conceal your disappearing act." Trevor snickered. He really thought Mattie's condition was kind of fun, in a weird sort of way. "I think this is going to work out just fine. Let's go!"

"I'm glad one of us is getting a kick out of all of this. You don't seem to grasp the seriousness of my situation."

"What's to grasp? We've got to get married by sundown. The Judge is downstairs; I'm in favor of marrying you and everything is ready to go. All you have to do is get down there and say 'I do' and all your body parts will reappear! I think you better do it soon though, because the sun is getting close to the horizon."

Mattie's head sputtered a bit as she adjusted her veil. She smoothed the long, white kid gloves that went clear up to her elbows and said, "OK…let's do this thing." She pushed Trevor ahead of her and they both started down the stairs.

"Make sure you stand to the right of me, Trevor, so the judge can't see the left side of my face and please hurry him along as much as possible."

"Don't worry; I will."

Mattie stopped abruptly. "Wait…we forgot the rings."

"What rings? I didn't have any time to buy a ring." For the first time, Trevor appeared to be a bit embarrassed about how unprepared he was for his own wedding.

"Wait here for a minute." Mattie ran back up the steps and into the bedroom. She dug through the pockets of her jacket and pulled out the small, brass box she'd found in the car. She hadn't had time to see what was inside, but whatever was in there would have to do. She hurried back to rejoin Trevor on the staircase. "OK, now I'm *really* ready."

Trevor took her by the right hand and wrapped it around his forearm. "I love you, Mattie. I'm a happy man. Life is going to be one terrific adventure with you. I'm glad you asked me to marry you."

Mattie smiled and gave Trevor a kiss on the cheek. "Whatever!" They continued down the stairs and on into the study.

Kash was standing by the bookcase with the Judge waiting for the bride to arrive. When he saw her he hurried over to block her left side from everyone's view until he got her over in front of the Judge. He stepped to the side of her and the Judge started the ceremony.

"Dearly beloved, we are gathered here in the sight of God, and in the presence of this company, to unite Trevor William Karington and Mattison Amber Bott in holy matrimony. Marriage was ordained by God in Eden and confirmed in Cana of Galilee by the presence of the Lord Himself, and is declared by the inspired Apostle Paul to be honorable among all men. It is therefore, not to be entered into unadvisedly or lightly; but reverently, soberly and in the fear of God."

"Judge…" Trevor interrupted quietly, "Can we get to the point a little faster?"

The Judge pulled his head back and blinked his eyes a few times in disbelief. "I beg your pardon, young man?"

Trevor continued whispering, "We really need to hurry this along Judge. Could you just give us the bare bones service and get this over with?"

The Judge looked at Mattie for some sort of an indication that she agreed, but she turned her head away every time he addressed her directly.

"Well…I guess I can if that's what you both want."

He glanced over at his wife who was shrugging her shoulders and smiling.

The Judge continued hesitantly. "It is your duty, Trevor, to be to Mattison a considerate, tender, faithful, loving husband. It is your duty, Mattison, to be to Trevor a considerate, tender, faithful, loving wife; to counsel, comfort and cherish him in prosperity and trouble; to give to him …

"Yes, yes," Mattie interrupted. "I will. Just say the words."

The Judge was visibly flustered by her outburst. Trevor chuckled softly to himself at Mattie's assertiveness. This was the spunky woman he had fallen in love with the first time he noticed her back in school.

The Judge quickly scanned down through his notes and continued.

"Let me charge you both to remember, that your future happiness is to be found in mutual consideration, patience, kindness, confidence…"

"We understand," Mattie and Trevor chimed in together. "Hurry!"

Lois was clasping her hands tightly over her mouth to suppress her laughter and Rainey couldn't stop crying. Most of her face was buried in a handkerchief that was becoming more and more saturated by the minute. Even Kash was having a hard time holding back the urge to laugh.

"Do you, Trevor William Karington, standing in the presence of God and these witnesses, solemnly pledge your faith to Mattison Amber Bott? Do you promise to live with her according to God's ordinance in the holy estate of matrimony; do you promise…"

"I do," Trevor said early. "Of course I do."

The Judge turned his attention towards Mattie and said, "Mattison Amber Bott, standing in the presence of God and these witnesses do you…"

"I do too," Mattie broke in.

By this time Lois and Rainey appeared to be out of control on the other side of the room.

The Judge shook his head. "OK," he said obediently. His sentences were now being read at high speed. "Then… by the authority committed unto me as a duly certified official of the court, I declare that Trevor William Karington and Mattison Amber Bott are now husband and wife. You may kiss the bride!"

The Judge took a deep breath and let out a long sigh as he dropped his body back onto the couch.

Trevor turned to Mattie, lifted the veil and puckered up for a nice kiss, but Mattie's mouth and nose had disappeared a couple minutes earlier and hadn't quite caught up with the Judge's declaration of marriage. He wasn't sure where to land his lips so he took his best shot.

"Lower, Trevor," Mattie whispered. "You're just a bit too high."

"Oh," Trevor whispered back. "Sorry." He aimed a little lower and felt her soft lips touch his for the first time and he melted inside. It was definitely 'love at first kiss' and all he wanted to do was stay right there for the rest of his life.

"That's good, Trevor," Kash said as politely as he could, patting him on the shoulder. "She needs to breath."

Trevor pulled back and saw his bride; face, head and all in full view, just in time for the sun to disappear below the horizon.

"We did it!" Trevor said. "I can't believe we did it!"

The bewildered Judge shifted his attention to the two hysterical women on the other side of the room. Between his wife, who was wiping away the tears from laughing so hard and Rainey, who was also wiping away the tears from crying so hard, it was impossible to tell who was doing what and for what reason.

“That was the strangest, fastest wedding I’ve ever performed in my entire career,” the Judge said in a bewildered state of exhaustion.

“That was the best birthday I’ve ever had!” Lois blurted out. “Congratulations, you kids. That was so much fun.” She went over and pulled the Judge up off the couch. “It’s time to go, Judge and let these kids get off on their honeymoon.”

The judge stood there staring blankly into space. “Yes, yes, I agree. I’ve got to go lie down. You kids can do the ring thing whenever you want…if you want. That’s up to you! Good luck to you both…you’re going to need it.” He handed Kash the marriage license on his way past and wandered out the door behind his wife who was stepping livelier than she had in years.

Kash had completely forgotten about the rings. “Oh Mattie, I feel bad we didn’t have your mothers’ wedding ring for you. Trevor could have had mine.”

“Mattie has a ring!” Trevor declared proudly. “She thinks of everything.”

Mattie flung thc trail of her dress out of the way and sat down. “Well, that’s not exactly the truth. I found a ring box way under the car seat when I was trying to find you a pen this afternoon.”

“Really?” said Kash. “I wonder whose it is. Let’s see it.”

Mattie held up the box to show everyone. Rainy gasped and stepped back flat against the wall.

"Don't open it!" she shrieked.

"What is it, Rainey?" Kash asked.

"It's the missing rings of Prather Mendell from the 14th generation of Sentinels. They've been missing for nearly two thousand years. They have special powers of their own and are dangerous! Where did you find them?"

"In the car…like I said. How do you know these are the rings of Preacher Mansell?"

"Prather Mendell," Rainey said clearly, "Not Mansell. There's a picture of it in the *Book of Ancestors*."

Kash walked over to inspect the box closer. "Would either of you mind if I took a few minutes to search through the Book of Ancestors to see if there's anything written about it before you open it up?"

Mattie looked at Trevor, who nodded his head in agreement. "I think that's a good idea, Dad."

"Let's leave them here while we're on our honeymoon, if that's alright with you, Mattie, and Dad can find out if it's safe to open it up by the time we get back."

Rainey peeled herself off of the wall and began hunting for something. "You kids will need a key to the house before you leave, though you'll never use it since the house responds to you anyway."

"Responds to us?"

"Well, to the current Trekker and Splitter."

"How so?"

Kash loosened his tie and walked over to the grandfather clock. "It's in here, Rainey." He opened the glass door and ran his hand up under the lip near the clock face. He pulled out the key and handed it to Mattie. "You can take it with you if you want, though you really don't need it. The house will unlock itself when you get within 10 feet of it anyway."

"How cool is that, Mattie?" Trevor said. "Do you want to take it with us?"

"No, I don't see any reason to do that. Go ahead and put it back in its hiding place and then we won't take the chance of losing it."

Kash slipped the key back inside the clock face. "I think Amber said the limo would be here around 8:00, which is in an hour. You two need to pack a few things before it gets here."

Chapter 16

The Rings

Kash shoveled some eggs off the platter onto Rainey's plate and then pushed what was left onto his own. "Boy, I don't know if I'll ever get used to getting up at the crack of dawn like you do."

"The day goes by too fast," said Rainey, "and it seems like there's never enough time to get all of the work done."

"Don't you think we could take a break this morning and go for a swim? It's supposed to be a beautiful day today."

"Maybe…maybe. I've got to finish fixing the weed whacker and then I could take a break...maybe."

"Man, you're such a slave driver, my dear auntie. I can hardly keep up with you."

"It's been nearly three weeks since the kids left. That's an awfully long honeymoon. When are they getting back?"

"They called last night to tell me they'd be coming home today."

"Did you look where I told you to?"

"For what?"

"The rings!"

"Oh, yeah…I found it. There wasn't much written about them though. I do know there should be two in there, but I haven't opened them yet to see. I want the kids to do it."

"So you think it's safe?"

"It is if they do it. If you or I did it, it would be dangerous."

Mattie and Trevor sat inside the outdoor gazebo where they leisurely ate their breakfast. The sun had barely come up, pushing some light through the breezeway. They were enjoying the garden atmosphere on the patio that was located in the center of the elegant, eighteenth century hotel. Three wooden balconies lined with rooms were guarded by freshly white-washed railings without end. The center court opened up towards the soft, blue sky above and a mild ocean breeze gently swayed the enormous palm leaves overhead.

"Oh, I hate to go back to the real world." Trevor said, stirring his spoon around and around in his oatmeal.

"What real world?" Mattie replied. "There's nothing real about our world. Everything we do is a fairy tale to 'real world' people."

"Well…I guess that's true. I really hadn't thought about it that way." Trevor sat quietly for a moment and said, "I really don't mean that anyway. I like our lifestyle. It's anything but boring."

Mattie folded her napkin neatly on her dish. "Did you already take the bags down to the car?"

"I did. They're in the car ready to go."

"I'm anxious to find out what Dad discovered about the rings so I can actually have one on my finger—whether it's a Mendell ring or some other ring."

Trevor smiled and took her hand. "That's right! I want guys to know you're taken. I don't like them flirting with my wife." He wiggled his eyebrows at her.

Mattie smiled and returned the sentiment. "The feeling is mutual! Finish your breakfast and let's go, shall we?"

They decided to take one last stroll through the center garden before leaving. Suddenly Mattie threw her arm up to block Trevor from taking another step forward. "Look…a blue footprint!" she said faintly.

Trevor quickly turned his head in every direction. "I don't see anything."

Mattie stood motionless. "I don't know what to do. I don't dare step on it; it scares me."

"Whatever you do, Mattie, don't step on it!" Trevor pulled her back a few steps. "You need to learn what you're doing before you end up somewhere lost in time."

"I feel the weirdest magnetic pulse pulling me. It's really strong!" she confessed. "It's almost irresistible to me, Trevor."

Trevor reached around her shoulder and anchored her body in under his. He cautiously steered her six feet away from where her eyes were fixed on the footprint. "Watch where you're stepping Mattie; whoever is sending the print may want you bad enough to send some more. We could be in real trouble if you stepped on one by accident."

They walked warily down the garden path, making a careful examination of every step. People who passed them mumbled softly to themselves, pointing at them as they chortled. Trevor and Mattie were so intent on avoiding a mishap that they hadn't noticed how many people were reacting.

By chance Trevor glanced up at one couple who had stopped to stare at them. "What are you staring at? Haven't you ever seen a blind person before?

The people were obviously embarrassed and apologized profusely. Mattie snorted and closed her eyes, letting Trevor move her forward slowly.

"You crack me up, Trevor."

They laughed quietly to each other as they recalled the encounter over and over until they reached the car.

"Why do you suppose I felt so drawn to the prints?" Mattie asked, still puzzled by how she reacted.

"I don't know," replied Trevor. "Do you still feel it?"

"Not as much now, but it's still there. I'll have to ask Dad about that when we get home."

"Come on, Rainey!" Kash called. "The water is really nice. You need a break!"

"Let me see if I can tighten this bolt first," she shouted, "and then I'll be right out!"

Rainey secured the lid on the dishwasher and stripped off her coveralls down to a pair of shorts and a t-shirt. As she started walking towards the beach, Trevor and Mattie pulled in. Kash came up out of the water, grabbed his towel and headed up to greet the newlyweds.

"Did you have a good time?" Kash inquired.

Mattie leaned over the top of the car and said, "We did, Dad. We had a blast. Thank you for the honeymoon."

"It was your mother, not me."

"It was both of you and we really enjoyed it, but a footprint appeared in the garden, Dad, and I didn't know what to do. It was pulling me strongly towards it."

"Oo-oo, that's got to be a pretty important Divvy; the stronger the pull, the more critical the need for help."

"It scares me to think of stepping on it. What if I went back there and got into trouble? I need to know what to do in different circumstances and quite frankly, I haven't got a clue!"

"Let me tell you something that will help you feel more secure. According to your mother, there's someone or something that's always with you and speaks to you – especially if you ask for help. It was like someone was whispering in her ear. She said that she had to learn to listen to it and recognize it, but that it's always there. The voice saved her life many times. It can forewarn you, show you things and make suggestions as to how to handle different situations."

"How am I supposed to practice hearing it if it only comes when I'm on a Divvy?"

"It's already with you now. It came to you when you Inherited; in fact, you've already used it."

"I have?" Mattie said. "When?"

"In the Chamber when you got back from your first Divvy. That's how we got away…remember?"

"Oh-h-h…yeah-h-h….I remember! It was like I could see everything that was going to happen in advance. But, I thought you said it was a voice?"

"It is, but Amber also said that it can be visions, feelings and kind of a sense of knowing. It can be lots of things!"

"That reminds me, Dad," Trevor interrupted. "Did you find out anything about the rings?"

Kash squeezed his hair dry in the towel and wrapped it around his waist. "Come inside," he said. "Rainey showed me where it was written in the book."

They all headed up to the Chamber in single file. When they reached the Chamber door, Kash stopped and turned to Mattie. "Open the Chamber, will you, Mattie? All you have to do is reach out and touch the handle."

Mattie stepped up to the door and touched the side of the knob with her fingers. There were a few clicking noises, three thumping sounds and the door swung open slowly all by itself. Kash walked through in a matter-of-fact way and Rainey followed. Mattie turned and grinned at Trevor who returned a smile of his own. He was getting such a kick out of all these new tricks his bride could do and he could hardly wait to see what came next.

Kash turned on the lamp that sat on the small, circular table where the *Book of Ancestors* sat. He flipped through several pages before stopping.

"Here it is," he said. "Rainey showed me where to find it. There's not a lot written about it, but I'll read you what there is." Kash pulled a chair over to the table, sat down and began to read.

Sentinel Entry:
14th Generation
Prather Mendell

I've guarded the rings for the greater part of a century and I'm getting too old and tired to continue. I suspect that I don't have much time left before I die. The "Interloper" from the future has nearly secured them twice. It would be devastating for all of us if he were to take possession of them.

Since only a Trekker that has Inherited in an even year, prior to a new century, along with his or her Splitter can safely wear the rings, I'm going to hide them from the world as best I can by having my Trekker pass them through several time corridors to different descendants. The 12th Trekker to receive them during their Divvy will retain them. That Trekker, whomever it may be, will be charged with the safe keeping of the rings and will be the only one aware of their secret location in time and space. May God guide and protect them in this most solemn duty until two worthy candidates can bear them on their wedding fingers once again."

Prather Mendell

Trevor sat up abruptly. "Mattie, it's an even year! Does that mean you're the one?"

"I don't know!" Mattie replied, "But, I wonder if the Interloper was the one who killed Mom? He must have tried to stop her from passing the rings on to me!"

"And me!" Rainy exclaimed, wheeling around. "I'll bet he was here searching for the rings."

"…and what is a Sentinel?" Mattie asked.

Rainey stood up proudly and said, "We…are a type of guardian for all of the Trekking tools, artifacts, and Chambers. Some of us are aware of our station and others are not. You can tell the Sentinels by their eyes. One will be blue and one will be green."

"Aunt Lila has eyes like that," Mattie quickly pointed out.

Rainey stood taller, if that was possible for a vertically challenged woman of her age to do, and declared, "Lila…is my daughter! Her father was killed in World War II and I had no way of providing for her after his death. My sister, your grandmother, said she and her husband would be happy to adopt her and set me up in the beach house as a nanny for the girls. It would be nice for Amber to have a sister and I could still be a part of my daughter's life; though we hid the fact that I was her mother for various reasons. She's the next Sentinel after I pass away, though she doesn't know it yet."

Kash went over to Rainey and laid his arm over her shoulder. "Those were difficult times for you, weren't they, Rainey?"

"They were," she admitted, "but they were wonderful times, too. The most important thing is that she grew up in the best family in the world and turned out to be as brilliant as her father."

"Yes, she did," Kash agreed, "and as beautiful as her mother, inside and out."

Rainey leaned her head against Kash and began to blush. "Thank you, Kash," she said shyly.

Mattie closed the *Book of Ancestors*. "He didn't say what the powers of the rings were. How can we find out and if the 'Interloper', as he called the guy from the future, is still after them. We probably should find out, don't you think?"

"There are unwritten legends; folklore that the Sentinels have passed down through the centuries," Rainey added. "I don't know which ones are true. I do know that the safest place for the rings is on the fingers of the eligible Trekker and his or her Splitter. Once on, they can't be removed until they both die or their fingers are cut off. I also know that you have to have both rings for the powers to manifest themselves. The biggest problem is that a detailed description of those powers has never been written."

"How could the Interloper use them then?" Trevor asked.

"If he were to wear both rings at the same time, one on his left hand and one on his right, he would become immortal. He could move both backward and forward in time without a Splitter. However, there is a nasty price to pay for wearing them if you're not the qualified Trekker or Splitter."

"What's that?" Mattie asked, visibly getting involved in the story.

"The Legend says that he will always be in pain; terrible pain when the sun goes down. Apparently the sunlight holds the curse back. Also, he'd have to cut off his own fingers to rid himself of the curse. The benefit is that he would be young forever and no one could stop him from doing terrible things in the future or the past."

Trevor's head lifted sharply to attention. What he had heard concerned him. "Does that mean the Trekker and Splitter will suffer for the rest of their lives, too… just to take advantage of a few powers that no one really has any record of?"

"No-no," said Rainey. "Actually it's the opposite. They can never get sick and they heal from any type of injury within minutes if the rings are within a close enough proximity. They will never age in appearance, and when they reach the ripe old age of 100 they will simply run out of time and die in their sleep."

Trevor sat back, relieved. "That's more like it! I'm assuming that Mom was the traveler that Prather's Trekker saw on his journey through several corridors."

"Apparently so..." Kash said thoughtfully. "I wonder why she didn't tell me about the rings."

"Because she Inherited in an odd year, past the middle of the century. Telling anyone would endanger everyone!" said Rainey.

"Like I said...this is an even year, Mattie. You could be the one," Trevor repeated.

"That's what I think," said Kash. "The legends all point to the two of you. How do you feel about that, Mattie?"

"Gosh, I don't know, Dad. This is all so overwhelming to me right now. When you think about it, it's pretty amazing that I reached under the car seat for the pen in the first place and felt the box instead. What if I hadn't felt it back there? I mean... it was wedged clear back in the corner. I was lucky to touch it at all!"

"That must have been why the car was broken into the morning of the picnic. The Interloper was searching for the rings. Your mother must have known he would do that based on your description when you Divvied back to her and told her what you saw in your dreams. It's all beginning to make sense."

"So, what do you think, Mattie...Trevor?" Rainey interrupted.

"It feels right to me," said Trevor. He was anxious to see them and get one on Mattie's finger. "Where are they?"

Kash got up and went over to the table where the *Book of Ancestors* rested. He slid his finger along the underside of the trim and released a hidden lever. A small drawer popped open revealing the worn brass box and a few other strange objects. He handed the box to Mattie and went over to stand by Rainey. "It's your choice, Mattie…and yours too, Trevor."

Mattie caught Trevor's eye and raised her eyebrows, searching for a response. Trevor gave her a nod of approval. She pushed her fingernails into the crack and carefully pried open the brass box. A puff of dust sprang out as she broke the seal and a soft golden glow followed from inside. There were two smooth, gold rings that were nestled side by side in a cushion of braided coral satin.

"They're both too big," Mattie noticed. "In fact…they're way too big for me."

Rainey chuckled to herself, nodding her head up and down. "That's part of the magic, my dear! They size themselves automatically to the wearer."

Trevor reached in and removed one of the rings. He took Mattie's left hand and held the ring in front of her wedding finger. He became serious as he gazed into her eyes. "With this ring, I thee wed. In placing this ring on your finger, Mattie, I pledge my love to you and it will be the symbol of my everlasting devotion." He slid the ring onto her finger.

Tears filled Mattie's eyes. When the ring reached her knuckle it shrank so fast it pinched a squeak right out of her. "EEK!"

Trevor jumped. "Did it hurt you?" If so, Trevor wasn't sure he wanted to put his ring on now. He massaged her finger and said, "I'm sorry."

"Oh…no…it didn't really hurt. It surprised me; that's all. Actually, it's a perfect fit!" Mattie took the other ring out and held it at the end of Trevor's wedding finger. "In placing this ring on your finger Trevor, you…are now…mine! I give you this ring as the pledge of my love and as the symbol of our unity and with this ring, I thee wed." She slid the ring to the end of his finger and with a *crack* it shrunk to fit him, too.

Trevor jumped again. "That was fun—kind of like getting married twice." He reached over with his left hand and took Mattie's left hand into his. The moment the rings came into contact a mist started swirling about them. They immediately pulled their hands away from each other and the mist faded instantly.

"What was that?" Trevor said.

"Your guess is as good as mine!" Mattie replied. "Rainey, I need to hear more about every legend you can remember. Let's talk after lunch and I'll record them in the *Book of Ancestors*."

Rainey's face turned anxious. She shook her head and started pacing in a circle. "No…no, no, no! We can't do that. They can't be written. The Interloper can read them and he already knows too much."

"OK…OK," Mattie said calmingly. "We'll just talk about them…how's that?"

Rainey stopped circling. "OK…" she said happily, shrugging her shoulders, "I've got to finish fixing the dishwasher." She marched out of the Chamber and Kash followed.

Mattie put the ring box back in the hidden drawer and closed it tightly. "I hope that'll be safe there. Whoever our Inheritor is will know right where to return the rings when we bite the dust." She winked and smiled at Trevor.

"You're such a sensitive woman," Trevor teased.

Mattie smiled. She walked over and slipped her arm into his. As they strolled slowly out of the Chamber together, the room turned off the lamp and the door began to close, mirroring their easy pace until it locked itself gently behind them.

Chapter 17

The Burglar

Lila was enjoying a wonderful dream where she was saving a pizza from a fate worse than consumption when her phone rang. She rolled over, slapping her hand down on the night stand trying to find the phone with her eyes shut.

"Hello-o-o?" she said, half asleep.

"Sorry to wake you, Ms. Graham. There's been a break in at the library. We need you to come over as soon as possible."

Lila was still groggy. She sat up in bed to see if it would help her clear her thinking. "What…what did you say?"

"This is Detective Farquarth, Ms. Graham. I'm at the library. Someone broke in about thirty minutes ago and set off the alarm. There's been some fairly extensive damage and I need you to come over to see if you can identify what might be missing."

Lila looked at the clock. It was five o'clock Friday morning and it was still pitch black outside. She wasn't particularly a pleasant person in the morning and was rather grumpy if awakened any time before eight. "I'll be right there," she said, and rolled out of bed to get dressed, mumbling as she went.

She threw a robe on and kicked her feet into her favorite bunny slippers on her way over to the vanity. She slid the drawer open, took out her gun, checked to make sure it was loaded and left for the library. When she arrived, there were several police cars parked at different angles around the entrance with their lights still flashing. From where she sat, she could see a crowd gathering. The door to the library had been pried open with something sharp. There were gouges all around the hinges. The top and bottom hinges were broken from the frame and the door dangled sideways from the one remaining in the middle.

As Lila approached the library, an officer stepped over to lift the door as high as he could so she could get through it.

"Sorry to bother you this early in the morning, Ms. Graham."

"I'm sorry, too!" Lila snarled. "Oh, gosh! They've destroyed the door. What else am I going to see destroyed in there?"

"The only other thing we could see damaged was the door to the basement. It's amazing they could get past that size of bolt without explosives. We were hesitant to go down because no one knows the floor plan of the room. If he's still down there, someone could get hurt."

"No one's going down there but me!" growled Lila. "That basement is absolutely off limits to everyone!"

"You seriously don't think we're going to let you go down there alone, do you?"

"I've got a gun. I'll be fine!"

Lila pulled a 9mm, semi-automatic pistol from the pocket of her dress, hunched down and pointed it towards the door. She had just started to creep forward when the officer grabbed her hand and carefully twisted the gun away from her.

"Whoa-oa-oa, Ms. Graham. You can't go down into a dark basement with a burglar swinging a hand gun like that."

Lila snapped her short, stout body to attention, facing the officer and said fervently, "I most certainly can! I'm a concealed weapons permit holder just like you are and this is my library!"

"Officer Dally, take Ms. Graham's gun and hold it for her. I'm going to call for the dog."

"Oh, no you don't! I'm not going to have a dog running around down there. He could damage some irreplaceable artifacts with a swish of his tail."

"The dog can sniff out an intruder with no risk, Ms. Graham—no risk to any of us, and she's trained to be extremely cautious."

"It's a dog, for heaven's sake. Dogs aren't cautious and they slobber all over the place."

"Listen, Ms. Graham…it's either the dog or me. Take your pick. "

Lila thought for a few seconds and leaned back against the wall with a sigh of defeat. "All right, but if that dog so

much as drools on the floor I'm going to have him put to sleep. Got it?"

"He's a she."

"What?"

"The dog is a female Ms. Graham."

"Oh…my…gosh," Lila huffed, "I'm surrounded by imbeciles!"

Officer Dally snickered as quietly as he could. The detective backhanded him on the arm before slapping the gun in his opened hand. "You stay here with Ms. Graham while I talk to dispatch…and nobody goes downstairs. Does everyone understand?"

Dally shook his head in a series of nervous nods. Lila folded her arms and shifted her weight to the other foot. She didn't like being told what to do, but without her gun she didn't feel secure in carrying out her original plan.

Five minutes later a big K-9 unit rumbled to a stop out front. The dog was locked inside and the crowd could hear her sniffing already. The detective talked with the trainer for a few minutes. He appeared to be nervous, shifting his weight from foot to foot several times during the conversation. Shaking his head, he opened the cage. Out jumped a shaggy haired, squatty little dog that began bouncing around like a rubber ball, sniffing everything in sight.

"For Pete's sake, Stan…," Farquarth said discreetly, "Pick 'im up and bring 'im inside."

When Lila saw the dog, she had a fit. "Your fierce police dog is a miniature Terrier? You're outa' your minds! That dog should be home sleeping on the foot of your daughter's bed, not searching for a burglar that could send him flying across the room with one swift kick!"

Detective Farquarth appeared to be a little embarrassed. "Our usual police dog has a lousy cold or something. Her nose is all runny and stuffed up. This is the best they could find under the circumstances."

"My gosh; what is the world coming to?" Lila snapped. "I'll bet this dog's name is Fifi!"

The detective ignored Lila's comments, trying to remain calm and professional. He let the dog down and aimed it through the door. "Go get 'em Spike."

"Spike?" Lila blurted out. "His name is Spike? I can't take this anymore." She started towards the office to see if anything else had been disturbed while the police, in her opinion, played cops and robbers.

"Wait…Ms. Graham. Is there a light we can turn on for Spike?"

Lila kept walking as she called back, "It's to the right, just inside the door, if you think it'll do that *mutt* any good."

The detective felt around the corner, flipped on the light and closed the door. He and Officer Dally pressed their ears up against it to listen. A minute later they were startled when Spike started barking violently. The men jumped back, looked at each

other and immediately pulled their guns. Officer Dally scurried over against the wall behind the door and Detective Farquarth backed up to the wall on the other side. Spike continued to bark and they could hear him running, sliding and knocking over all kinds of untold treasures. Spike growled and yelped once in a while and occasionally they would hear something shatter. Their eyes grew bigger, not sure whether they feared running into the burglar or being present upon Lila's return. Finally, all was silent. The detective cautiously opened the door a crack and out shot...Spike. Both officers were taken completely off guard and fell backwards on the floor, firing their weapons into the ceiling. Spike was chasing a mouse as fast as his short little legs could churn. The next thing they knew, he had slammed headfirst into the opposite wall, letting out a yelp. The floor was too shiny and slick to offer any traction for Spike to follow the mouse's maneuvers, and the rodent got away. Lila came running out of the office with intimidation written all over her face. Her arms were flying everywhere.

"Get out! Get out of my library, you imbeciles, before I murder you both! And take that screeching rug rat with you!"

"You'd better calm down, Ms. Graham or I'll order you off the premises and do whatever I see fit," Farquarth snapped back at her.

Lila stomped her foot on the ground in anger. "It's obvious my plan was the best plan!" she fired back at him.

"You need to cool off, Ms. Graham, before you blow a gasket. We still haven't searched the interior of the library and the burglar could still be in there. Now...if you're going to

remain on the premises—which is against my better judgment—you need to stay in your office until we can sweep the rest of the building."

Lila had an idea. She quickly agreed with conditions. "Alright, do what you must; however, you've got fifteen minutes before I head for Judge Whipple's to get a restraining order against the police department."

"Oh, give us a break, Ms. Graham! The judge isn't going to issue you a restraining order against us," Farquarth taunted. He was getting impatient.

"You've got fifteen minutes," Lila retorted, staring him down with squinting eyes.

Farquarth signaled to his back up team to move into the interior and spread out. "You stay in your office, Ms. Graham. Or else!"

"Or else what, Detective?"

"Or else you'll be escorted off the premises and I'll pursue obstruction of justice charges. Do you understand me, Ms. Graham?" Now he was staring at her with beady eyes.

Lila didn't say a word. She spun around and headed for her office.

The police disappeared into the main library. The moment they were gone, Lila got another gun out of her desk drawer in her office and headed for the basement. She pushed back the broken bolt and closed the door behind her. No one

was going to keep her from doing what she knew must be done. She marched down the stairs to the basement, pointing her gun all over the place while issuing some pretty colorful threats as she went. If there was a burglar still down there, only heaven could help him now. When she rounded the corner she could see that some tables were turned over; books were lying around all over the floor; lamps were turned upside down; bulbs were broken and there were little brown boxes everywhere. Lila sat down on the steps, leaned her chin on her hands and dropped her elbows onto her knees. It was a disaster! Without a doubt it was going to take her a solid week to clean up the mess before she could determine whether anything was missing or not.

Then she caught a whiff of something awful. It smelled like a mouse had died behind the wall. She put the gun back in her pocket, thinking that whoever had been there was gone and walked over to open one of the air vents to help circulate the stale air. When she turned around she stood face to face with an older man who hit her over the head with one of the vases she had been protecting. She slumped to the ground, unconscious.

Mattie brought the *Book of Ancestors* down from the Chamber and sat down by Rainey in a comfortable leather couch that faced the fireplace.

"I assume that you've gone through this book before, Rainey."

"Not for many years," Rainey said. "I haven't seen it since your mother and father moved into Benten after your grandparents disappeared."

Rainey scratched her head agitatedly and picked something out of her hair that Mattie really didn't want to see.

Mattie looked back at the book and continued, "So, you don't think that there is anything at all written about the power of the rings inside the book?"

"I KNOW there isn't," Rainey replied with certainty.

"Alright then, would it be acceptable to take a few notes on a separate piece of paper and burn it later?"

Rainey tipped her head backwards and rolled it to the left, away from Mattie for a few seconds. Rolling it slowly back to the right she said perkily, "I suppose that'll be alright— if you'll promise to burn it!"

"I will," Mattie replied. "I promise."

"Well, then, these are the legends of the powers of the rings. Number one you already know. They cannot be removed until your death or be taken from off of your hand. Number two, they have protective powers and healing powers. Number three, it is said that they can take you beyond the maps boundary."

"What does that mean…beyond the maps boundary?"

"I really don't know. I'm just telling you what the legends are. I can't help you with the interpretation of them and I'm not even sure that they're true."

"OK. Go on then," Mattie insisted.

Rainey leaned back on the armrest and brought her feet up onto the couch to get more comfortable. "Let's see. I remember my father talking about the Splitter actually being able to travel back through time with the Trekker for brief periods. Also, the Trekker can move forward in time, but not very far. I think he called it 'accelerate,' or something like that."

"Why would I want to move forward in time?"

Rainey tipped her head, showing signs of impatience.

"Oh…I'm sorry," Mattie said apologetically. "Go on."

"The rings are supposed to be able to lift you up in the air together and move you great distances. Also, there was something about talking to the dead. There has never been much said about that one, though. You'll have to find out for yourself." Rainey became distracted, picking at her toes.

"Is that it?"

"I think there might be more, but I can't remember right now. I'll tell you when I think of them. Is that alright?" She smiled at Mattie, then patted her on the head and left the room.

Mattie chuckled to herself quietly as she watched Rainey practically dance out of view. "*Hmmm…that was entertaining,*" she thought. She enjoyed Rainey's simplicity, but their conversation wasn't as helpful as she had hoped it would be. "*Where on earth do I begin?*"

The police came out of the inner library satisfied that no one was inside. Farquarth went to the office to discuss the next move with Lila, but she wasn't anywhere to be found. He followed the other policemen outside, expecting to see Lila out there, but instead found her assistant, Marlene Skinner, standing at the bottom of the steps, frightened out of her wits.

"Where's Ms. Graham, Marlene?" demanded the detective.

"How should I know? I just got here," she chattered back nervously.

"Didn't you see her come out?"

"No. I didn't even know she was here. I came in early to do some cataloging."

Suddenly it occurred to him that Lila must have snuck back in while they were sweeping the inner library. He yelled for help to go find her. "Come on, men! Ms. Graham's gone back in on her own; the stubborn woman."

"Wa-a-ait a minute, detective. You guys can't go down into that basement. Lila has some kind of special document from the judge that gives her the right to prevent anyone else from entering the basement," insisted Marlene.

"She might have been attacked by the burglar down there! She may be hurt, or even dead by now. Certainly the judge isn't going to enforce that document under these circumstances."

Marlene's eyes opened wide at the thought of what Lila may be facing, but still didn't back down. "I wouldn't be so

sure about that, Detective," Marlene warned. "She's pretty thick with the judge."

"All the more reason to get down there and make sure she's alright."

"It's your neck, Detective," Marlene taunted, in a high voice, making it clear that this was a warning from someone who had been there and done that herself.

Farquarth hesitated for a moment and then signaled the men to follow him in. Once inside, he stopped at the top of the stairs and called out, "Lila, are you down there?" There was no response. His first inclination was to run down the steps with guns blazing, although he hesitated at the thought of having to face Lila if nothing was wrong. His second inclination was to send the dog back in, but dismissed that thought quickly when he remembered what happened the first time. Finally, he decided he'd better get down there and face any possible consequences with Lila. He started creeping down the steps, listening closely for any noise that could signal trouble.

Lila was beginning to stir. She painstakingly got back to her feet with the help of a chair that had been toppled over during the 'Spike fest'. She shuffled over towards the stairs, stopping occasionally to catch her breath. She heard heavy breathing in the stairwell and pulled the gun out of her pocket to protect herself. Luckily, she yelled out a warning to whoever dared be present in her basement. "I've got a gun! You'd better not be there by the time I am!"

"Lila, it's Detective Farquarth. Lower your weapon!"

Marlene had followed the policemen and was standing in the doorway. When she heard Lila's voice, she turned and ran frantically back into the office and sat down at her desk, staring at the doorway and waiting for Lila to appear.

"Detective, you better get yourself out of this stairwell or I'll have your pension," Lila threatened.

"Don't threaten me, Ms. Graham. You went against my authority and I can see you've received a nice bump on your head for it. You're lucky that's all you got. You could have been killed!"

"Hog wash!" Lila said, defiantly.

Farquarth's face flushed with anger. "I think he's still down there and I'm taking the men in."

"I have a court document that gives me complete authority over who comes and goes in this basement. You better think of another way to get him than going down there, because it simply is not going to happen!"

Officer Dally stepped around the three officers that were shielding him from Lila and said timidly, "I've got a few tear gas canisters in the squad car and a couple of gas masks. Why don't we bomb the room and flush him out. Then no one will have to enter the room and when he comes out, we can take it from there!"

"That's not a bad idea, Dally," Farquarth acknowledged. "Go grab em', would you?"

Farquarth pressed the men back up the stairs and into the corridor. Lila went into the office to sit down for a few minutes while Dally ran out to the car to get the equipment.

When Marlene saw Lila stumble into the room with pieces of the vase still in her hair and a tiny stream of dried blood on her forehead, she hurried over to help her sit down.

"What happened, Lila…what happened? Do you want me to call an ambulance?"

"I'll be alright Marlene. Just call my sister. She's out at the old beach house in Seaport. You'll find the number in my Rolodex over there." Lila pointed to the counter and laid her head down on her desk, moaning, "What a night. What a horrible night…ohhhhhh..."

Rainey was on the floor working on the dishwasher when the phone rang.

"I'll get it!" Rainey yelled, tossing the screwdriver back into the bucket. "Hello?"

"May I speak to Amber—please?"

"She's not here right now. May I take a message?"

"Tell her that someone broke into the library early this morning and her sister was hurt. She…"

That was all Rainey needed to hear to start falling apart. She dropped the phone and ran to the garage, nearly knocking Kash over on her way out.

"What's wrong, Rainey? Rainey?"

He saw the phone dangling from the wall and could hear a muffled voice saying, "Hello? Hello?"

He picked up the phone and asked, "Who's this?"

"This is Marlene Skinner from the library. Ms. Graham asked me if I would call her sister for her. There was a break in at the library this morning and she's been injured. Is Amber there?"

Kash realized that Rainey was headed for the car and would be gone before he could catch her if he didn't hurry. "OK…we're on our way. It'll take us several hours to get there. You need to get her some help. Now! Thanks for calling," he added politely. He slammed the phone down into the cradle and ran out the front door to catch Rainey… who had already backed her antique truck into a tree. He hurried over to open the door, trying to calm her down. When he gripped the handle she jerked the truck forward, pinching his fingers. He pulled his hand back in pain, flipping it sharply to stop the sting. Rainey drove down the road at a reckless pace. Mattie and Trevor heard the commotion and came running out to see what was going on.

"What happened?" Mattie asked. "Are you alright?"

Kash was jumping up and down, cradling his hurt fingers with his other hand. "Lila was injured during a break-in at the library this morning. Her assistant just called the house trying to find Amber. Rainey took the call and flew out of here to go help before I could stop her. She's going to kill herself, or someone else, before she ever gets there. She hasn't driven anywhere beyond the property in more than twenty years." Kash

put his fingers in his mouth and began sucking on them, trying to lessen the pain.

"What should we do?" Mattie asked gloomily.

"I'll go start the car," responded Trevor.

"No..." Kash said, pulling his fingers out of his mouth. "We've got to be smart. There's no time for error."

"Meaning?" Mattie questioned flatly.

"We have to test the power of your rings. But first, you need to Half-Parallel to Rainey and stop her somehow."

Mattie immediately locked in a Half-Parallel as far as she could see down the road and was gone. Kash went in with Trevor to formulate a plan while he ran his throbbing fingers under some cold water.

After several transfers, Mattie spotted the truck about a mile away as it was running another car off the road to get on the freeway.

"To the truck bed," Mattie commanded. She landed in the bed of the old truck with several bags of weeds, a shovel, and a hoe that was located right below her hip. It was the first bad landing she had experienced and she let out a scream. Rainey heard the thump in the back of the truck and when Mattie screamed she thought she had run over someone. She jerked on the steering wheel and the truck went into a spin. Fortunately, she hadn't yet picked up enough speed to enter the freeway. The truck came to a stop when it hit the bushes along the embankment. Mattie jumped out of the truck and started

banging on the door for Rainey to unlock it and let her in. Rainey was totally dazed. She sat motionless in the driver's seat, lost in her own world of worry. When Mattie couldn't get her attention she ran around to the other side where the window was partly down. She reached in and unlocked the door. After a few minutes, she was able to convince Rainey to change places with her so she could drive them back home.

"Everything will be alright, Rainey. Trevor and I will use the power of the rings to get to Lila and help her. It'll save hours of driving and you can rest assured that we will take good care of Lila for you. Maybe she'd consider coming out for a visit. We'll ask."

Her words calmed Rainey down and Mattie backed the truck down the on-ramp and drove back to the house.

Kash opened his notebook and sat down with Trevor at the dining room table to start formulating a plan. "Let's review all of the powers of the rings that Rainey was able to recall." He ran his finger down the notes Mattie had written. "According to Mattie's notes, you should be able to transport great distances together. It doesn't say how, though!"

Trevor sat back and ran his fingers through his hair. "Are you thinking that both of us should go back to Benten together to help Lila?"

"Yes, I do! I think that's the only way any of us could get there soon enough to do any good. But the question is how do you do it?"

"Maybe it's the same procedure as the Half-Parallel. We'll have to experiment with it a couple of times in close range where we'd be safe. Maybe Mattie will have to hold a mental picture of the location in her mind or something; I don't know," Trevor rambled.

"Yeah, that's a good thought," Kash said, folding the notebook. He twisted his head towards the window. "It sounds like Mattie just drove up. Let's see how she feels about it."

Mattie was comforting Rainey as they walked towards the house. Kash opened his arms to Rainey as she approached.

"Everything's going to be fine, Rainey. Lila's assistant didn't sound shaken up at all and I'm sure she would have said more to me if it was serious. Why don't you come in and rest. Mattie and Trevor can use the rings to get there in seconds. It would take us five or six hours to get there by car."

Rainey saw the reason behind his thinking and began to calm down. She walked over to Mattie, hugged her, and said, "I trust you, Mattie. Please take care of my little girl." She backed away slowly, keeping her eyes locked on Mattie. "Before you go, I feel like it's important for me to tell you about the other entrance to the basement of the Library."

"OK..." Mattie said supportively. Her eyes flickered towards Trevor. "We're listening."

"Behind Lila's store at the outskirts of town is a storage shed that conceals the entrance to the tunnel of artifacts. It leads into the basement of the Library where the soul box's are kept."

Mattie wasn't quite sure what relevance that might have for her at the moment, but she took Rainey's advice seriously. She stepped towards Rainey and took hold of her hands. "Thank you, Rainey. You're so thoughtful."

Rainey nodded her head as she fought back the tears. Finally she turned to go to her room to rest and wait.

"Come on, you two. Let's go outside for a couple of test flights where I can watch." Kash pushed opened the screen door and walked out to the field; stopping about thirty feet from the house. Mattie and Trevor followed.

Chapter 18

The Boost

"I think you're going to have to hold a mental picture of the location in your mind, Mattie, and then put your rings together." Kash pointed to the pigeon washed rocks at the end of the beach and said, "Try a few test flights across the field to the rocks over there."

Mattie slid over in front of Trevor, leaning her back against his chest. She extended her right hand down to her side and opened her hand towards him. "Take my hand Trevor."

Trevor slipped his hand into hers. "Now what?"

"Let me get a picture in my mind and then I'll say the location when I grab your left hand." She stared at the top of the rocks, then blurted out, "No-no, I better think about a less dangerous area and try to 'boost' there first, in case my focus or aim is off."

"That's a cool word…'boost'. Did you just make that up?" asked Trevor, then added, "and someplace soft and wide open would be good for me."

Mattie smiled and squeezed his hand. She turned her attention towards a spot out in the middle of the field, and closed her eyes.

"Wait!" Trevor interrupted. "Don't you think you ought to keep your eyes open so we don't run into anything on the way?"

Mattie laughed and said, "Do you think I'm going to be able to see the lawn at the library in Benten from here if my eyes are open? I've got to be able to see a picture of it in my mind."

"I think that's right, Mattie," Kash agreed.

Mattie stared at the ground, deep in thought. A moment later she glanced up at Trevor; her eyes filled with anticipation and said, "Ya ready, Trev?"

"Ready when you are, Mattie." Trevor bit his lower lip and closed his eyes tightly. Mattie smiled at how cute she thought he was, closed her eyes and stood silent for a few seconds more. She reached for his left hand and the moment the rings came together the mist started swirling.

"To the field..." Mattie said and within a split second their bodies were jerked straight up into the air about 200 feet off the ground, shifted about 40 feet to the east in a geometric pattern and then pulled back down to earth in the exact location Mattie had envisioned.

"OK, Mattie…I'm ready. You can start any time you want."

Mattie grinned as she continued to hold his hands.

"I'm ready, Mattie. Let's do it," Trevor repeated impatiently.

Mattie pulled away to get a good look at him when he opened his eyes. Trevor hesitantly opened one eye at a time. When he saw where they were he hunched down quickly towards the ground like he was still anticipating a hard landing.

He looked up at Mattie and yelled, "We did it, Mattie! I didn't feel a thing! That was awesome!"

"Yeah, that was pretty cool, wasn't it? I didn't feel anything either" said Mattie. "Let's do it again with our eyes open this time, shall we?"

She stepped back in front of Trevor and took his hand again. She focused on a spot near the rocks and all she said was "boost". Up they went into the air again, then moved in a straight line to the space directly above the target and down they went…right on the mark.

"Oh…holy mackerel," Trevor said, dancing away from Mattie. "You are one fun wifie!" He clenched his fists and jumped around Mattie in a circle, whooping and hollering. Mattie stood there laughing; enjoying the show.

"We'd better get back to Dad and get on our way to help Lila," Mattie said, trying to bring Trevor back to the reality of the situation at hand.

They 'Boosted' back to where Kash was waiting for them without any trouble at all.

"Did you see that, Dad?" Mattie asked.

"Was there something different that you experienced? It resembled a Half-Parallel to me, except there were two of you doing it. I didn't see anything unusual. What was it like?"

Mattie explained what they had experienced and added that they could see every inch of the 'Boost'.

"Is that what you're calling it? Boosting?"

"Mattie made it up and I kind of like it," Trevor boasted.

"It just sort of came out," Mattie admitted. "Where do you think we should try to Boost to get to Lila that would be safe, Dad?"

"On the south side of the library might work. There are some bushes that you used to play hide-and-seek in when you were little. Remember?"

"Yah—that would be a good place. Since the bushes have filled in and the library pushes up against that embankment no one would see us arrive."

"You better get on your way then. I think it'd be a good idea to focus on places that are in the open air until you can play around with 'Boosting' some more. No one knows whether you can go through objects or not, so you better play it safe."

"We will Dad."

"Do you have any money with you?"

“I do,” said Trevor. He liked the feeling of being Mattie’s provider and protector. It made him feel manly.

“OK…good luck. Call me when you get there.”

Mattie turned to Trevor and said, “Are you ready Trev?”

Trevor nodded his head in rapid succession. Mattie could see he was nervous because he kept biting his lower lip and wrinkling his brow. “I’m ready!” he said hesitantly. “Let’s do it!”

They stood side by side and clasped right hands. Mattie thought of the library area she wanted to boost to, took Trevor’s left hand, and said “to the library” and they were gone.

Lila heard Dally coming in through the front doors and went to join them in the hall.

Farquarth grabbed one of the other officers by the arm and said, “Jefferies, go get Spike and let him run one more sweep.”

Lila perked up immediately. “You leave Fifi out of this. He’s done enough damage for several decades. No Fifi! Let’s just stick to the plan.”

“Well, I really think it would be a good idea to send him in one more time.”

“He’s too much of a liability. You should see the damage he caused chasing that stupid mouse.”

"Oh, alright—let's get this over with," said Farquarth. "Give me a mask, Dally, and I'll toss in a canister"

"Remember, you don't go past the end of the wall," Lila warned, "or I will have your badge!"

"Yeah, yeah…"

Lila put on the other gas mask and followed closely behind the detective. The way she was waddling down the steps with the mask on she resembled an old pot-bellied penguin headed for the beach. The policemen at the top of the stairs started snickering as they watched her laboriously descend each step. When they reached the bottom Farquarth moved in close to the wall until his arm could fling the bombs around the corner without exposing himself. He popped the top of the first canister and slid it on the floor as hard as he could into the room, immediately followed by the second. The room filled with white smoke. They stood breathlessly still, listening to see if they could hear any coughing, choking, or gagging sounds on the other side of the wall. But, to their disappointment, there wasn't even a sneeze.

To the detective's surprise, the smoke cleared rapidly as though it were instantly sucked out of a vent. He turned back to Lila and slowly removed his mask.

"That was weird." Dally said, standing on the upper landing. "What happened to the gas?"

"I da-no!" Lila muttered clumsily through her mask. "Bt ru sta-ear! No peeging aroun ta coana."

"You can take off your mask, Lila," detective Farquarth said. "There's no gas left."

Lila pulled off her mask and tossed it back up to Dally. "I know that. If he's in there he'll be asleep by now anyway and I'll drag him out. You stay here!" She repeated firmly. "I meant it when I said I'd have your badge if you as much as stick your nose around the corner."

Farquarth was irritated by Lila's bossy nature, but he nodded his head in agreement anyway. Lila disappeared around the edge into the room. It was just as she suspected. The intruder had moved on through the tunnel and must have left the exit open at the other end, rapidly sucking out all of the tear gas.

"The coast is clear here," Lila called. "I'll be right up to turn off the lights on the way out."

Officer Dally removed his cap to scratch his head. "I don't get it!" he exclaimed. "How could he have gotten away?"

"Your guess is as good as mine, Dally," Farquarth replied.

"Do you think he got out after he hit Ms. Graham over the head, when we were still searching the main room?"

"Possibly, but I want you to take the men and search the rest of the library one more time—and be thorough."

"Yes, sir," Dally replied crisply. He signaled the backup teams to split up and cover the interior again, including the children's section and the main office.

When everyone finally emerged from the building, Detective Farquarth ordered the door to be boarded up until the damages could be repaired. Satisfied that no one was going to try and go back into the library, Lila got in her car and drove to the tunnel exit at the edge of town.

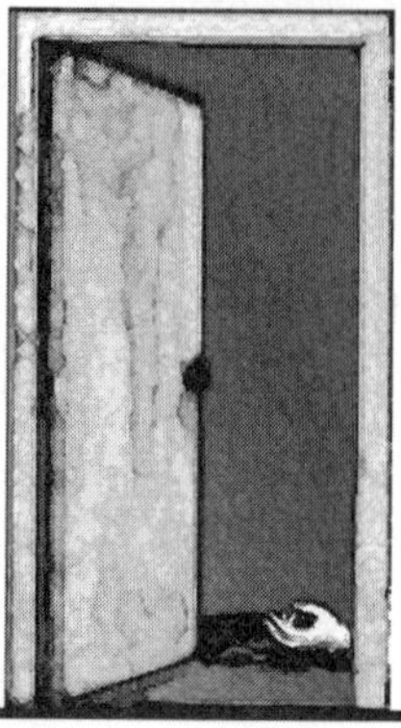

Chapter 19

The Second Chance

"Ugh! Your memory of this place wasn't quite accurate!" Trevor said, trying to push his way out of the bushes.

"Well, it has been a while since I played hide-n-seek here. Things do grow and change you know. Come on." Mattie moved quickly around to the front of the library where people were still gathering to see Jerry Wilson, the town fix-it-man, board up the front doors. "Has anyone seen Lila?" she called out. "Anyone?"

No one had a clue where Lila had disappeared to. Detective Farquarth was leaning against his car writing out a report.

Mattie walked over and stood in front of the detective. "Excuse me, officer."

Farquarth lowered his pencil. "Can I help you, ma'am?"

"Yes, I'm looking for my Aunt Lila."

"Um-m, she was here a few minutes ago. I don't know where she went."

"Oh dear, I hope she's alright. I heard she was injured."

Dally butted into the conversation. "Not bad enough to slow her down. She's one tough old bird!"

"Do you have any idea where she could have gone?" Trevor asked. "We've come a long way to help her."

"No idea!" Farquarth replied and returned to his report.

"I saw her get in her car and tear out of here headed that way." Dally pointed towards the outskirts of town. "She only left a couple of minutes ago. Maybe you can catch her if you drive fast."

"Drive….fast?" Trevor said. Mattie elbowed him in his ribs to stop him from saying any more.

"Thank you. We'll do that," Mattie said, and pulled Trevor with her as she walked into the crowd. "Listen, Trevor, I've got to see if I can catch her. I know she drives a red Honda Accord and the road out of town isn't that busy. I should be able to see her from a distance. I'll 'Parallel' ahead if you'll wait for me here."

"Alright; maybe I'll snoop around and see what I can find out."

"I'll be back soon." Mattie gave him a quick kiss on the lips and disappeared.

"M-m-m, m-m-m, m-m-m. I do like that!" Trevor said happily to himself and headed back towards the detective.

Mattie did six Half-Parallels down the road and still couldn't see anything. She paralleled down and back a few side roads and finally ran out of ideas near a convenience store that stood alone about a mile out of town. She walked in to inquire if anyone had possibly seen Lila's car drive by.

Inside, she looked around the store that appeared to be empty. "Hello?" she called out. "Is anyone here?"

A curly headed, middle aged woman with leathered skin popped up from behind the counter chewing a huge wad of gum with her mouth wide open. "Where'd you come from?"

"I'm just out for a walk. My aunt was supposed to meet me a few minutes ago. Have you seen anyone in here recently?"

"Out fer a walk clear out here? T-s-s. Not likely."

Mattie ignored the woman's rude demeanor. "She drives a red Honda. Maybe you noticed it parked outside?"

"I ain't seen nobody fer over an hour," she said curtly, sliding the cabinet door open to pull out a mint. She spit her gum at the garbage can that was nestled in the corner at the end of the counter, about ten feet away. She lifted her hand in the air, swishing her two fingers forward, indicating she'd

made the shot. She popped the candy into her mouth and asked, "What's er' name?"

"Lila Graham," Mattie replied, somewhat repulsed by the terseness of the woman.

"Lila? Heck, Lila owns this place." The woman came alive. "She's probably out back doin' whatever she does back there. You say she's your aunt?"

"Uh-huh…I did."

"My condolences!" The clerk said boldly. "That woman scares me!"

"Yes, well thanks." Mattie looked around. "Is there a back door I can go through to see if she's out there?"

The cashier bowed her head and lifted her hand towards the hallway that led out back. "Be ma guest!" she said lazily, grabbed a magazine and plopped her oversized load down on an overburdened stool behind the counter to read.

Mattie opened the door slightly to see if she could see Lila. She pushed it wider and wider until the supply building was in full view on the other side of the ally. It was left wide open and to Mattie's horror she could see a chubby hand lying on the floor in a pool of blood in the doorway. Lila's car was the only one back there parked next to the building. She hurried over, hoping it wasn't her. It was dark inside, so she bent down to feel if there was a pulse in the wrist until her eyes adjusted. The hand was cold and stiff. There was no heart beat to be found and as her eyes adjusted she could see that it was Lila.

She was lying in a pool of blood with a hole in back of her head. She could see something about the size of a softball further inside the room and reached over to pick it up. It was a rock that was covered with blood.

Suddenly Mattie heard the most heart-stopping scream she'd ever heard in her life that sent shocks running through her entire body.

"Ah-h-i-i-i-i-i! You killed her!" The cashier had apparently followed her out to get some more hotdog buns and saw her stooping over Lila's body. Assuming Mattie had killed Lila, she ran back into the store, locked the door behind her and ran for the telephone to call the police.

Mattie immediately set the Half-Parallel and sped away from the scene. A minute later she was back at the library hunting for Trevor.

Trevor was difficult to see since he was sitting on the lawn with some people eating a breakfast burrito they had offered him. This was a big event for such a small town and many of the rubberneckers came prepared with a picnic to stay the whole day if the action continued that long.

Trevor's mouth was quite full when Mattie located him. She gave him a look of disapproval, making Trevor feel self-conscious. He got up as quickly as he could, saying thanks to his new friends for the food, spewing a bit of egg out of his mouth here and there.

"Don't talk with your mouth full, Trevor; I need you to come with me right now," Mattie said sternly.

"Thanks again for the burrito," Trevor said as Mattie pulled him off balance by his shirt. "I'll see you later." He turned his attention towards Mattie and mumbled, "What's the rush? That wasn't very nice of you."

Mattie kept walking back to the location they had originally boosted to. "Lila's dead!"

"What?" Trevor forced the rest of his food down. "How?"

"I think it must have been the Interloper. We've got to try and go back in time together as far as we can. According to Rainey, the legends say the rings can move us back a few minutes.

"How many minutes?"

"I don't know."

"Do you have any idea how we do it?"

"I'm guessing, but maybe we do this along the same line as Boosting. Before we try it, let's Boost to where Lila is and hide in the bushes."

They took each other by the hand and Mattie imagined landing inside the bushes next to the storage building where Lila was. She took Trevor by the left hand, narrowed her eyes and wrinkled her brow slightly. "To the bushes," she said in a solemn tone, and they were gone.

Trevor landed in the middle of a large willow bush and Mattie landed near the outer edge on flat ground.

Trevor batted the shrubs away from his face. "Did you do that on purpose because you were irritated with me for eating that sandwich?"

Mattie pulled him towards her to help him get out. "I wouldn't do something like that because I was mad at you…I'd strand you in the trees!" She teasingly poked her finger in his ribs and twisted it gently.

Trevor chuckled and buckled his body towards her hand. Then he frowned, brushing her hand away. "Don't do that…I'm ticklish!"

Mattie raised her eyebrows mischievously.

A voice in the distance drew their attention back to the situation with Lila and they both went silent to listen.

"She's over there, officer, and the young woman that did this got away. I was lucky she didn't try to get in the store and kill me since I'm the only witness."

The policeman stooped down to get a closer look. "Did you actually see her do it?" he said, picking up the jagged, bloody rock with a loosely held rubber glove. He turned it around a few times and then stuck it in a plastic bag.

"No, not 'xactly, but there weren't nobody else around…" The cashier admitted.

Mattie turned to Trevor and whispered, "Come on. Let's go deeper into the trees and see if we can make this work."

They walked into the foliage until they felt like they were out of hearing range and started experimenting with thoughts and words to see if they could do a shift in time using the rings. They stood together like they did in the Boost and Mattie said, "Double-Divvy 15 minutes." But, nothing happened.

"Let's try a left handed high-five and see if that does anything. It seems obvious that we at least have to connect the rings." Trevor suggested.

"That sounds ridiculous. It can't be that simple," Mattie said, "but, I guess it's worth a try. Do you think I need to say anything?"

"Let's try it without any words, since Rainey said that she didn't know how far back in time the rings would take us anyway. Maybe it's just a set amount of minutes or hours and that's it!"

They faced each other, raised their hands and slapped them together in a high-five. The rings magnified the cracking sound from their hands and they felt the mist engulf them. The scenery started whirling, melting into a whirlpool of color as it swirled around them. Mattie turned her head away from Trevor to watch the movement and caught a glimpse of someone coming towards them in the spinning background. It was her mother. Mattie was stunned. At a distance she could see two other people before the spinning stopped.

"Trevor…did you see them?"

"Yeah. Who were they?"

"The woman coming towards us was my mother!" Mattie's heart started pounding. She felt faint and had to sit down on the ground.

Trevor knelt down beside her. "So she's not dead?" He tipped his head and shook it slowly. "She must be trapped in time!"

"That must have been what the legend meant by 'beyond the maps boundary.' She exists beyond the charts of our time frame. I want to see her again. Maybe we can find a way to get her back?" Mattie asked, hopefully.

"We probably ought to worry about that later, don't you think? Right now we need to correct the situation with your aunt," Trevor reminded her. "I wonder how far back in time we moved. It felt like things were swirling for maybe about a minute."

"Let's go see if Lila's car is out there."

They walked back over to the edge of the thicket and pushed the bushes aside quietly to take a peek. Lila's car was gone, but the storage door was still open.

"Do you smell that?" Mattie asked Trevor. "It smells like burning skin."

Trevor was already plugging his nose. "Yeah, it stinks, bad!"

The bushes rustled on the other side of the drive and a clean cut, elderly man appeared out of the bushes. His movements were quick and quite fluid for someone his age.

"Look," Mattie said, "over there! He looks like he might be about 65 years old. I'll bet that's him. Look at his clothes." Mattie spoke in hushed tones. "I've never seen anything like that."

His face looked angry. His clothes shimmered and mirrored his surroundings. They made it difficult to distinguish him from the background, except for his bare head and arms.

"He's much older than I thought he'd be."

"Yeah, me too!"

Suddenly they heard Lila driving down the alley towards them. The sound of the car approaching startled the man back into the shrubs. Lila pulled up to the building and got out of her car. It was obvious she hadn't seen him duck out of sight, because she slammed her door and started walking briskly towards the structure without hesitation. She stopped abruptly about half way there and twirled back around to return to the car to get her gun.

"Oh great..." Trevor whispered. "She's got a gun! That complicates things."

Before Lila emerged from the car with her gun, Mattie saw the man reach out of the bushes, pick up a large, jagged rock and pull back into his hiding place. She recognized it as the murder weapon she had picked up by Lila's body. Lila started walking back to the open doorway more cautiously. She held the gun in front of her nose pointing it straight

ahead. She stuck her head inside the door and felt around for the light switch. Mattie was planning to do a Half-Parallel into the bushes and flatten the Interloper before he emerged, but she was too late. To her surprise he appeared out of nowhere standing over Lila's head holding the rock, ready to strike Lila from behind.

Mattie ran at them yelling, "Lila…watch out!" Her warning startled the Interloper and Lila, too. He whipped his head in Mattie's direction. Lila swung the gun around, getting off a haphazard shot. He staggered backwards, set a Half-Parallel and mumbled, "To the woods" and was gone.

Mattie skidded to a stop in the loose dirt. Trevor plowed into her from behind, grabbing her arms to hold them both up.

"He did a Half-Parallel, Trevor! Did you see him?"

"You bet I did. How's that possible?"

"I don't know. Maybe I should try and follow him."

She lifted her arms into position, but Trevor grabbed them, pulling them down sharply.

"No…I don't think that's a good idea. He could be waiting for you. We'll face him again later, anyway."

Lila was stunned. She had absolutely no idea what had happened. She'd never seen anything like this in her whole life. She took several stutter-steps backwards until she felt the support of the building against her shoulder and

started shaking. Mattie and Trevor approached her cautiously because she still had the gun and was visibly jumpy. When they got close enough for Trevor to get a hold of the gun he carefully removed it from her trembling hand, bringing her back to reality.

"Thank you for the warning," Lila said, still shuddering. "He probably would have killed me if you hadn't been here."

"For sure you would be dead!" Trevor blurted out boldly.

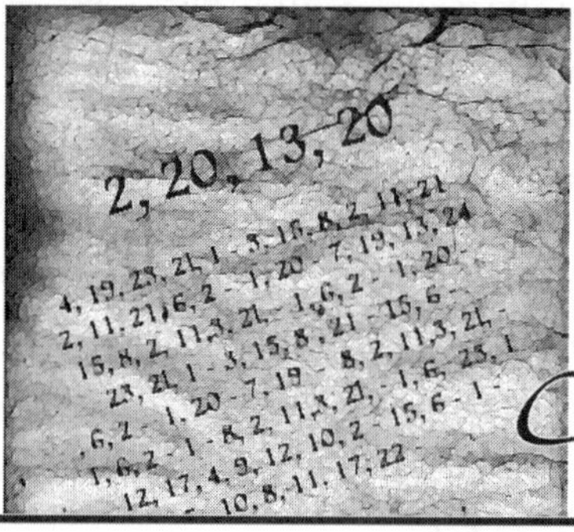

Chapter 20

The Kash-Napping

Lila stared at Mattie. She began to realize that the person who had saved her was her niece. "Mattie? You are Mattie, aren't you? I haven't seen you in more than ten years."

Mattie reached out to Lila and gave her a big hug. "It's good to see you again. I've missed you since..." Mattie caught herself, realizing that what she was about to say could possibly stir up some hard feelings again.

"…and I you." said Lila. "I've missed you and your parents more than I realized." She pushed Mattie away from her to get a full view of her. "You're all grown up! Boy, you look like your mother!" Lila paused for a moment, "Where did you come from? Your timing couldn't have been more perfect; you saved my life!"

"Aunt Lila, I want you to meet my husband, Trevor Karington. Trevor, this is my favorite aunt…Aunt Lila. We were married recently and came in on the bus from Seaport to visit with you. When we arrived in town, everyone was pretty

excited. People told us there was a break in at the library and you had been injured. One of the officers said you had headed this way and he'd be glad to drop us off at the 7-11. He said you owned the place and might be here. The cashier inside said you were probably in the back. When we came back here to say hi we saw that man standing behind you with a rock in his hand," Mattie explained quickly, trying to not arouse suspicion.

"Thank heavens you did. I will never be able to repay you," Lila said gratefully.

Trevor saw something half buried in the dirt on the ground where the stranger stood. He bent down to pick it up and noticed a few smatterings of blood while he was there. "You must have hit him, Aunt Lila. There's some blood on the ground right here." He pointed to several drops of blood that had been flung in a half circle.

"What did you find, Trevor?" Mattie asked.

Trevor stood up and opened his hand to blow the dirt off of the object. He appeared to be dazed. Staring at it he said, "You're never going to believe me, Mattie."

"What is it?"

"It's our ring box."

"*Our* ring box?"

"Yes!" Trevor blew it off again and stuffed the box in his pocket. "We'd better get back as soon as we can. I hope nothing has happened to Dad or Rainey."

"Rainey? Rainey's still alive?" Lila responded, surprised at hearing the name. "I haven't seen her in years. She was your mother's and my Nanny when we were growing up. I love that dear little lady. She's a bit crazy, but wonderful! Why would they be in danger?"

"There're a lot of things we need to explain to you Lila…" Mattie said, "…and I wish we had time to stay and visit like we planned. I don't mean to be vague, but we'll have to come back another time. Would you mind dropping us off at the bus station in town? We've got to leave right away."

"I'd be happy to dear. I wish you could stay. Let me lock this door and I'll take you where ever you want to go." Lila secured the door and drove them back to Benten.

"If you'd drop us off at the bus station that'd be great," Mattie repeated. "I'm sure you've got a hundred and one things to do after the break in and all. We'll give you a call and see if we can come and visit you later. Next time, we'll give you some warning that we're coming."

That reminded Mattie that she hadn't called her Dad like she said she would. After Lila dropped them off and they all said their 'goodbyes' Mattie found a pay phone and called home. The phone rang and rang.

"No one's answering?" Trevor asked.

Mattie shifted her weight several times. Her mind was racing with awful possibilities concerning her father and Rainey. "We've got to find a secluded spot and Boost home immediately. The interloper may have hurt them going in to get the rings."

They walked around the corner of the bus station into an alley and slipped behind an empty bus when they were sure no one was watching.

"Hang on tight, Trevor, I'm not sure exactly how the area lays out behind the shed, but I'll do my best."

"Please try to keep me out of the middle of the bushes. I got scratched up enough on that last landing"

"Oh, wah! Poor baby!"

"I'm not your Guinea pig, I'm…"

"…*Boost!*" Matte exclaimed, and they were gone.

They landed several feet behind the shed in open territory.

"…the most important person in your life!"

"Sh-sh-sh…listen!" Mattie whispered. "I can hear voices in the distance."

Trevor peered cautiously around the corner of the shed to see who it was. As far as he could tell there wasn't anyone out there.

"See anyone, Trev?"

"No, but I hear them. It sounds like maybe it's coming from inside the house."

"Let's go around to the back door."

Mattie and Trevor snuck around back and went in through the kitchen. As they crept in they could hear Rainey in the entry pleading with someone to take her instead of Kash.

"Please bring him back—you can have me instead." Rainey said.

A man's voice echoed down the hallway. He sounded like he was having a hard time getting out his words. "I…want those rings…you old hag." He took several breaths and then said, "Tell them if they don't…hand over the rings…when I return at midnight…I'll kill her father, too."

Trevor slid one of the kitchen drawers open and grabbed a knife. They heard a slapping sound and a thud. That was it for Trevor. He threw open the door and bolted into the hallway yelling as he went. He saw Rainey lying on the floor rolled into a ball, crying.

"Where'd he go?" Trevor shouted angrily, running out the front door waving his knife from side to side. He exploded back into the house, darted into the study and back out to Rainey. When he was satisfied the man was not there he stopped to question her.

"It was the Interloper," Rainey said weakly. Mattie helped her up off the floor. "He came a few minutes after you left and made me open the Chamber for the rings. He held a gun to Kash's head and I didn't have any choice. When he saw the rings were gone he went crazy and started pushing Kash around. Finally he pushed me down on the floor and dragged Kash out of the room. By the time I got out into the

hall they were gone. I don't understand how he got away so fast with Kash."

Mattie helped her over to a chair. "So this was the second time you saw him today?"

"Yes, but Kash wasn't with him this time. He was holding his arm when he arrived and his sleeve was soaked in blood." She put her head in her hands and shook it back and forth. "Oh, I don't know what to do…I don't know what to do! He said if you didn't deliver the rings by midnight tonight, when he returns, he's going to kill Kash, too."

"I wonder who else he's killed for these rings?" Trevor said tensely. His mind was engaging the horror of having to cut off his finger and worse—Mattie's finger to save Kash. "I'd rather die than cut off your finger, Mattie."

"No one's going to cut off my finger or yours either, for that matter. I think I know where he's taken Dad and we've got to find out how to get him back if there's a time thing attached to this."

"Where is he and how would you know?" Rainey asked.

"He's taken him beyond the maps boundary."

Trevor's face lit up, "Of course…that's how they got away so fast!"

"I don't know how he's doing it, but I'm gonna go see if the *Book of Ancestors* has any clues. There's gotta be somethin' in there."

Mattie dashed up the steps with Trevor close behind her. She touched the knob and the door swung open promptly in response to the hurry she was in.

"Wow…that's so cool!" Trevor said as he watched the door fly completely open. "Exactly what are you trying to find?"

"Exactly? I don't know exactly!" Mattie placed her hand on the book to open it. "But, probably the words 'beyond the maps boundary' are involved." The instant she said that the book opened itself up, pushing her hand away. It flipped through dozens of pages until it flopped open on page 132. The numbers 2, 20, 13, 2 appeared at the top and a bunch of numbers appeared below as if it were in a paragraph format.

Trevor turned the book towards himself, mumbling something as he slid the book closer. "It's a kid's code. We used to play with it all the time when I was in junior high. The number two is a 'B', 20 is a 'T', 13 is 'M' and we're back to a 'B'. B, T, M, B…Beyond the Maps Boundary!"

Mattie turned and threw her arms around Trevor so tight that it squeezed the air out of his lungs.

"Wheeeez—Maaattiiiee, not so ti-i-i-ght!"

Mattie released her grip, allowing Trevor to catch his breath. "Sorry, honey. I forget that I have extra strength since I Inherited. Help me make a key for the alphabet so we can both work on it to save time. You start from the beginning and I'll start at the end and work backwards."

The Interloper stumbled out of the time keeper and dropped to one knee, holding his bleeding arm. He'd lost enough blood during the Divvy to make him dizzy, adding a third source of damage to his already weakened condition. His body was smoldering from the time transfer and his face appeared older and more haggard than it did before he left.

A sleek young woman with dark, cropped hair staggered out of the Splitters box and grabbed the man by his arm. "Don't get blood on that expensive Persian rug, you moron, or they'll know we've been using the Chamber for sure. If they find out…you're through! Get up and move…now!" With as much extra energy as she could muster she yanked him up and shoved him through the small opening that was hidden behind the encircling curtains.

He stumbled through the gap and fell forward, jamming his shoulder into the banister that stopped him from plummeting to the ground below. "You've got a cold, tough heart, Missy," the man said feebly as he dug his heels into the floor to scoot himself higher up against the railing. He pulled up his sleeve to get a better look at his wound.

"Don't give me any of your lip, old man, or I'll leave you to shrivel up in the sun like the rotting piece of meat you are."

"You need me!" he said, trying to rally enough energy to sound forceful.

"I don't need you, you old bag of bones. I can wait a few years for the twins to grow up and the rings will be mine anyway. Now do what I tell you without getting smart with me or you'll never know what it feels like to be young again." She pulled the wall panel back into place and dragged herself over to a basket of rags that sat in the corner of the landing. Pulling out the cleanest cloth she could find, she bunched it into a tight ball and threw it at his head. "Here, Bayne! Wrap this around your arm. It'll stop the bleeding. When I get my strength back I'll help you clean it up and get it bandaged."

After several minutes she had regained enough strength to move around the area unrestricted. Bayne was still lying against the rail, his head rolled back, eyes closed, moaning, while holding the blood soaked rag against his wound.

"Interloper…t-s-s-s. You're pathetic!" the young woman said with disgust, standing over his tired, pain filled body. "That fancy name they've given you belongs to me." She bent down and pulled the dripping, red cloth away from his arm. "The bullet passed clear through." she said, sticking her finger in the hole.

"Ah-h-h-h…" Bayne yelled. He grabbed her hand and threw it away from him as hard as he could. "What's the matter with you, girl? Haven't you got a single drop of kindness in your entire, hateful body?"

"You're such a wimpy old man," she retorted. "Stop your whining! We've got to get out of here and get you cleaned up. You've got to be ready to go back again tonight to get the rings." She slung his arm over her neck and lifted him to his feet.

"You stink. I can hardly stand to be near you after a Divvy. Each time you return you come back more putrid smelling than when you left. Why don't you make some effort on your own to get down the steps?" She smirked at the thought of how much easier it would be to toss him down the steep stairwell and clean up what was left of him afterwards. "Come on Bayne…" she snapped and proceeded to roughly lug him from step to step until they reached the bottom.

"Stop for a minute, please!" Bayne pleaded. "I can't go any further."

"If we don't get this thing cleaned up you're gonna' get an infection in it. Hold on until I can get you back to camp. You should be getting some of your strength back soon and that'll help both of us."

A few minutes later they emerged from a tunnel that surfaced deep in the woods. She pushed away the brush they had used to camouflage the entrance. An old, thrashed motor home, where Bayne lived, sat alone in the middle of the thicket. It was in terrible condition. Most of the siding had been stripped off, leaving bare wood and wires exposed to the weather. She ripped open the bent screen door and pushed Bayne up the steps until he was inside. He dropped down on the couch to rest while she went into the bathroom to get some supplies. The tan carpet that led down the hallway was almost black. The curtains were jagged from rotting in the sun through the years; the toilet and sinks were so grimy that you could scrape the scum off with a half bitten fingernail; there were pans and dishes lying all over the place; filthy bedding and dirty clothes cov-

ered most of the floor and the bare mattress exhibited rips where the springs popped through and stains of every size, shape and color covered the surface. She opened the cracked mirror on the medicine cabinet and pulled out some rubbing alcohol. She yanked down a box of gauze and tore open the top to pull out several squares. She stuffed the first aid tape dispenser in her armpit and carried the supplies back to Bayne to clean up his wound.

"Why can't you do anything right, you old fool?" she said, walking down the hallway, "You've nearly ruined your sleeve this time."

"Is that what you're most concerned about," Bayne responded angrily, "the condition of my costume?"

"Shut up Bayne, before I stuff this gauze in your mouth." She pulled his shirt up over his head, opened the lid to the bottle of alcohol and before he knew it she poured it into the bullet hole. Bayne arched his back and screamed in pain. "You little witch! Some day you're going to regret that." He sprang up off the couch and ran over to the sink to splash some cold water over the wound.

"See…" she said, pleased with herself. "That got you up and moving. Now maybe we can get you ready to go back for the rings. If you'll hold still this won't hurt…much."

It wasn't long before they had the information translated.

"It looks like something's missing, Mattie."

"Yes, it does. Let me read it out loud and maybe we can figure it out."

"Beyond the Maps Boundary is the core of all time; no road maps are written, no directions you'll find. Captives may live and forever will last, 'til the ring bearers see them in flight to the past."

Mattie paused to think. "We did that when we went back in time together to save Lila, remember?"

"Uh-huh…I do."

Mattie continued, "*Ingress and egress can only be gained by a piece of the soul and the full given name. If the egress delayed passes midnight you'll see, that the captive must wait one more year to be free. The Book will give notice, the tell-tale sign, announcing the entry at the exact entered time. A full Trekker and Splitter must link to make three, hold the soul, say the name, which will then set them free.*"

"There, that's the part that's missing. How can a Trekker and Splitter be three?" Trevor shook his head. "What does it mean by 'three'?"

"Let me finish this," said Mattie and continued.

"There can cross only one at a time from the core, while the rest linger on and must wait for their door."

"Three…what do you think it means, Mattie?"

"It could mean a number of things. Maybe we're supposed to say the words three times; the name three times; do it at 3:00; find a third person…" Mattie's face lit up as she stood up slowly. "That's it! We need a third person. I wonder if we need a Sentinel." Mattie ran out of the room to get Rainey.

A few minutes later Mattie returned with Rainey to show her the translation and get her input. Rainey read through the riddle and sat quietly for a minute to think.

"I think you need a third person, Mattie."

"That's what we thought, too," said Trevor, "and Mattie thinks it's supposed to be a Sentinel."

"That makes sense to me. There have been other instances where Sentinels were an important part of the formula."

"What do you think it means by 'a piece of their soul,' Rainey?" Trevor asked.

"That would be something that contained their DNA, like a fingernail or a lock of hair. A finger print would also work because it's unique to them."

"How would you get that? There might be people in there from centuries ago," Mattie said, sounding disappointed with the answer. "That would be impossible!"

"Not really," Rainey said, "Do you remember seeing page after page of recorded Divvy's in the *Book of Ancestors*?"

"Yes," Mattie replied.

"The names and dates of the main objective or person the Trekker was summoned to help is always listed in the *Book of Ancestors* and a sample of their DNA is brought back with the Trekker for safeguarding following each Divvy. For the past 100 years or so, those boxes have been sent to this address and the Sentinel here forwards them to the library in Benten. The head librarian, who has always been a relative within the family, catalogs them and files them for safekeeping. Every Trekker, Splitter and Sentinel since the beginning of time has their own records that are kept in the book as well as a DNA sample stored for each of them in the basement of the library, too."

"So...if I understand you…we have to locate the sample for Dad before we can bring him back; is that right?" Mattie thought for a moment and asked, "Why can't we just take a sample of hair from his comb in the bathroom?"

"That's a good question. We can't do that because the sample has to be set apart by a Sentinel within 72 hours of receiving it. We can't use old samples to summon the person in any space or time frame. If the sample is not set apart it is considered desecrated and is useless."

"That means we have to get back to Benten and get Lila to let us in so we can find Dad's soul box."

Rainey closed the book and strolled over to one of the time keepers and ran her finger along the top edge of the armrest. "Lila is a Sentinel, too. She'd be the one to use once you get there."

"But Lila doesn't know she's a Sentinel," Trevor said solemnly. "She won't know what to do."

"I don't know what to do either—exactly," Rainey reminded them. "You're going to have to experiment as it is. The only thing that concerns me is that Lila can become difficult if she gets overwhelmed. She can get downright belligerent!"

"I know," Mattie said. "I can attest to that, but we don't have much choice. It'd take you hours to drive back to Benten and we don't have that much time to waste."

"That's true. You and Trevor could get there in a heartbeat."

Trevor walked over and picked up the book. "Do you think we should take this with us?"

Rainey took the book from Trevor and set it back on the table. "You won't need it. All you need is the full given name, the DNA sample and the three of you linked together somehow. Figuring it out is what will take up most of your time. You know your father's full given name and Lila will supply the rest."

"That makes sense to me," Mattie said. "Let's get outside and Boost to Lila's back yard. I know it well and there's probably no one there."

They all went out on the beach to get set for the Boost. Mattie slid in front of Trevor and took his right hand.

"Oh," Rainey interrupted, "I forgot to ask you if Lila was hurt badly. I got sidetracked when the Interloper showed up."

"No, she's fine." Mattie smiled at Trevor, leaving the rest of the information unsaid. "It was just a bump on the head."

"Thank goodness!" Rainey shouted. "That's a relief." She clapped her hands above her head and stepped away from the kids. "Be careful, you two, and give Lila my love."

"Will do," said Trevor.

Mattie winked at Rainey, took Trevor by his left hand and said, "Boost!"

Rainey jumped and chuckled. "I don't know why that kind of stuff still startles me after all these years," shc mumbled to herself as she walked back towards the house.

Chapter 21

The Perfect Specimen

Mattie and Trevor popped in right on the mark. Unfortunately, Mrs. Schnettle was pruning her tree on the other side of the hedge and saw them appear out of nowhere. When she screamed, it threw her off balance and she fell sideways off the ladder, plummeting head first into the hedge. By the time Mattie and Trevor could locate the direction of the continued screaming all they could see were two legs kicking frantically in mid-air.

Mattie snorted and slapped her hand over her mouth. Trevor grabbed her by the arm and dragged her with him as he ran around to the other side of the house. By the time they got there they were laughing so hard they had to sit down.

"Oh, my gosh. That was priceless!" Trevor said, laughing hysterically as he rolled onto his back while holding his stomach that was beginning to hurt.

Finally, after several minutes of being totally out-of-control they settled down. "I wish I had a camera," Mattie said,

snickering. "That picture could come in handy some day. Too bad!"

They got up and went around front to see if Lila was home. Her car was gone, so they boosted back over to the side of the library where they had gone before.

"Much better landing, Mattie; thanks for keeping me out of the bushes."

"I had a better picture to go by this time. Makes a difference, doesn't it!"

"Yeah, it sure does. Maybe we should be traveling with a camera so you can get a clear picture if you ever need to return some other time down the road."

"Not a bad idea. Let's go see if we can find Lila."

Grrrrrooowwwwwwlllleeeeeeeeooooiiiiiiiiiii.

"What'd you say, Trev?"

"That was my stomach. I'm starving!"

"Maybe we can order some take out after we find Lila. Look…there she is."

Lila was standing with Detective Farquarth, helping him finish his report. Everyone could see that the detective was about fit to be tied. Lila was an obvious source of irritation, yet he couldn't seem to get rid of her.

"Aunt Lila, can we talk to you for a minute?" Mattie called out.

Lila stopped talking to the detective, which gave him noticeable relief. "What are you two doing here? I thought you were going to catch a bus back into Seaport?"

"We were," Mattie said, scrambling for a story. "Er, a, I was able to get Dad on the phone and everything is fine. We need to talk to you though and it's kind of urgent."

"Well, of course," Lila said. She turned back to Detective Farquarth and asked if he could spare her for a few minutes.

"Take all the time you want, Ms. Graham. I'm long since done with this report." When Lila turned her back to talk with Mattie, Farquarth discreetly slipped into his patrol car and left before she could change her mind.

"Hmm. Strange man." Lila said, stepping into the shade of a large, oak tree. "My, it's warm today. I hear it's going to rain though. That would sure be a nice change." She pulled out a clean, white hanky from her purse and wiped the perspiration from her brow. "Now, what's so important?"

Mattie hadn't had time to listen to a weather report for a couple of days and was beginning to feel panicked inside. "Can we go someplace private to talk?" Mattie said, glancing at the sky that was indeed showing a few signs of cloud formations. "Preferably inside somewhere."

"Yeah, someplace with food," Trevor added.

Lila loved food! She considered it to be the American dream. Besides, it was lunch time; the perfect excuse to eat.

"Betty's Café has great fish and chips—that have any interest to either of you?" She pointed across the street to a small diner that appeared to be one of the original buildings in Benten. Several large windows made up the front of the café. The bright colored advertising covered nearly every inch of glass, utterly restricting the view to the street from the tables inside. In front there were three small tables arranged closely together on the sidewalk, draped neatly with red and white checkered tablecloths. A large red and white striped canvas awning stretched over all but half of the last table on the end, providing shade for most of the customers.

"Oo-oo yes; it interests me," Trevor said. Without delay he spun around and led the way toward the sidewalk café. "Is that OK with you Mattie?" he called back as he crossed the street, dodging a couple of cars in his path.

"I guess it'll have to be," Mattie said, drawing out a one sided smile.

Lila could see she already liked this young man of Mattie's. They had a love for food in common. She started her body moving as fast as she could in Trevor's direction. Mattie followed a couple of steps behind, frequently glancing up at the sky.

"Shall we eat outside?" Lila called to Trevor.

"NO! Er-r, I'd rather not if no one objects," Mattie blurted out.

"I'm OK either way," said Trevor.

"I'd rather eat outside in the shade," Lila said. "I'm stuck inside all day and it's going to cool off soon with the clouds moving in."

Mattie bit her lower lip to keep from saying something that might set Lila off. She figured she could run inside if the lightning started. Unfortunately the two tables closest to the door were taken and they were forced to sit on the end, where half of the table was exposed to the sun.

Trevor noticed that Mattie was getting a bit edgy. "I'll sit in the sun," he said. "You ladies can sit under the awning."

As thoughtful as it was for Trevor to offer to sit in the sun, she knew he didn't realize that she acted like a gigantic lightning rod and was more often the cause of the thunderstorm than not. It would be safer for everyone to hug a 70 foot metal flag pole in the middle of an empty field during a lightning storm than to sit within 20 feet of her. He knew the story about her mother; however, only a few weeks of being in the family could never be enough time to comprehend the danger of it all. She wondered if they had a basement in the restaurant that would provide the 'Double-Down' she would need to survive. Out of the blue she thought of the library.

"Aunt Lila, is there another way into the library other than the front door that's been nailed shut?"

Lila became suspicious with such an odd question. "No!" she said emphatically. "Why do you ask?"

"I was just wondering!" Mattie reacted, without any further thought of what she might answer.

Lila became distracted by the waiter that had emerged from the café with three glasses of ice water and the menus. He was a tall, lanky, sixteen year old boy, overflowing with nervous energy. "Hi guys…." he said, shuffling out the menus as he walked around the table. "My name is Cody. I'll give you a minute to look over the menu and I'll be right back to take your orders." He disappeared back into the café after checking to see if anyone needed anything at the other tables along the way.

"You say the fish and chips are good, Aunt Lila?" Trevor asked, loosening his belt in anticipation. "I'm so hungry I could eat a bald headed, freckle faced kid!"

Lila chuckled at such a description. She really liked this young man of Mattie's and could relate to him easily. Her eyes became almost dreamy as she described the delectable qualities of Betty's Old Fashioned English Style Fish and Chips. "It's the house specialty!" she said in a lilting voice. "They have the most delicate crust made with a beer batter that's to die for."

Trevor leaned closer to make sure he heard every word of Lila's description that was having a big influence on his watering mouth.

"The owner selects the fish fresh daily himself from local fishermen." Her hands danced in the air as though she were casting the line herself to catch these perfect specimens. "They are consistently light and flaky; made from the most delicate cod…." Her tone changed to a critical whine, "…not that parasite laden halibut." She paused, drawing in a slow,

deep breath. "...and with the malt vinegar and a dash of salt...it practically melts... in your mouth."

Trevor's mouth watered from the description Lila gave. "I'll have that!" he said promptly.

Mattie rolled her eyes at how absurd they both acted over fish. She had lost her appetite since hearing the weather report and the urgency to find a way to bring her father back was weighing on her mind heavily. She was also concerned about how she was going to solicit Lila's help. It irritated her that Trevor was so focused on his stomach and insensitive to her misery. In fact, she was getting down right perturbed and the clouds that were gathering at a faster rate created a lump in her throat.

Cody strolled back over to the table. He took the traditional teenage boy waiter position, shifting his weight mostly to one leg and slumping over his notepad with pencil in hand. "Are you ready?" he asked.

Lila didn't hesitate a second. "Yes," she blurted out, sitting up straight to guarantee there would be enough air in her lungs to rattle the order off in a single breath. "I'll have your fish and chips, extra sauce; a large order of fries and a strawberry-pineapple milkshake. For dessert I'd like a piece of your mud pie with extra ice cream, a drizzle of caramel syrup and a cherry on top. Hold the nuts!"

Mattie heaved a sigh of impatience. She felt like the whole afternoon was going to be wasted on eating a tub full of cholesterol, while her dad's fate rested in her hands alone. She

could envision everyone running and screaming in less than five minutes when the lightning began its relentless pursuit as it did with her mother only three weeks prior. As far as she could make out, Trevor had disconnected his brain entirely and was truly *out to lunch*!

"Ditto for me…" Trevor followed without delay, "except I want double the nuts!"

Cody turned towards Mattie, "And you, Miss?" he asked with his nose still in his notepad.

"Nothing for me," she said curtly.

"Oh, come on, Mattie, you need to eat something. We've got a lot of work ahead of us today." Trevor unfolded his napkin and placed it politely on his lap as though they hadn't a care in the world.

"I'm not hungry," she said shortly. Her head felt like it was going to burst from the rage that was building inside.

Trevor and Lila appeared to be in another space and time. The transparent, sporadic cloud cover was beginning to be more opaque as it slowly packed in from the edges. Mattie's stomach was flip-flopping inside and she was beginning to feel nauseated. Trevor placed his hand on her knee to stop her from subconsciously bumping it up and down under the table in a nervous reaction. She glanced his way and continued her gaze towards the sky. When he saw the concern on her face he realized how thoughtless he had been. He actually allowed his stomach to overrule his reason, which wasn't entirely unusual for him. He turned towards Lila, who was casually nursing her

cold glass of water and tried to correct his inconsiderate behavior with respect to Mattie's feelings. He abruptly put the question out there that Mattie had been stewing over and didn't know how to approach Lila with since they got there.

"Lila, Mattie and I need your help on a dreadfully serious, dangerous matter. Will you help us?" Lila's trance was shattered by the intensity of his request. The water that was being squeezed soothingly through her parched lips, rerouted itself instantly, shooting out both corners of her mouth. Trevor snatched the napkin off his lap and wiped his face dry from the spatter as he continued, "Sorry, Lila. We really have a serious problem and need your help desperately."

Mattie flinched in response to the first crack of lightning in the distance. She was terrified. Trevor's demeanor became even more passionate as he observed the growing stress on Mattie's face. He realized Mattie was in serious danger! He had totally spaced out regarding the fear Mattie must feel from the thunder overhead and the ruthless approach of the not so distant lightning.

"I'm sorry…" Mattie said abruptly, glancing back towards the library. "I've got to go."

"Go where?" Lila asked. "We just got here!"

Cody was making his approach towards the table with his arms full of food when Mattie launched herself out of her chair. Her shoulder came up under Cody's arms and sent the tray, dishes, food, and drinks flying through the air in every direction. Lila threw her arms up, pulling the chair off balance.

She tipped backwards in to the bushes that lined the front of the café; unable to get back up on her own. Trevor reached for the closest plate to see if he could rescue a few pieces of fish from landing on the pavement, reluctant to let such promising delicacies go completely to waste. The milkshakes strung out across the customers at the next table. Most of the mud pie landed on top of Cody's head, gradually drizzling tiny, golden rivers of caramel down his face. The finale came when one of the cherry halves landed squarely on top of Lila's left eyelid, forcing her to close both. Mattie took off for the library straight away. Lila's unobstructed eye opened slightly into a fearsome slit. Her face pinched out a repugnant scowl as the tension escalated inside of her.

Chapter 22

The New Killer Skill

Crack! The lightning struck the ground in the middle of the street only 15 feet behind where Mattie had been a few seconds before. It sent everyone at the café running and screaming for cover. Trevor pulled Lila out of the bushes and hurried her inside where the noise level was almost unbearable due to the screams of both men and women alike.

Shock ran through Mattie's whole body with the impact of the lightning. She felt like she was already dead! Frantically she scanned the property for an outside entrance to the basement of the library. Suddenly she remembered her father talking with her mother a few months ago about something called a Full-Parallel when they didn't know she was in the room. At the time, she had no knowledge of who she was and what she could do. She brushed off the information as if it were a science fiction movie they were discussing. If she recalled correctly, the traveler they were talking about could move through solid objects to a location they envisioned within a hundred yards.

Having learned how to do a Half-Parallel, she now realized that the traveler must have been her mother and herself. As far as she could remember, the only place she had been in the library was on the main level. She'd never seen the basement and it would be far too chancy to try and land down their without a visual of the layout. The rain started abruptly as if it were a solid sheet of water, making her stumble as she ran desperately to move out of open view where she could test out the new ability before she was hit by the lightning. She lifted her arms up into what she thought a Full-Parallel would look like in comparison to a Half-Parallel and envisioning as clear a picture as she could remember of the domed entry inside the library said, "To the corridor…" and disappeared. The execution of the new ability produced a booming sound like a jet breaking the sound barrier, which echoed through town. That alone caused the remaining stragglers on the streets to fall to the pavement in terror. Mattie saw the fiber of the tree that stood between her and the building as she passed through it at an incredible speed. Within nanoseconds she recognized the inside of the brick, mortar, wood frame and insulation as she accelerated through each layer, coming to an abrupt stop in the middle of the lobby. Mattie immediately collapsed to the floor. The Full-Parallel had a much different effect on her than the Half-Parallel. She was extremely weak and her legs refused to lift her aching body off the ground to move her over to the basement door. There was no time for her to try and gain any of her composure because she knew that she was still in danger and had only seconds to put enough substance between her and the lightning to break the affinity it had for her. She needed the extra layer of ground cover the basement offered, and she needed

it immediately. She started dragging her body towards the entry, expending the remaining energy she had left. Remembering the Half-Parallel, she set herself for a shift to the top of the stairs. Luckily the door was opened enough to see the landing to help her make the move.

"To the landing…" she said feebly. Her body shifted to the top of the stairs in a slow, but steady sliding motion; unlike the quick transfers she had become accustomed to. Still, she did get there without much effort at all. "To the basement," she softly whispered as she set another Half-Parallel. Her powers were too depleted to lift her completely up off of the steps, exposing her dead legs and limp body to a rhythmic beating with each drop. By the time she reached the basement she was entirely exhausted from the pounding. She lay motionless, unable to even blink her eyes. At least she had made it safely to the Double Down and was deep enough in the ground to be protected from the high voltage attraction that had been stalking her outside.

People were running wildly through the café, climbing on tables, knocking over chairs, making it more dangerous to remain inside and be trampled rather than face the storm outside. Lila was frozen with horror. Trevor anchored her to his body and moved her back through the entry until they were once again on the patio, huddling under the awning together.

"Lila, is there another entrance to the library?"

Lila remained huddled down against Trevor, silent, unable to think or speak. Trevor tried several times to get an answer from her and finally slapped her face sharply to try and wake her up. Lila's round, fleshy faced jiggled from the shock of being hit. Her eyes couldn't have been any larger if they had been stretched and sewn wide open by a skilled plastic surgeon. Trevor shook her by the shoulders as he tried one more time to get an answer.

"Lila, I've got to get into the library. It's a matter of life and death for Kash and Mattie."

This stimulated Lila's awareness more than anything and she started to lift herself up to meet Trevor eye to eye.

"Mattie and Kash are in danger?" she sputtered, still trembling from the shock of her unconventional lunch.

Trevor helped her to her feet and righted one of the tipped over chairs for her to sit on while he continued his plea.

"I don't know where to begin, Lila. All I know is that you are the key to saving this family from certain death."

Lila closed her eyes, scrunched her nose and started crying in a squeaky, high-pitched whine. "This has been the worst day of my life. First I'm called down to my library that has been broken into. Next some idiot hits me over the head and damages half of the most treasured area of my library; Fifi destroys the other half; I shoot some maniac out by the store; he disappears into thin air; and you two show up. I have perfectly good fish and chips thrown into the gutter; cherries plopping in

my eyes and now…" Lila began to gain her composure. Anger took over and she started yelling, "…and now—you're telling me I have to save Mattie and Kash because they're going to die if I don't do something." She clenched her chubby fists together and shook them in the air. "You people are crazy!" Lila was clearly becoming more focused.

"You are the only person in the world who can save this family now," Trevor pleaded, "please listen to me; there's not much time."

Lila pushed him away and started across the street as fast as she could; holding her forearm over her brow to see if she could locate her car through the pouring rain. "My family is insane!" she screamed over and over again until she disappeared inside her car, slamming the door. She drove away recklessly, leaving Trevor in a stupor.

Mattie lay motionless in the dark on the cold, cement floor. She didn't have enough energy to even open her eyes. All she could think of was Trevor and what she would say to him if she could possibly live through this, which brought some comfort.

Chapter 23

The Mental Connection

Trevor stood helpless under the awning, wondering what he should do next. He hoped Mattie had escaped the lightning and was inside the library, though he wasn't sure how she could have gotten in there. His next thought was of Rainey. If Lila wouldn't help them they'd have to find a way to get back to Rainey. With the thunderstorm, Mattie wouldn't be able to "Boost" them back; they would both die through the transition. Trevor felt a deep, sickening panic inside and began to hyperventilate. He stumbled back to the chair he had straightened up for Lila and sat down. He tried to shift his thoughts to something else to help him reduce the tension when he heard a quiet voice repeating the words, "*Help me, Trevor—please help me!*" over and over, increasing in volume. He swung his head in every direction in an attempt to locate the source of the voice. There wasn't a single person left on the streets anywhere and they would have to be speaking directly into his ear for him to hear them whisper like that. Gradually the voice became louder and clearer as if someone were carrying on a conversation while sitting right in front

of him. Stranger still, the voice was beginning to sound like Mattie's.

"Help me, Trevor. I feel like I'm dying. I need you. Why won't you come and save me!"

Trevor stood up, confused and frantic. He remained lifelessly still, holding his breath as though his motionless body would help him listen better.

"I feel cold inside, Trevor, and I can't move. Please help me. "

He felt like running, but didn't know where. He began pacing the sidewalk, listening for any kind of a clue as to where she was.

"I wish we had had more time together without all this chaos in our lives. You deserve more than I've given you...I'm sorry..."

His heart was pounding in his chest and he started hyperventilating again. He felt helpless and irrational, like he was losing pieces of his mind with every passing second.

"I wish you could hear me Trevor. I love you so much. I want your arms around me more than I want to live right now. It's like the library is a thousand miles away from where I imagine you are."

"*The library!*" he thought. "*You're in the library?*"

"*Yes!*" replied the voice. "*You can hear me?*"

"*...and you can hear me!*" he thought with a rush of joy. "*I'm coming Mattie...hang on. I'll have to break into the storage shed that Rainey said leads to the Library. I'll go as fast as I can.*"

"*I don't know if I can last that long. I've never experienced anything so completely draining and I feel like I'm slipping away. Hurry!*"

Trevor started running down the middle of the street towards the edge of town. His movements were deliberate and smooth with a dash of fear, reminiscent of his high school track days. The rain was beginning to let up, making it easier to move without difficulty. Five minutes later he slid to a stop in front of the storage shed behind the convenience store. He glanced quickly around at the base of the building where he remembered seeing the Interloper drop the rock he was going to kill Lila with.

"*I'm at the storage shed, Mattie,*" he thought, trying to send her encouragement to hang on. "*I'll be there in a few minutes.*" But, there was no answer; only a dark, heavy silence. "*Mattie...can you hear me?*" There was only silence in his head. Trevor felt a cold chill sweep through him. His eyes started watering at the thought of losing her. His hand began slamming the rock hysterically against the handle. The pounding noise drew the attention of the clerk inside. She pushed the back door open to see where the racket was coming from and saw Trevor trying to break the lock.

"Hey…you get away from there," she yelled, "or I'll call the cops." When Trevor didn't show any sign of stopping she vanished back inside the store to make the call.

Seconds later the handle gave way and hung loosely from the screw that remained partially intact. He grabbed the knob with both of his hands, twisting and yanking on it until he finally jerked the bolt out of the frame. He flung the door open, flipped on the light and quickly scanned the room. In the far corner of the room he saw another door that was half way open. He wound through several large stacks of buns, pickles, crackers, candy bars, and potato chips before reaching the entrance to the tunnel. He turned the lock and pulled it shut behind him to slow down the police that were sure to follow. He sprinted down through the tunnel, passing thousands of small brown boxes that neatly lined the walls from top to bottom on both sides of the passageway. Every once in a while he'd pass an unfamiliar object he didn't recognize, raising his curiosity to new heights, but he didn't dare stop for fear he would be too late to save Mattie.

Mattie was barely breathing by the time he reached her lifeless body, lying at the foot of the stairs. He placed his hand on her head, brushing away the hair that was covering her face. He leaned in close to listen for a breath and she began to stir.

"It's me, Mattie, I'm here." He scooped her up into his arms and held her tight.

She drew a slow, deep breath and lifted her head higher on his shoulder. "I knew you'd come for me," she said, releasing the remaining breath gently.

Trevor could feel his own strength growing and passing through his body into Mattie's. He could sense her recovery was becoming more rapid with each breath. As Mattie's strength

returned she reached her arms around Trevor and hugged him back. It felt wonderful to rest in his strong, muscular arms for a few minutes more. Her aching, limp muscles felt strong and agile again. The rings had kept their promise by snatching her from the clutch of death and restoring her to full health and energy.

"Thank you, Trevor. I thought I was going to be dead before you could get here. I've never felt so completely zapped of life before. That Full-Parallel is a scary trick!"

"What's a Full-Parallel?"

"It's something I heard my parents discussing a couple months ago and it was my only option to escape the lightning. I had to try something…anything! It moved me through solid objects and dropped me on the spot I was thinking of in the lobby upstairs. I wonder if I would have died if you hadn't saved me." She snuggled her head into his chest, breathing a sigh of satisfaction and relief.

"I hate to bring this up again, Mattie, but I have some bad news."

"H-m-m-m?" Mattie said softly, enjoying the moment.

"Lila freaked out and took off in her car. I don't know if we can reason with her after all that's happened. She totally lost it after you left." Trevor leaned back against the wall, pulling Mattie with him. "Do you think we should try and find your dad's soul box ourselves and drive back to Seaport? Rainey could complete the triangle."

"I'd draw the lightning to the car. I can't be above ground for more than a few seconds at a time until the clouds can dissipate entirely and that'll take hours. We don't have hours to wait."

"I don't understand how the Interloper can drag people beyond the maps boundary." Trevor pulled himself in a more upright position and Mattie sat up.

"I don't either, but we don't have enough time to find out right now. Our only hope of getting him back before midnight lies with Lila." Mattie stood up and rocked her head from shoulder to shoulder, loosening her neck, which was still stiff from the beating she had taken on the stairwell. "I think your idea about locating dad's box is a good place to start. I'll look around if you'll go and call Rainey. Tell her to get out of the house. Maybe she should go stay with the Judge and his wife until it's safe. I'm afraid the Interloper will return while she's still there."

"OK, I'll be right back." Trevor bounded up the steps and disappeared through the open doorway. Mattie started shuffling through the boxes. One by one she replaced them back on a shelf as she read them. The more she went through, the more she realized how impossible the task was. There were literally hundreds of near-identical boxes covering the floor. It would take all night to locate the right one, if it was in this group at all, and they still needed to convince Lila to help them complete the triangle. Mattie leaned against one of the shelves. She fought the deepening despair that was building within her. Trevor jumped back down the steps covering several at a time

to join the search and found Mattie standing amongst the pool of brown boxes.

"What's the matter?"

"This is impossible! We'll never be able to find Dad's soul box before midnight without Aunt Lila's help." Mattie took a quick breath. "Great! The police are swarming outside the storage building; I can see them in my mind. We need to get out of here now."

"How do you propose we do that? The front door is boarded shut and the alarm will go off if we open any of the windows."

"We could try a Full-Parallel together?"

"Oh yeah, and kill us both! We might as well *Boost* up into the thunderstorm together and go out with a bang!"

"No! The rings will protect us and we could move underground to the Time Chamber so I wouldn't be exposed to the lightning again. It would be the ultimate Double-Down."

"Hmmm, that does have some reasoning in it. How do you see us going about this one?"

"You stand behind me and slide your arms up under mine. Put your palms together in front of me. I'll set the Full-Parallel on top of your arms with my palms open to connect the rings together. We shouldn't feel any pain and the Full-Parallel will transport us through the earth; basement to basement."

Trevor stepped behind Mattie and reached his arms around her waist. He rested his chin on her shoulder and snuggled his cheek up against hers.

"Not now, Trevor…" Mattie said sweetly. "Let's stay focused on the jump."

"OK…" Trevor responded, somewhat disappointed. He pushed his palms together with his arms parallel to the ground. She rested her arms on top and pressed her palms to the back of his hands. The rings started to vibrate when they touched and the swirling mist lifted them a couple inches off the ground.

"Oh-h-h-h…here we go," Trevor said with a touch of excitement in his voice.

"To the Chamber!" she called out and they vanished together. A harmonic vibration shook several more brown boxes from their shelves and the room was filled with papers tumbling through the air like feathers blowing in a gentle breeze.

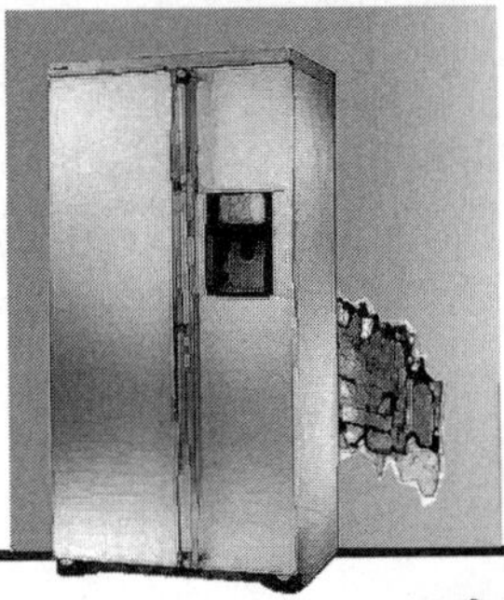

Chapter 24

The Recruitment

Mattie and Trevor watched all kinds of rock formations, sewer pipes, electrical wiring and tons and tons of dirt pass through their vision before arriving in the Time Chamber.

Upstairs, Lila was sitting at the kitchen table fretfully sipping a strong cup of Chamomile tea to calm her shattered nerves. She was still shaking from the traumatic events at the restaurant as she hovered over the steaming liquid, cradling it between both hands. To her further distress the whole house started to shudder with the arrival of her unwelcome guests who were making a landing in the Chamber she knew nothing about. Fearing it was another earthquake she threw her head back and forth frantically watching the ceiling to see if it was going to collapse. She glanced down at the cup in time to see a thick stream of tea rise in the center, separating a single drop of fluid at the top, ultimately slopping over the side. The hot tea burned her hands and she let go of the cup, allowing it to shatter on the tile below.

When they finally landed, Mattie and Trevor stumbled over a box that had fallen into their path due to the uproar their arrival had produced. They fell to the floor together; Mattie landing first with Trevor following; smashing her from on top.

"Oh...you need to move Trevor." Mattie said, squirming to get free.

Trevor rolled off to the side, rubbing his elbows which took most of the impact from their fall. "I feel like we should be wearing protective padding for these trips of ours," he said. "I wonder if we'll get luckier with our landings as we get more experience—or if it's always going to be this miserable."

"I don't know. I hope we get better at this stuff, too. These bad landings are getting old!" Mattie hushed Trevor. "Just a sec..." She lifted her head up towards the stairs. "Lila's in the kitchen. She's a nervous wreck!"

"That's how she was the last time I saw her."

"We've got to find a way to get her down here. Got any ideas?"

Trevor stretched back out on the floor gazing at the sparkling jewels on the ceiling while he thought. "Did those stairs lead into the house at one time?"

"Uh-huh. They used to take you through an opening behind the fridge, but Dad plastered it shut before we left for Seaport."

"I guess we could tear down the plaster and go in through there."

"I'm afraid Lila would completely lose it if she heard someone coming through the wall and then we wouldn't get anywhere with her."

Trevor stood up and walked around the room. "I know you can't be above ground for very long until the storm clears, but could you transport me up there and drop me off? That way I could go in and try and reason with her."

"Probably, but you'll need to get back to me as soon as you can, because when I come back down here by myself it'll wipe me out like it did when I Paralleled into the library alone."

"I know and that bothers me. Can you think of another way?"

"No, let's just do it. We'll have to take our chances; we're running out of time." They set a Full-Double Parallel to the living room and Mattie returned to the Chamber where she buckled to the floor to wait.

"*Are you alright Mattie?*" Trevor thought.

"*Too weak…to think,*" Mattie thought back. "H*urry!*"

Lila felt a brief rumble like an aftershock of the earthquake and then heard a thud in the other room. The

combination sharpened her awareness, restoring some focus. She hurried over to the stove and opened the bottom drawer. Pushing aside several pots she finally pulled out the biggest, heaviest frying pan she could lift. Raising it above her head to protect herself she crept towards the swinging door that separated her from the intruder. Adrenaline flooded her veins preparing her to flatten whoever it was that dared enter *her* house uninvited.

"Lila," Trevor called out from the other room. "I need to talk to you. Please, please, please help us!"

Lila lowered the pan, swung the door open and stepped into the living room. "Oo-oo, you have a lot of guts, young man."

He saw the pan in her hand and turned pale. "Mattie's dying in the basement and I've got to get back to her. I need your help."

"There's no basement in this house," Lila objected sternly.

"Yes, there is, and you've got to help me get down there. We can't waste any time."

Trevor ran into the kitchen. Lila's eyes tracked every inch of his movement as he past her until he disappeared through the swinging door. When she got to the kitchen she saw Trevor sliding the refrigerator away from the wall.

"What are you doing? I really like you, but you act like you belong in an asylum."

"There used to be an opening behind here that leads to the basement. Do you have a hammer?"

"Now…what is it about me that makes you think that I would go find you a hammer to help you tear my wall apart?"

Trevor stood up to face Lila. His jaw was set and his determination was visible in his face. "Aunt Lila, I don't know what makes you such a bitter woman and I don't much care. You need to take a leap of faith with me here or lose your entire family—mother, sister, brother-in-law, and niece…everyone that loves you…within the next several minutes." He continued to stare into her eyes with conviction.

Lila visibly softened. "My mother?" she said, somewhat confused. Her eyes flickered away from Trevor and back, searching for further information that would explain the inclusion of her mother in the list.

"Rainey is in as much danger of being killed as Kash is, and if Mattie dies in your basement because you're so wrapped up in your own selfish world of bull-headedness you'll lose them all!"

Lila stood in the middle of the kitchen stunned, confused, and getting more irritated with every word Trevor said. She wanted to know more, but wanted him to shut up and leave her alone, too. For the first time in her life she felt like her world was completely falling apart. "My mother?" she muttered again.

"Oh, for heaven sakes, Lila! Wake up!" Trevor marched over to the cabinets to search through the drawers, hoping to

find a hammer or something big enough that could help him break through the wall. In the second drawer he spotted a meat tenderizing mallet. He grabbed it and returned to face the wall on the other side of the refrigerator. He took a full swing, which barely punctured the plaster. Lila dropped the pan and moved away from him in disbelief. Trevor beat on the wall until he created a hole about the size of a dinner plate. He dropped the mallet and started kicking the edges, exposing more and more of the room with each thrust of his foot. After several strikes he gripped the larger pieces of the fractured plasterboard, pulling it away until the opening was big enough for him to get through. He crunched down and slid sideways into the Chamber and disappeared from Lila's view. Lila inched her way warily over to the opening and stuck her head inside. The room was dimly lit, but she could see Trevor on the floor holding Mattie in his arms, talking to her softly.

Mattie lay motionless, already appearing dead to Lila and her eyes started to fill with tears. "What have I done?" She wailed as she stepped inside and made her way over to Trevor trying not to touch any of the strange objects as she went. By the time she got there she could see that Mattie was beginning to stir; bringing a warm feeling of relief to her heart. For the first time in years she felt like she had a family again and all she wanted to do was protect them, no matter what kind of crazy things were going on around her. Mattie sat up as Lila was kneeling down by Trevor.

"Mattie…I…uh…" Her throat felt like it had a lump in it the size of a lemon and she couldn't speak.

Mattie reached up and squeezed Lila's arm. "It's alright Aunt Lila," she whispered, "I know this is totally overwhelming for you and we don't have a lot of time to fill you in..."

"...but we'll try!" Trevor said kindly, finishing Mattie's sentence.

Chapter 25

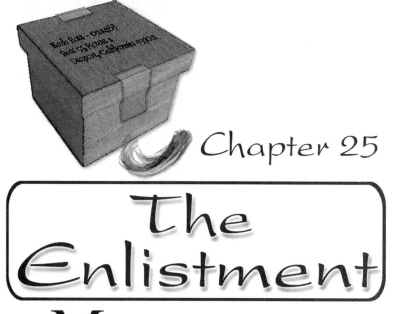

The Enlistment

Mattie and Trevor spent the next two hours explaining the events of the last several weeks. It was important for them to build the type of informational groundwork Lila would need to help her stand firm through the trials and strange events that were certain to pop up in the near future. To their surprise, she accepted the wild tale without too many questions. She turned to Trevor and asked, “Why did you include my mother in the list of people that might die? She’s been gone for years. In fact, you made it sound like Rainey was my mother.”

Trevor hadn’t realized that he had let Rainey’s secret slip while he was chewing her out. His eyes flickered over to Mattie’s for help before glancing down at his hands for a diversion.

Mattie took a deep breath and told Lila about her real father and how he’d been killed in World War II, leaving her mother without a way to support herself and her new baby. She

lovingly explained about the decisions that were made and the reasoning behind them. She described how hard it was for Rainey to give up the rewards of being her mother and how she was willing to sacrifice her own desires to give her daughter a happier, less complicated life. "As your nanny, she could still be like a mother to you. She could raise you with a sister and insure a stable parenting environment while she carried on her duties as a Sentinel."

Lila sat silent. Mattie glanced at Trevor wondering if she had broken the news satisfactorily.

"So I'm a Sentinel by birth!" Lila twisted her head and sat up.

"Yes and that's why you're the key. Trevor and I are only two thirds of the trio needed to move beyond the maps boundary and bring Dad back before midnight."

Lila slowly glanced around the room, stopping briefly on each of the objects that held a new position of importance to her. She finally understood why her parents willed the house to Amber and why they could never disclose their secrets. In truth it explained a whole host of mysterious events throughout her life that had troubled her, bringing reason to their existence. "I'm in!" she exclaimed boldly. Her enthusiasm was a relief to Mattie. "Where do we go from here?

"We have to find Dad's DNA box before we can attempt to enter the core. We'll need it to bring him back with us," Trevor explained.

"What's a DNA box?"

"They're all over the place in the basement of the Library," Mattie explained. "Every Trekker, Splitter, Sentinel, including each person that was the focus of a Divvy since the beginning of time has some kind of container that protects their DNA in case…" She paused in thought. "Wait a minute. That's it!"

"What's it?" Trevor said.

"The day Mom was killed, the Interloper broke into the car searching for the rings. He also took samples of hers and Dad's fingerprints. There was chocolate powder on the stick shift and crumpled Scotch tape on the floor. That's how you take a fingerprint. That works like a DNA sample and he must have used it to pull him into the core, the same way we're going to use it to bring him back!"

"But wouldn't it have to be set apart before he could do that?" Trevor reminded her.

"If he comes from the future, there must be a Sentinel there, dedicating his samples." Mattie refocused her attention to her dad. "Right now, we have to figure out where Dad's DNA box is so we can go get him."

"That's easy!" said Lila with a grin. "I never did know what it was, but it's in my desk in the library. I kept it close to me because…" Lila hesitated and then boldly confessed, "Because Kash has always held a special place in my heart. You see, I was in love with him too, but he was already deeply

in love with your mother. I guess the *bitter* woman you accused me of being came into existence at their engagement. It was never Amber's fault; it was my pettiness that drove us apart. Finally, when Mom and Dad gave her the house, I used it as my excuse to hate them both."

Mattie and Trevor were stunned. They didn't expect Lila to open up like that. It explained a lot of things to Mattie about the family that never made any sense to her either. She knew everything was going to be all right now.

Lila let out a long sigh of relief, "Whewww, it's good to get that off my mind. Oh, that reminds me—a box came to the library a few weeks ago that had Amber's name on it, too; written in her own hand writing. I didn't put two and two together on the handwriting until just now. I kept her box up in my desk with Kash's. Why would she send herself a current DNA sample?"

"It must have something to do with bringing her back as well," Mattie said thoughtfully. "She must have known that there was a space in time, 'beyond the maps boundary' as the book refers to it. Dad said he could see her crying from across the field and the tears were a glowing, fluorescent blue. Since a Trekker's tears can heal people I'll bet that she was betting her life on the fact that if she were crying when the lightning struck her it would keep her from dying. She was probably guessing that it would move her into the core of time instead."

"That's why we saw her when we moved back in time together to resurrect Lila," Trevor added. "That was quite a gamble!"

"Resurrect me?"

Trevor smiled, shifting his weight. "We did!" he exclaimed proudly. "The Interloper killed you with the rock the first time. We did a Double Divvy of sorts and stopped him the second time."

"Oh my…" Lila's head was swimming with so many new stories. "I guess I should thank you again for saving my life…or…bringing me back to life!" She blinked her soft green and blue eyes a few times and shook her head in bewilderment.

"What are families for?" Mattie said. "I'm sure you'd do the same for us!"

Lila beamed. It was nice to feel important to someone again.

Mattie's thoughts returned to the rescue effort. "We need to get back to the library and get Dad's soul box. I can't go outside as long as it's raining and I need Trevor to do a Double Parallel with me to get me there without complications. Can we meet you inside the tunnel to the library, Aunt Lila?"

"Absolutely! I'll leave right after you do and meet you over there."

"I don't know if you should be in the room when we Parallel. I have no idea what happens when we depart and I don't want you to be hurt."

"Well I can tell you the house shakes fiercely, so…you've got a point. I think I'll leave. See you over there in

a few minutes." Lila gave Mattie a hug and hurried out of the Chamber.

Trevor snuggled up behind Mattie and hugged her himself. "I do love you, Mattie. My life was boring before you came along." He gave her an extra loud kiss on the cheek and set the Parallel. Mattie set the Double-Parallel on top of his arms and pressed the rings together. "Back to the library basement…" she said, and they instantly began retracing their underground journey.

Chapter 26

The Reunion

It didn't take Lila five minutes to get to the entrance of the tunnel where the police were swarming around the door. Countless trails of water streamed down their rain drenched ponchos, as they tried to figure out what happened and where the criminal had gone. The first thing out of Lila's car was her umbrella that popped open automatically above the roof, providing shelter from the rain. Lila stood up underneath it and closed the door.

Detective Farquarth approached the car, tromping his way through the mud. "Ms. Graham, you seem to be drawing nothing but trouble today."

"Well, Detective, this one is all in the family. My nephew had an emergency and needed some equipment inside the building. He couldn't get a hold of me, so he broke in to get what he needed. He called and explained afterwards and suggested I come down to secure the door until he could get back to fix it. I'll take it from here. Thank you for your prompt, professional services…all of you!"

Farquarth scratched his chin and looked around at his colleagues. He'd never known Lila to be this nice. "I see…thank

you for explaining things to me so patiently, Ms. Graham." He squeezed his lips together tightly; raising his eyebrows. "Well—people, I guess it's a false alarm." He flicked the back of his hand up and down a couple of times and said, "Let's go!"

After everyone had left the alley, Lila told the cashier to close up the store and sent her home for the night. She went inside the storage unit and shuffled towards the back. As she reached in her purse to get her key, the door opened from the other side where Trevor stood waiting for her.

"There you are. Are you ready?" Trevor asked, with a hint of enthusiasm in his voice.

Lila smiled at his boyish charm. It felt good to smile again. "I'm ready. Where's Mattie?"

"She has to stay below ground until the storm passes."

"Oh that's right. It's going to take me a while to get all of these things straight in my head."

"We better get started."

Lila stopped to lock the door and then led the way down the tunnel.

"Haven't you ever wondered what some of this stuff is, Aunt Lila?" Trevor asked, curious himself.

"You know, I've seen these things for so many years that I've just subconsciously gone through the motions of keeping them stored, cleaned and safe. I wonder now though!" She chuckled to herself under her breath.

A few minutes later they reached the main room of the basement where Mattie was picking up boxes to help Lila with the mess.

Lila appreciated Mattie's gesture to help. "Don't worry about those dear. I'll have to arrange them by their catalog numbers to get them back in the right order and that'll take a while. I'll have plenty of time later. Let's get this problem solved with your dad first." She continued walking towards the stairwell. "I'll be right back." A few minutes later she returned with Kash's box. "Here it is."

Mattie and Trevor stood in the least cluttered area of the room and beckoned Lila to join them.

"Now what?" Lila asked.

"We're not sure," replied Trevor. "It may take some time to figure things out."

"May I have Dad's box, Aunt Lila? I'm pretty sure I need to hold the sample itself in my hand when we bring him back." Mattie carefully opened the box and pulled out the lock of hair. "Look how dark it is."

Lila became melancholy. "That was sent many, many years ago when we were all young. I'm telling you, your dad was a tall, dark, handsome man. There were a lot of girls in love with him—not just your mom and me."

Mattie grinned at the thought of her father being in such demand by so many women and closed her fingers tightly around the youthful sample. "Let's try holding hands. Maybe it works

like an electrical circuit, channeling our energy in a continuous circle.

They stood in a circle and clasped each other's hands. Several seconds passed without any sign of them changing locations.

"In everything else we've done with the rings they had to touch each other," Trevor reminded her. "Wouldn't you think they probably need to touch on this type of transfer as well?"

"Good point." Mattie quickly lifted her left arm up and stuck it out in front of her. "Trevor put your left hand on mine and Aunt Lila, you're going to top us off." The moment Trevor's hand touched Mattie's the mist began to swirl out from the rings. Lila snickered and Trevor's eyes sparkled with excitement. When Lila laid her hand on top, Mattie shouted, "Beyond the maps boundary!" and the room became a blur. Harmonious chords filled the air and an overwhelming sense of peace moved through their bodies. A sense of joy engulfed them and they were instantly free from the tension they had been in. The everyday concerns that were common to mortality were gone and they felt lighter than air. As the whirling slowed, they could make out images of people dressed in all white clothing. When the mist stopped they found themselves standing amongst family and friends that had long since passed away. Mattie scanned the faces to see if she could see her father. Kash emerged from the crowd to see what the excitement was. He was dressed in the same clothing that he was wearing the last time she saw him. As she continued to look through the crowd, she began to pick out others that were dressed in clothing from different eras.

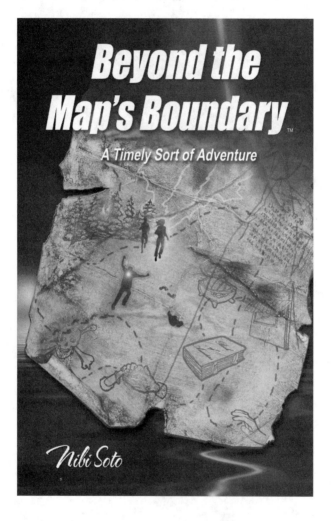

About the Author

Nibi Soto

Nibi grew up along the Wasatch Mountains of Utah, in the Great Salt Lake valley. She has three advanced degrees and a diverse background with many prestigious awards in a wide variety of fields from college and professional sports to art, music and writing.